PASS IT ON!

In the [REAL LIFE] series, four girls are brought together through the power of a mysterious book that helps them sort through the issues of their very real lives. In each of these stories, the girls find the mysterious RL book exactly when they need it. Each girl leaves the RL book for someone else to find, knowing it will help the next person who reads it.

While the RL book is magical, this book could be left in the same way for the next reader. Maybe this book needs to be read by someone you don't even know, or maybe you already know of someone who would really enjoy this book. Simply write a note with READ ME on it, stick it on the front of the book, and then get creative. Give the book to a friend, or leave this book at your church, school, local coffee shop, train station, on the bus, or wherever you know someone else will find it and read it.

No matter what your plan, we want to hear about it. Log on to the Zondervan Good Teen Reads Facebook page (*www.facebook. com/goodteenreads* — look under the Discussion tab) and tell us where you left the book, or how you found it. Or, let us know how you plan to "pass it on." You can also let your friends know about Pass It On by talking about it on your Facebook page.

To join others in the Pass It On campaign, pick up extra copies from the [REAL LIFE] series at your local Christian bookstores and favorite online retailers.

Other books in the Real Life series:

Motorcycles, Sushi & One Strange Book (Book One)

Boyfriends, Burritos & an Ocean of Trouble (Book Two)

TOURNAMENTS, COCOA & ONE WRONG MOVE

[REAL LIFE]

book three

NANCY RUE

ZONDERVAN®

ZONDERVAN.com/
AUTHORTRACKER
follow your favorite authors

ZONDERVAN

Tournaments, Cocoa & One Wrong Move
Copyright © 2010 by Nancy Rue

This title is also available as a Zondervan ebook.
Visit www.zondervan.com/ebooks.

Requests for information should be addressed to:

Zondervan, *Grand Rapids, Michigan* 49530

Library of Congress Cataloging-in-Publication Data

Rue, Nancy N.
    Tournaments, cocoa & one wrong move / Nancy Rue.
       p.   cm. — (Real life ; bk. 3)
    Summary: When a knee injury and a subsequent mistake threaten to end her
basketball career, athletically driven Cassidy finds support in the most unlikely
places — including a room filled with juvenile delinquents and the pages of an old
book labeled "RL."
    ISBN 978-0-310-71486-6 (softcover)
    [1. Athletes — Fiction. 2. Wounds and injuries — Fiction. 3. Christian life — Fiction.]
I. Title. II. Title: Tournaments, cocoa and one wrong move.
PZ7.R88515Tp 2010
[Fic] — dc22   2010023289

Published in association with the literary agency of Alive Communications, Inc., 7680 God-
dard Street, Suite 200, Colorado Springs, CO 80920. www.alivecommunications.com

Cover design: *Rule 29*
Cover photography: © iStockphoto
Interior design: *Patrice Sheridan & Carlos Eluterio Estrada*

Printed in the United States of America

10 11 12 13 14 15 /DCI/ 23 22 21 20 19 18 17 16 15 14 13 12 11 10 9 8 7 6 5 4 3 2 1

CHAPTER ONE

It was the best night of my life, it was the worst night of my life.

I think we read a book in Junior Honors English that started something like that. I couldn't tell you the title now. I usually forget stuff like that the day after the test.

Anyway, that night Honors English was the last thing on my mind. So was AP Chemistry and the crush I had on the guy who bagged my mother's groceries. All I was thinking about was basketball.

Specifically the fourth quarter of the game against Monument Valley High, which we had to win to take the county title. Actually, which *I* had to win. When Monument Valley called a long time-out — like, all of a minute long — Coach Deetz pulled us *all* into what he called a "puddle" (a "huddle" to any other coach), but his beady browns zinged to *me* at the end of every question. I was used to it.

"What's the score, ladies?"

"Sixty-eight, sixty-eight," Kara said beside me.

A half dozen of my best friend's blonde curls had escaped from that messy bun thing she always did with her hair for games, and they were sweat-plastered to her temples. She could shoot with deadeye accuracy like nobody in El Paso County, but when the score got this close she usually choked. Reason number one why Coach's eyes kept flicking to me.

"And how much time is left on the clock?" he said.

"A minute thirty seconds," M.J. Martinez said, her voice so gone you could barely hear her accent.

The Trident gum Coach always decimated during games peeked raggedly out from under his left incisor. His eyes landed on me again. "What's going on, Cassidy?"

Behind us the crowd was stomping on the bleachers in rhythm with the pep band, a backbeat for the heaving breathing coming from the four girls around me in the puddle—M.J. and Kara and Hilary and Selena. The outer ring of fifteen who hadn't played this quarter looked on, envious and un-sweaty in their green warm-up jackets. We five slurped water and dripped on the gym floor and bent over, pressing our knees with our hands. Everybody was looking at me just like Coach was.

"Okay—" I said. "We have to stop passing to Kara and expecting her to make the jump shots."

Hilary's red head snapped up. "But she's our best—"

"She misses one more layup and I'm taking her out," Coach said.

I didn't look at Kara. Didn't have to. Her baby blues would be tearing up about now.

"She's tired," I said, instead of the truth, which was that she was about to freak. I turned to Selena. "If you could get on that Number Twelve chick and keep her away from me so I can get to the paint, that would work."

Coach chewed his gum at us, eyes the size of BBs. "You have ten seconds left. Anybody gonna argue with that?"

The skin over Selena's cheekbones stretched until you could almost see through it. "If I cover her any closer I'll foul her."

"So let her foul *you*," Coach said. "You know how to take a charge." His eyes tightened. "Look, you can't start playing a powder-puff game now. Get in there and clear a path so Cassidy can take it to the hole. What do you want, Cass?"

"Half-court trap," I said. "M.J. and Selena on Twelve as soon as we get her over to the corner. Make her go for a skip pass, you guys."

"And you'll intercept it," Coach said.

"Or *I* can," Selena said.

Coach shook his head. "They have a nasty edge—you break it and let Cassidy take the shot. Clear?"

Selena nodded, of course. We all did. But when I thrust out my hand and everybody stuck theirs out with me, I could see her swallowing like she had a marshmallow in her throat. That was her pride going down. Kara, on the other hand, grabbed onto me like she was about to fall off a tall building.

"Defense on three!" I said.

M.J. did her usual hoarse-because-I've-been-yelling-for-an-hour "Uno—dos—tres," and all of us screamed, "*Defense!*"

The ref's whistle pierced the air, and Coach tugged on his supposedly lucky Mickey Mouse tie and faked a smile. He hadn't *really* smiled since the season started, and I knew he wouldn't again until we dumped a bucket of Gatorade over his head at the end of state finals—which he promised we could do when we won. When. Not if. There was no "if" with Coach Deetz.

I started to follow the team onto the court, but Coach hissed, "Brewster." I turned to face him while I continued backing slowly toward the sideline.

"Do what you have to do," he said.

Translation: "It's all on you now."

Why would he even bother to say it? It always was.

It wasn't that I had brought the Austin Bluffs High School varsity girls' basketball team through an undefeated season single-handedly. We—all of us, even the second team—were like a well-oiled machine for three quarters of every game. The newspaper and the local TV station called our first team the UN because we had M.J. the hard-driving Hispanic, Selena the focused Asian, Hilary the fiery Irish girl, Kara the shooting Scandinavian queen, and me, the white-bread captain. But it didn't escape the team that somehow when it came to the fourth quarter, it was like I was the only one out there.

I didn't have any more stamina than anybody else; I was breathing like an asthma patient at the moment, and my muscles were practically screaming, "What are you thinking? We're dyin' here!" So that wasn't it. My mother said it was my "mojo." My father said—

Well, never mind what my father said. If I went *there* right now, we could forget about the Gatorade baptism ever happening. I didn't even chance looking up into the stands, where Dad was at that very moment probably throwing an embolism. I wasn't sure exactly what that was, but my brother's med-student girlfriend had said it about him when they told him they were moving in together. You get the idea ...

The Monument Valley team apparently got a butt-chewing from their coach during the time-out, because when the refs finally finished wiping the sweat off the floor and the ball was thrown in, they took to the court like a swarm of bees.

On steroids. Number Nine—a wiry African American with two inches on my five foot nine—was immediately all over me. I managed to dribble in front of her but she stuck close to my behind. I could hear Coach Deetz—and probably my father—screaming at the ref, but no whistle blew, not even when I felt the not-all-that-subtle push in the small of my back. Why did Selena have her panties in a bunch about fouling these chicks? People were getting away with full-on groping out here.

Pressure makes perfect. The words took shape in my head before I even told myself to think them. *Other people fall apart—you come together. Simple as that.*

My breathing slowed down and I could feel myself coming into focus. Now all I needed was for Selena and M.J. to come together too. I should have gone over the play with them once more, especially since M.J. was a little ADHD. Now I couldn't exactly yell "Half-court trap!"

M.J.'s dark eyes darted around helplessly as I continued toward the half line, where once I crossed there was no going back. No way I could point to where I wanted her to go with Nine all up in my dental work. I finally barked, "M.J.—corner!"

I hated sounding like a pit bull, but at least she got it and moved to the corner of the attacking half of the court. That drew the nasty Number Twelve over there, which was perfect. Nine stole the ball from me and passed it right to her.

Immediately M.J. was on her, those wonderful brown arms of hers working the air. Coach Deetz always told her to

"Remember the Alamo, Martinez!" A racially sensitive man, our coach. Selena didn't join her like I hoped she would, but Hilary, bless her, did, red hair escaping from her ponytail, freckles oozing sweat. The two of them trapped Twelve so she couldn't dribble out. Okay, so they *had* heard me. This was the team I loved.

Twelve only had five seconds to hold on to the ball before she did something with it, and I pretty much knew she was going to try for a skip pass.

Tennies squealing across the boards, I sprinted down the court. Kara was diagonal to me. I assumed Selena was behind me somewhere, hopefully keeping Nine from chasing after me and climbing up my tailpipe. I turned in time to see Twelve raise both arms over her head, pale and long and flexible as cooked pasta, and make a long lateral pass. Right into my path.

I jumped for the ball and let it settle into my hands with the leather-smacking sound I lived for. I immediately passed it to Kara, who dribbled it all of two times while I took off toward the goal.

Opposite lower corner, Kara, I told her with my eyes. *Just like in practice.*

She made the quick transition like the pro she totally could be and passed the ball high and toward the lower corner of the backboard. Even as I focused I could hear the crowd moan because they thought she'd missed the shot. But the ball went right where I wanted it to go — right where I could catch it as I pulled myself straight into the air, right where I could twist and make the basket without ever touching the ground. *Cassidy Brewster Wins It with an Alley-Oop,* the headline would say.

I heard it swish, making my second-favorite sound on earth. Then came my most favorite — the unanimous surprised cry as the buzzer blasted. Seventy to sixty-eight in the last seconds.

All of that rippled through my mind before gravity started to pull me down. And just as quickly it was all jolted out. Somebody else was there, below me. I felt her heat as I twisted to avoid coming down on top of her, and suddenly I was Gumby — all my limbs hyperextending and taking off on their own.

When my right foot landed without the left, I felt a pop in my knee, and then the shiny court floor slapped me in the face. I just lay there while my team celebrated around me and the crowd screamed "Cassi-DEE, Cassi-DEE," and the pep band burst into the Austin Bluffs fight song, trombones pumping as if the star player *weren't* lying in a crumpled heap on the ground.

I rolled over and looked up the legs of the person I'd slid down in my graceful path to the floor. They weren't the lithe limbs of Number Twelve. These were way more slender and way more familiar.

"Selena!" I said. "A little help!"

But it was Kara who crouched over me first. "Cass, you okay?"

I nodded, because I wasn't really in pain. Ticked off, yes, but not hurt.

Not until she hauled me up and I got to my feet—and collapsed like I was trying to stand on top of Jell-O.

"Cass—*what?*"

"What's going on?" Coach was there, bumping Kara aside as he went to his knees beside me.

"I'm fine," I said. "Seriously. My knee's just weird."

Coach muttered something religiously profane under his breath and yelled, "Somebody get the doc!"

"No, I'm okay," I said. "Let me just stand up—"

I pushed his hairy arm away—something I wouldn't have done if my head hadn't been going into panic mode—and struggled to my feet again. This time I tumbled before I even put my full weight on my right leg. This time a whole tangle of hands got me to the ground.

And this time I didn't get up.

*

"I don't see any swelling," Dad said. "It's probably just a strain. We'll put some ice on it when we get home."

Jimmy Sanchez, our trainer, gave him a polite-looking nod, but he mostly just kept putting his hands on my knee joint. I could see it in his narrow eyes: *And where did you go to medical school, Mr. Brewster?*

My father wasn't a doctor. He was an attorney, although not an especially interesting one. He worked on publishing contracts—stuff like that. You would have thought at that moment, though, that he'd gotten his MD from the University of Colorado, the way the two vertical lines were digging a trench in the skin between his dark eyebrows. And the way he was firing questions at me.

"How much pain are you in, on a scale from one to ten?"

I propped myself up on my elbows on the table they'd stretched me out on in the hall behind the gym and shook my head. "Two—maybe three."

"If it were serious she'd be hurting worse than that," he said to Jimmy.

I think that was what he said. I was more interested in the crowd that was still cheering in the gym. The pep band was on their third playing of the *Rocky* theme. I should be out there with my team, celebrating our title.

"I'm not going to swear that's what it is," Jimmy was saying to Dad, "but I'd get her to a doctor if it starts to swell."

"She's tough. A little ice, a little ibuprofen—she'll be good to go."

Jimmy looked about as convinced as a ten-year-old on Santa's lap. "I want you to try to put weight on it again, Cassidy," he said. "If it's—"

"Look, I think we've already established that she can't walk on it yet." Dad's blue eyes and everything around them were coming to a point like a drug-sniffing dog. It was weird how eyes that pale could get that intense. Even Jimmy, a nurse practitioner specializing in sports medicine, shrugged and backed off.

"Take the crutches then," he said. "I'll get you an ice pack."

"We've got one at home," Dad said. "You can hop out of here, can't you, Cass?"

"Home?" I said. "The whole team's going out to celebrate."

"If you want to play next week, they'll have to celebrate without you." Dad nodded me off the table. "I'll cook you a steak."

"Rest, ice, and elevation," Jimmy said. To the air. Because

my father already had his long fingers curled around my arm and was helping me hobble one-legged to the door.

"Thanks, Jimmy," I said over my shoulder.

"Don't mention it," he said back. But his eyes were glowering straight at my dad.

It wasn't that my father was some kind of monster. He definitely didn't look like one. He was tall. Pretty thin except for the slight paunch that he could totally get rid of if he'd do something besides direct my athletic career. His hair was all white, even though he wasn't *that* old, and with his goldish skin, it was sort of striking. That was what my friends' mothers would say when they first met him: "Your father is so striking." After they got to know him, they didn't say much about him to me at all. Nobody did.

By the time we made it halfway down the hall, Coach opened the double doors from the gym and herded the team through them toward the locker room. Most of the team dodged around him and headed for me. I supported myself with the wall and grinned.

"You're okay!" Kara said. Most of us had lost the ability to squeal like that at age six. Not my Kara. She could seriously pierce your eardrum.

"Not okay enough to go out partying, if that's where this conversation's headed," Dad said.

"Then we'll bring the party to you!" That came from Hilary, who hadn't been around my father enough to know you didn't tell *him* what was going to happen. Although she was pretty much known for blurting stuff out and then folding all her freckles into a smile and getting away with whatever came from her mouth. Even Coach didn't yell at her. That much.

"We'll pick up pizza and drinks," M.J. said. "Who's got money?"

"Not me," Selena said—though I was sure she did. Her father *was* a doctor. She was probably the only daughter of a plastic surgeon who actually went to public school. "I'll drive, though."

The usual complicated process of figuring out who was

riding with whom drowned out any protest my father might have staged. Coach took him aside, which gave me a chance to grab Kara.

"Will you ride with me, *please?*" I said. "I'll owe you."

She didn't even have to ask why. I had long ago decided that was the definition of a best friend: somebody who knew the things you hated and would make sacrifices so you didn't have to suffer through them. It was the same reason I always invited her to spend the night with me when her older sister came home from college, so she didn't have to go shopping with her. Kara hated shopping. I hated riding home from games and practices alone with my father.

But even having Kara sit in the front seat of the Escalade with my dad, babbling on about how I stole the county title right out of Monument Valley's hands, didn't save me entirely.

"It was a total alley-oop," Kara said, twisting around to look at me propped up in the backseat.

"Barely." Dad looked at me squarely in the rearview mirror. It wasn't just the snow falling that made me wish he'd keep his eyes on the road. "If you'd missed it, they would have had it. There was nobody there to rebound. My question is, how did you let the score get that close in the first place? You could have outplayed that entire team."

By "you," he meant "Cassidy," not you, the Austin Bluffs varsity girls basketball team. What was Kara—roadkill?

I didn't answer. I had come to accept that the raw material that made up me came from my father. He was six foot five and played basketball in high school and college, and until I started playing when I was ten, his idea of a good time was shooting hoops at the gym with his other I-could-have-played-pro-ball buddies. That I could see myself doing someday. What I couldn't do was give it up to live through my kid and watch her play my game for the rest of my life. I would still get out there and dribble and pass and shoot. And I wouldn't use the car as a moving interrogation room she couldn't just jump out of to get away from me.

I'd considered that more than once.

*

We could barely see Pike's Peak for the snow that was turning the cars in the driveway into hulking white mounds when we pulled up to the house, but I could tell that one of them was my mother's Jeep Liberty. It was nine thirty. She should have been at the studio, gearing up for the ten o'clock news, especially with a storm blowing through. Although, come to think of it, snow in February in Colorado Springs wasn't exactly a breaking story. Still, the head meteorologist never missed a broadcast. I could prove that by the number of my games she'd missed. Like every one that wasn't played on a Saturday, which was most of them. We were sort of even, though. I rarely saw her gigs at six and ten, either.

She greeted us in the garage when Dad drove in. She was still in her television clothes and on-camera makeup, and her long-in-front, short-in-back hair was sprayed into a helmet. None of it hid the "Trent, what the Sam *Hill*" in her bluer-than-blue eyes.

"Imagine my surprise when the entire athletic department showed up at the front door," she said as Dad lowered his window. "A little something you forgot to mention on the phone?"

"I didn't know you were coming home."

"You didn't think I would?" Her eyes shifted to me in the backseat. "Cass, are you okay?"

Kara squeaked out a signature squeal. "She rocked, Mrs. B! You totally missed it—she scored the winning point with, like, zero seconds to go."

Mom had already opened my door and was now peering in. "How bad is it?"

"It's not," Dad said. His glare in the mirror was probably meant for both of us. "You didn't need to come home, Lisa."

"Evidently I did." She directed those blue eyes—the only thing I inherited from her except our blonde hair painted with honey, which I personally thought looked better on her—toward the headlights that beamed up the driveway. "Is this the opposing team arriving now?"

"It's probably the food," Kara said, and scrambled out of the car to go pretend she needed to help Selena and M.J. and Hilary with the pizza. There was only so much family tension even a best friend was willing to put up with.

I'd have split too, if I could have done it without my knee collapsing under me. I'd stretched my sweatpants over it, but as far as I could tell it still wasn't swelling. It just felt weird, like I might be able to bend my leg in the wrong direction if I tried.

"Get some ice, Lisa," Dad said.

The quills immediately rose along the back of my neck. I usually found an excuse to be gone by the time one of their conversations got to the him-ordering-her-around stage, so I wasn't sure what was going to happen next. Like I said, under any other circumstances the Frenemy would have me out of there.

The Frenemy had been my constant companion since I was about seven—that prickly sense of anxiety that sickened me when I was learning fractions or square roots or irregular Spanish verbs, or following my friends into the bathroom to gossip, or anything that didn't involve a layup or a free throw. I knew exactly when I started calling it the Frenemy. Until then it was just The Prickly Thing or The Prickly Thing with Quills the Size of Knitting Needles. But the summer before eighth grade I heard somebody on a tell-everything-about-celebrities show—one of those women with eyebrows like perfect apostrophes and voices that go up at the end of every word—referring to some of the loser-girl stars as Frenemies. They're pretty much always together but can't stand each other. And I thought, "That's The Prickly Thing. It's constantly there and I hate it, but I think it's what keeps me from showing everybody how terrified I am." That's why I fell in love with basketball—because the Frenemy didn't play with me. She sat on the sidelines and, unlike my father, she didn't scream instructions. She didn't know anything about the game.

But she was fully operational now as I watched my parents exchange glares over the front seat. My mother broke the evil spell first.

15

"Which knee is it, Cass?" she said.

Before I could even point to it, Dad gave a hissy sigh and said, "If you would just get some ice ..."

Mom disappeared and I somehow climbed out of the car and hopped toward the door to the house with my father at my elbow. He put his hand on the doorknob, but he didn't turn it.

"I'm not saying it doesn't hurt, Cass," he said. "But you can't play any game unless you can take a little pain."

"It really doesn't hurt that much," I said—for about the twentieth time.

He got a smile in his eyes. "That's my girl. So, we won't let this turn into a bigger issue than it is."

"Right," I said.

He used the word "issue" a lot. Actually, at the moment my only "issue" was him.

But that disappeared the minute I got inside the door and the team started chanting "Cassi-DEE, Cassi-DEE." I was on the big leather sectional sofa in the family room with my knee encased in ice and my foot propped up on pillows like the Princess and the Pea before I could get them to stop.

"We're a team," I said. "We *all* rock."

"Okay," M.J. said from her perch behind me on the back of the couch. "We do."

Kara put a slice of pizza with pineapple and Canadian bacon—my favorite—on a paper plate on my lap, but I looked instead at the second team, lined up on the stone hearth across from me with longing in their faces.

"*All* of us," I said. "Emily, you're totally the free throw queen."

"True," Hilary said. "You just need to get fouled more often."

Emily's face blanked. "Really?"

"No, doofus!" M.J. bonked her on the head with an empty water bottle.

Emily grinned and ducked and turned the color of a pepperoni. She was a sophomore and still pretty much all arms and legs, but I was working with her. We were losing M.J. and

16

Hilary after this year, and Emily could maybe fill one gap. At least on the court. I didn't like to think about them graduating and breaking up the UN.

"It didn't matter how much I got fouled, it never got called." Selena was sitting on the floor, legs folded in their usual perfect girly-girl bow. "I think every one of those refs needed glasses."

"It's not like they're not watching you," I said. "Everybody watches you."

Beside me, Kara gave a variation on her squeal.

"What?" M.J. said, tapping her with the bottle again.

"Will Mathers was watching you."

"How would you know that?" Hilary said. "You were supposed to be focused on the game."

"I was!"

Yeah. While we were actually in play. But during time-outs it was nothing for Kara to be checking out the stands to see who was with whom. If it hadn't been for me dragging her into basketball when we were in sixth grade, she'd probably be a cheerleader right now. Nothing wrong with the rah-rahs, but what a waste of her athletic ability that would have been. It was a good thing I had some serious influence on Kara.

"Okay, speaking of hot guys," said Jennifer, one of the second-team girls. She was craning her neck forward, head lowered like a great white heron. We, of course, all leaned in.

"Were we talking about hot guys?" Kara whispered.

Jennifer slanted her eyes toward the kitchen. When I followed with mine, I let out an industrial strength guffaw.

"That's Cassidy's brother," M.J. informed her.

"So? He's still a hottie."

"An engaged hottie."

"Still ..."

Still nothing. My twenty-three-year-old brother might *look* like dating material—we're talking Brewster-blue eyes, chiseled-out features, and Dad's once-dark hair, which probably meant he was someday destined to be "striking." But in my opinion, he had all the charm of a parking meter. What his fiancée, Gretchen, saw in him was totally beyond me.

"Hi, Aaron!" Kara called to him — because she would have thought Saddam Hussein was wonderful if you just got to know his heart.

I suppressed an eye roll when he actually stepped down into the family room and surveyed the group. They were rewarded for their attention with a half smile. Big throw-up.

"Close game," he said. "You pulled it out."

"Were you *there?*" Jennifer said.

That was my question. Aaron in a gym was like me at a fashion show.

"Yes, he was there." Gretchen, my future sister-in-law, looped a long, graceful arm through his and gave him an I-won-this-round smile. I guess. Actually, Gretchen smiled the way models on the front of *Cosmo* do, lips parted like something smelled funny. Of course, she *was* standing next to Aaron.

"I told him he needed to support his sister."

Everybody looked at me, so I tried not to let my lips fall open. Most of the time, Gretchen acted like she had too much to do to notice that Aaron even *had* a sister. Aaron himself was always saying she never even took the time to delete her text messages or throw away moldy leftovers. Interesting how *she* could get away with being "messy."

"Congratulations, by the way." She gathered her thick, pale brown hair into her hand and let it drop to her shoulders. "I have a question, though. Are you, like, actually having fun out there? I mean, you all just look so serious."

Ohmygosh. She was like Aaron's clone. Of *course* we were serious. Some of us had scholarships riding on games like that. A recruiter from the University of Tennessee, Knoxville had already been to see me play. The Lady *Vols* . . . although obviously the significance of that would be lost on both of them.

"So I heard you messed yourself up," Aaron said to me. "Gretch wants to see it."

"Ick!" Jennifer said

"She's a doctor, Einstein," M.J. said. She was apparently in charge of dispensing all my family details to the uninformed. It occurred to me that Jennifer had never been to my house before. I was going to have to fix that. If you didn't play together off the court, you weren't going to play that well together on it.

"I'm not a doctor yet," Gretchen said as she picked her way among the bodies to get to me. "I'm only a third-year med student."

There was an impressed silence as Kara scooted over and Gretchen sank onto the couch beside me. I handed somebody else the ice and proceeded to roll up my pant leg.

"It's no big deal," I said. "It doesn't even hurt that much. I felt worse when I had that concussion last season—"

A unanimous gasp cut me off. That and the Spanish profanity that slipped out of M.J. Every eye was on my knee, and mouths were gaping in horror—because it was swollen to three times its normal size.

"I think you've blown your ACL," Gretchen said.

"Is that bad?" I said.

The way she looked at me, she didn't even have to answer.

CHAPTER TWO

hey don't know for *sure* it's my ACL," I said to Coach. "I get the results of the MRI back this afternoon."

Coach Deetz glared out onto the practice court like he hadn't heard me, like he was totally focused on the team doing suicide sprints—or not doing them. But even when he yelled, "You're slackin' off, Kara. Irish—what are you, backing up? Any faster and you might actually start moving!" I knew he was chewing on what I said right along with his Trident gum.

"What exactly did the doc tell you?" he said between chomps. "And no editing, Brewster."

I resituated the crutches, which had been rubbing my armpits raw all day. "He said my knee is too swollen and the muscles in the back of my upper leg are too tightened up for him to do, like, the usual movement tests to tell if my 'anterior cruciate ligament' is messed up." I slanted him a look to see if he was impressed. He wasn't, so I went on. "That's why they had to do the MRI yesterday, which is like being in a coffin, by the way. Dude—did you see the way M.J. just made that cut? Awesome!"

Coach gave a grunt. "Did you hear a pop when you fell?"

"Kind of. Mostly all I could hear was everybody screaming." I nudged him with my crutch. "We won the title—or did you miss that?"

He finally pulled his little beady browns away from the team and let me see one of his "that's very cute, Brewster" looks. The shaved head, the bullet eyes, the allergic-to-smiling lips were never that intimidating to me. Not when I considered all the little things he did with his face. I'd caught onto that freshman year, and I kept seeing new ones all the time.

"You've had jelly for a knee ever since," he said.

"Yeah, but I didn't have that much pain until it started to swell, and that didn't even start until like an hour later."

I didn't add that the doctor had said that was typical for a torn ACL. For once I agreed with my father. We shouldn't make a bigger "issue" out of it than it was.

"Anyway, I'm a fast healer," I said. "I should be able to at least play in the state tournament, even if I have to miss district."

"Look, Cass—"

"Whoa—did you see Emily pull away from Hilary? She is gonna be killer next year. Wait—are you thinking of putting her on first team while I'm out? That's what I was thinking—"

Coach put his whistle in his mouth and blew. "All right—layup drill."

I watched them form two lines, and for the first time since sixth period started, I ached to be out there. Suicide sprints I could live without, but this was team stuff. I should be in the middle of it, with my practice shorts bagging around my knees like theirs were, wiping my face on my shirt the way they were doing, with my hair, too, all sticking out of its bun like scarecrow parts.

"Sit, Brewster," Coach said. "Get that thing elevated."

"I can't see that way, Coach," I said. "I'm fine—I've been sitting all day."

"Sit."

I did. It was harder to tell if Kara was making her shots now—

"Look," Coach said. To his hands. In a very un-Coach-like way that yanked my eyes off the court. "You play this game like it's been pre-programmed into you. It's like you could play basketball before you ever set foot on a court."

The Frenemy was suddenly there, which was weird, since she almost never followed me into the gym. It was also weird that Coach was laying all these compliments on me.

21

"You get every skill the first time I show it to you. I can charge you, hurl a ball at you, guard you like a gorilla, and you handle it without batting an eye."

"Um, thanks," I said.

"You're a gifted athlete, Cass, and I'm not gonna let you throw that away."

"I wasn't planning on it."

"Good."

He blasted the whistle and shot up from the bottom bleacher. "All right, let's step it up!" Sneakers squealed—and so did Kara, out there in her pink high-tops. Coach pulled a folded newspaper from under his clipboard and tossed it at me. "Did you read the article?"

"Yes."

"Read it again."

He took off with a sneaker squeal of his own. The Frenemy scraped her quills down my backbone like fingernails on Styrofoam. Okay—*what* was going on?

The *Colorado Springs Gazette*, which had landed lopsided in my lap, was folded to the story Mom had read to me the morning before in the doctor's office waiting room. *BREWSTER LEADS AUSTIN BLUFFS TO COUNTY TITLE*, the headline read. Next to it was a picture of me in midair, swishing the ball into the net. Ten seconds before I crashed and burned. Right now that same picture was hanging from magnets on our refrigerator door—right where my father could point out the errors in form I was displaying. I really didn't want to read this again.

But the difference between Dad pointing something out and Coach doing it was like the gap between T-ball and the Colorado Rockies, so I blew out a big puff of air and started in. I was only a sentence into it when I realized Coach had highlighted several things in yellow: "There is a precocious sophistication to Cassidy Brewster's game. She knows how it's supposed to be played—with poise, balance, and elegance ..."

Dude, they made me sound like a ballerina. At least it didn't say *for a player so young*. I was glad when the sports reporters stopped doing that, although I still didn't see myself as "poised"—at least not off the court. In every picture I ever saw of myself when I wasn't playing basketball, my lips were big and out of control, my smile was stupid-sloppy, and I had enough eyebrows for my entire team. Unlike my mother's, my cheekbones were not chiseled. In the mushiness of my face, I couldn't even find them. It was a good thing you didn't have to be *Seventeen* magazine material like Selena to be an athlete.

The article continued. "Brewster is an excellent shooter, a precise passer, and a willing team player with an aggressive, attacking style. With natural leadership, she inspires the Austin Bluffs players to well-orchestrated offensive patterns."

I turned the paper over on my thighs. The Frenemy parked herself squarely in the middle of my chest. So, what was with Coach loading all this praise on me? He always expected more from me than he did from the rest of the team, but as for pumping me up—usually all he did was tell me not to get a head so big he couldn't close it in a locker if he had to. I should have basked in this. Instead, it was freaking me out. At the moment, Kara had nothing on me.

Out on the court, Selena stood outside the paint and netted a nice shot that didn't even hit the backboard and barely swung her ponytail. Except that she could just as easily have missed it. She should have passed it to Kara, who was in prime position for an easy layup and who needed the practice in faking out a defender—although there wasn't one, because Emily wasn't where she was supposed to be. I'd have directed her if I'd been out there. Coach blasted the whistle. Now he was going to, and it wouldn't be pretty.

I hiked myself up and ignored the throb in my knee as I crutched myself out onto the court.

"All right, look here," he was already saying to the tops of their heads as they all bent over at the waist, breathing like locomotives. "We're gettin' higher in the competition, and the skills are gonna even out. It's not about who can shoot now—" He pointed a look at Selena until her face came up. "It's about

23

pride, courage, and a willingness to put your body in harm's way. I'm talkin' character — and toughness. I want to see some Cassidy Brewster aggression out here — because she isn't gonna be there to bridge the gap."

Backs straightened and gazes shook themselves out to land on me. Kara looked like somebody had just slapped her.

"Is she out for the rest of the games?" Hilary said.

Coach didn't answer, which was an answer in itself. I shook my head, but everybody suddenly seemed to be staring at my knee in horror, as if a possible torn ACL were a contagious disease.

"We don't know that yet!" I said.

"The point is, you have to be able to do this with her or without her, you get me?" Coach stared them all down until heads bobbed. "All right, I want to see some primal aggression out there. Emily — stop guarding like you're tending a house plant. Selena — this is not a one-woman show."

He attacked the whistle again and they jolted into action — all except Kara, who was patting her pockets like she was looking for her cell phone so she could text me. I wanted to mouth to her that it was okay, but Coach was nodding me toward the bleachers, a place my crutches didn't want to take me.

"The state tournament's not for two weeks," I said to him as the tennis shoes squealed behind us. "I'll be ready to play by then — right?"

He planted one hand on the waistband of his baggy sweats and rubbed his nose fiercely with the other. It was his "why are you arguing with me right now?" look, but I didn't care.

"I'll do whatever it takes—"

"You said you weren't planning to throw your career away."

"Right, so—"

"To me that means that if being out for the rest of the season means you can play for the rest of your life, you'll make the right choice."

The Frenemy started a full-out attack. "So that means missing *all* the postseason games? Even All-State — if I made it?"

"There was no 'if' about that—"

"Was?" I said.

Coach jerked his chin at the newspaper I'd left on the bottom bleacher. "I'm not the only one who sees what you're capable of. And I'm not going to let you risk a shot at the WNBA for a high school tournament."

"But it's not just about me!" I said. "What about the team?"

"You don't think they can pull it off without you, Brewster?"

No, I didn't. And from the way he sent his gaze out over the court, he didn't either. We five knew where each player was supposed to be without having to look. We had our own private hand signals. We even knew who was due for PMS when.

"We're a *team*," I said. "We're the freakin' UN —"

"See what the doctor says." He put up his hand, and then he turned again to the court. I knew *that* look. He was done.

But I wasn't. I so wasn't.

*

Sixth period was called Basketball Conditioning, and it satisfied our PE requirement. The real practice was after school, and I had to miss it that day because Dad was picking me up to go to the doctor. I watched for him through the snow-flecked glass from inside the front door of the school so he wouldn't come into the gym. There was always something about seeing him with Coach that made Dad seem like even more of a Doberman pinscher than usual.

Don't get me wrong, Coach was intense too. He could yell until his veins popped up like blue tubes under his neck skin. I guess he tended more toward a rottweiler. But for him it was like, "Here's what you're not doing. Now go do it and later we'll have a pizza." Dad never yelled — or offered rewards of food. With him it was like —

It was like me getting into the car that afternoon and him starting in.

"How's the pain level?" he said.

"Maybe four," I said.

"So, better than this morning."

No, but I didn't feel like hearing a lecture on what I must

have done wrong to drive it up to its current six. I had run out of Motrin before lunch.

He switched on the wipers to slap away the flakes from yet another snowstorm that had blown in just to annoy him—or so you would have thought from the trench between his eyebrows.

"I looked it up online, Cass," he said. "If this is a torn ligament, you can beat it with physical therapy. I've already researched a couple of people to interview. One guy's in Denver, but if that's what it takes, that's what it takes."

He reached over and squeezed my good knee, and I felt a lump come up in my throat. He really could be decent at times—

"But here's the thing—it's like I was trying to tell you Tuesday night. Being a great athlete, not just a good one, is about going beyond exhaustion. It's about being the intimidator—not the intimidated. You can't let this thing beat you. You're going to have to get in there and fight it—and that means not shrinking from the pain."

As usual, I wasn't sure what I was supposed to say. But if I didn't say *something*—

"Are you hearing me at all? Because I'm not saying this for my own benefit."

"Yes," I said.

He fired up the defroster with an impatient flick of his wrist. "That's it? Just 'yes'?"

"I'll do whatever it takes," I said. Just to get you off my back.

And yet that wasn't entirely true. I would do it because I couldn't *not* do it. I didn't just play basketball for my father, although he was the one who got me started when he put the hoop and backboard up on the front of the garage for my brother. Aaron never touched it, and my mother thought it was an eyesore, but the first time I dribbled up to it and dropped a ball through that hole, I was hooked.

I was ten years old.

There wasn't a team for my age in Colorado Springs at the

26

time. Dad practically had to go to the mayor to get me on the one for eleven-year-olds, and by then I was dribbling backwards, forwards, sideways—making seventy percent of my free throws, scoring from eight feet out—and guarding my six-foot-five father.

I was five foot four then, and I hadn't even hit my growth spurt yet. But I wasn't all arms and legs like those stick figures you draw when you're three, with the limbs coming straight out of the head. That was kind of how the other players looked.

I played center my first year on the club team. It was, literally, a whole different ball game playing with an entire team, as opposed to scoring against my dad and anybody else he could drag onto our driveway. But I picked it up fast, and any thought I ever had about any other sport faded in the face of my love affair with that orange leather ball.

The team only practiced three days a week and had one game a week, but I was out there under my own net every morning before school, every night after, and most weekends. I heard my mother tell my father I needed more balance in my life. My father told her I was basically an athletic prodigy. Aaron said I was messed up in the head. All I knew was that when I was going for a rebound or faking out a defender, the Frenemy didn't exist. That had to mean it was what I was meant to do—which was what they were always talking about in church. Finding God's purpose for your life. I had mine.

So, no, my dad didn't make me play basketball, and he wasn't going to have to force me to do physical therapy. No—what he did was squeeze the joy out of it.

*

Of course, there wasn't much joy to be squeezed out of an orthopedic surgeon's office. Not when the doctor looked you right in the face and said, "The news isn't good, Cassidy. You've definitely torn your ACL."

I blinked at him, took in his perfectly round glasses and his fuzzy red-blond hair that thinned over the top of his head, and wondered if he'd ever loved a sport. I couldn't imagine it, or he wouldn't have said it, like, "Your season's over. Your team's doomed. Tough break."

"How long will it take to heal?" I said.

"It won't." Dr. Horton folded his arms and leaned against the counter. "Once it tears it has to be reconstructed."

"Physical therapy can do that?"

"No — surgery does that. Physical therapy teaches you how to walk again afterward."

He unfolded one arm to point to a wall poster of a bunch of muscles crisscrossing each other and went into a long explanation of how the anterior cruciate ligament works and what it controls — while I fought to keep the Frenemy from hurling me to the floor in a fetal position.

Surgery? Somebody might have mentioned that in the last two days, but I hadn't heard it. All I heard was how hard I was going to have to work to get back in the game, how I was going to have to intimidate the pain and not let it beat me. How had I missed the part about being cut open on an operating table?

"I have to have surgery?" I said into the babble that was still going on over the poster I didn't care about.

"It can be treated non-operatively," Dad said.

"Sure," Dr. Horton said. "But you'd never be able to participate in sports again like you do now. Even with intensive physical therapy, if you play with an unstable knee, the damage to the meniscus and the articular cartilage could lead to severe arthritis and destroy your knee joint at a young age. You'd be looking at several knee replacements in your adult life."

He didn't need to tell me all that. He had me back at "you'd never be able to participate in sports again like you do now." I was already nodding, though with a lump the size of a softball in my throat.

"It's not going to be a big issue, Cass," Dad said. "So don't start stressing."

Dr. Horton shook his head. "Actually, it *is* a big surgery. We're talking about completely rebuilding a ligament with — "

"Okay," I said. "When can we do it?"

He nodded toward my exposed knee, whose cap was still

28

buried under puffiness. "Not until the swelling is resolved, which could be two to four weeks, maybe longer."

"Weeks?" I said. That would put us right in the middle of the state tournament. If I couldn't play, I at least had to be there to help on the sidelines. No way I could wait that long.

"You're going to have to have better range of motion before we go in," the doctor was saying, "and those thigh muscles have to be firing well. That's not going to happen with this swelling."

The trench between Dad's eyebrows had turned into a canyon. "Can you explain to me how this happened to an athlete in peak condition?"

"Perturbation."

Oh. That cleared it up.

Dr. Horton turned to me. "Somehow you were thrown off balance the instant just before the rupture."

"So you're saying she landed wrong," Dad said.

Naturally it would be my fault.

"It's like stepping off a curb awkwardly because you've been jostled," the doctor said, demonstrating with his hands, "only at full speed and force. Your foot didn't hit the floor the way you planned, did it?"

"It didn't hit the way it usually does," I said. I would rather have talked about cutting into my kneecap with a scalpel. This conversation was going to give my father endless stuff to lecture me about before we even got to the car.

"If, for instance, you had your plant leg in front with your knee locked, the way you guarded it kept you from flexing it, and more than likely you came down flat-footed. It's a classic situation — happens to girls in basketball and soccer all the time, no matter what kind of shape they're in."

Dr. Horton looked at Dad, but my father was calculating my leg with his eyes. Maybe I could catch a bus home.

*

As it turned out, the Frenemy kept me from hearing most of what Dad said on the ride to our house. The snowstorm also kept him from saying everything he wanted to, I was sure. So while he scowled at the windshield and crawled us through traffic, I tried to breathe through the anxiety without sounding like I was hyperventilating. It was already my own careless fault that I'd gotten hurt—to paraphrase my father. I didn't want to add to that by "starting to stress" over this surgery that just wasn't a "big issue," no matter what that specialist with the medical degree said.

Besides, Aaron's Saturn was parked in the driveway when we got there. Dad was the least of my worries when my brother was around. Maybe they'd get into it about the wedding or something and I could escape to my room.

I thought I was in luck. Gretchen was setting the table in our kitchen, and Aaron was opening containers of takeout Chinese, and there was a candle burning on the counter. They obviously wanted something badly from Dad, and they were more likely to get it with me out of the way.

I put the crutches into high gear and was swinging through the kitchen when Gretchen said, "Where are you going, Cassidy? We thought we'd have a family dinner."

"Mom's not here," I said, stupidly. Mom was never there for dinner. She was getting ready to tell all of Colorado Springs that it was snowing again.

"Eat with us, okay?" she said. "And then you can go do whatever."

She had her hair all bunched up in her hand, ready to let it drop to her shoulders in that thing she did, and her very round, very liquid gray eyes did look sincere. This was the second time she'd acted like I might actually count. I didn't feel that much like eating, but I nodded and parked my crutches and sat at the table.

"We picked up brown rice, white rice, and fried rice because we didn't know what everybody would want," Gretchen said.

I forced myself not to roll my eyes. "You'll want the brown, of course," I said to Aaron. "And could you pass the fried to Dad?"

I smiled sweetly.

Gretchen stared at Aaron. "Why didn't you know that?"

I didn't tell her that it was signature Aaron not to know

what anybody in his family liked except himself. She'd figure that out soon enough.

"You were right, Gretch," Dad said.

"About?"

"Cass's knee."

"ACL?"

He nodded, his mouth as grim as Oscar the Grouch. "We're looking at surgery and physical therapy. But she's never been one to back away from a challenge, so ..."

He nodded hard enough to give himself whiplash and reached for the moo goo gai pan. I hated it when he talked about me like I wasn't even in the room. And when he referred to "we" when it was actually "me" he was dissecting. And when he—

"So you really messed it up," Aaron said. To me. "How much physical therapy are we talking about?"

Gretchen pondered a piece of cashew chicken poised between her chopsticks. "Probably six to nine months. Depends on how extensive the surgery is."

"I don't know about 'extensive'—but I can tell you right now it's going to be 'expensive.' Great." Aaron tossed his own chopsticks on the plate.

"What's 'great'?" I said.

Gretchen put her hand on his arm.

"*What?*" I said.

"This is probably going to mess up you getting a scholarship too." He rubbed his thumb and forefinger together. "How much more do you think you can squeeze out of Mom and Dad before you're done?"

"Yeah, that was my plan—to hurt myself so I could take my parents down financially. Are you *serious?*"

Gretchen was wringing Aaron's arm by now, but I could have told her it wasn't going to stop him. He and I had been fighting practically since the day I came into the world and challenged his role as the anointed one. Even in photographs of us together when I was an infant, it looks like he's thinking, "I don't want my picture taken with *her*. She's messing it up." In his view, I had been messing it up ever since.

31

Gretchen raised her hand. "Can I say something?"

"Absolutely," Dad said.

She put her fingers around *my* arm this time. "Athletes come back from ACL injuries all the time. And just to keep it in perspective, there's no reason why you couldn't get an academic scholarship. Aaron says you're bright."

Aaron stopped in mid-bite. "Just for the record, I never said that. I said she takes honors and AP classes, and in this family it's not like she has a choice. No offense, Dad."

"None taken. You're absolutely right."

"Yeah, well, you can't get a scholarship for physical therapy. And insurance only covers, what, eighty percent? Over a nine-month period, that's got to run you into the tens of thousands—"

"It's not like it's coming out of *your* pocket." I had long since abandoned my chopsticks, my plate, and my appetite and was pushing myself away from the table.

"Yeah, Cassidy, it is." Aaron's eyes snapped over to Dad. "You want to tell her or you want me to?"

"I don't want anybody to tell me," I said. "I'd rather go do AP Geometry than hear it, actually." I seized my crutches and then glanced at my father. "May I be excused from the table?"

Dad waved me off while Aaron squinted at me. Gretchen seemed to be looking around for an arm she hadn't squeezed yet.

"I want her focused," I heard my father say as I hurled myself through the family room. "I'll deal with this other thing with you privately."

"This 'other thing'?" Aaron said.

Gretchen must have wrung the lifeblood out of his wrist because I didn't hear anything else, except my almost-slam of the door to my room. It was the closest I was allowed to get to a door-related expression of anger in our house. The fact that my knee wouldn't even let me flop into my green fake-leather beanbag chair just made me madder.

I had dragged the beanbag in from the Goodwill pile in the garage when I turned twelve and the Frenemy took up permanent residence in my being. I think my father had the "chair" in his bachelor pad before he and Mom were even married, and she thought she was going to get rid of it while he was out of town on business. I commandeered it as the perfect place to do battle with myself without making a sound.

Since it was now impossible to throw myself into it and beat it with my fists, I stretched out on the bed instead—and felt like a stick with a heartbeat. There was nothing I could do to stop the Frenemy from surging right up my backbone with her guilt-producing quills.

Great. Wonderful. Excellent. You landed wrong. You ripped out your knee. Your team's going to bomb without you. And, as if that weren't enough, you're now costing your parents tens of thousands of dollars—which gives your brother all the proof he needs that you are what he's always said you were: messed up.

I struggled up to prop myself on my elbows. That last part I didn't get—at all. Why did Aaron care so much about Mom and Dad's money? He had his scholarship or fellowship or whatever it was that was completely paying for grad school. His fiancée was going to be a doctor, for Pete's sake. If she made even half as much as Selena's dad, they were going to live better than my parents in a couple of years.

I let out a grunt as I sank back into the pillows. Maybe he was worried about his inheritance. Maybe he was thinking they'd die suddenly and he could live off what they left him and not have to work. Dude—Mom and Dad were only in their forties. If I didn't know my brother better, I'd think he was planning to bump them off. That would be way too messy, and he didn't like messes. That was why he didn't like me.

A tap on the door sent the Frenemy quills into a frenzy again. That would be Dad, coming to finish what he hadn't gotten around to in the car.

"Yes?" I said, trying to sound as if I were deep into a geometry theorem.

"Cassidy, it's me," Gretchen said. "Can we talk?"

I was so glad it wasn't my father I actually smiled when I told her to come in. She slipped in and shut the door soundlessly behind her and did a quick visual inventory of my

T-shirt quilt hanging off the end of my bed, my bulletin board bursting with photos and notes and certificates and all other things basketball, my open dresser drawers belching out all the clothes I'd rejected that morning because I couldn't get them over my leg.

"Have a seat," I said, "if you can find one."

She chose the corner of my four-poster bed and hooked one arm around the pole. I suspected she was leaving the other one free in case she wanted to squeeze my arm. She was obviously going to be one of those touchy-feely doctors.

"I guess you're wondering where that whole thing with Aaron was coming from," she said.

"Where it usually comes from," I said. "He thinks I'm 'messed up.'"

"Actually he doesn't," she said, voice lowered like we were planning a conspiracy. "He might not say it, but he's proud of you."

"Whatever," I said. This chick was going to be in our family for a long time. I didn't want to start out by telling her she was a whack job if she believed that.

Gretchen did the hair thing, and I watched the mass drop to her shoulders. "That business about the money just now — there's more to it than you know."

"Uh-huh."

"Aaron and I want to buy a house — we've found one that's perfect, in fact — and your parents were going to give us the money for the down payment as a wedding present."

The essential word there was obviously "were." That was the second time today the past tense had sent knitting needles through my heart.

"And now they're not because of my medical bills," I said.

"That's a possibility." Gretchen spread a long-fingered hand on her chest. "Your dad says he doesn't have all the data yet."

I could just hear him saying that. How many fathers would refer to their daughter's crisis as 'data'? If Gretchen thought this was making me feel better, she needed to consider a career change.

I shrugged. "So what does Aaron want me to do? Even if I don't have the surgery, I'm still going to have to do physical therapy—unless he expects me to tool around in a wheelchair for the rest of my life."

Gretchen leaned forward. Here came the hand onto my arm. "Aaron is still wallowing around in the problem. He does that. But meanwhile, I might have a solution. I think I can help you in a way that will get you and I both what we want— *and* get Aaron and your father off you."

I felt my eyes narrow. "What 'way'?"

She tightened the squeeze. "I have an idea, Cassidy. But we're going to have to keep it strictly between us."

"You mean, keep it a secret from my father?" I laughed bitterly. "Like that's going to happen."

"I get that," she said. "But I can help you gain a little independence here."

I couldn't help warming up to that. In fact, it was all I could do not to give her the nod right then. Except that I couldn't imagine pulling off anything that didn't have my father's fingerprints all over it.

"So what do you say?" Gretchen nodded as if I'd already agreed.

"I'll have to think about it," I said.

And then I did. All night long.

CHAPTER THREE

I was still "thinking about it" first period Monday morning. In theory I was listening to a lecture by Mr. Josephson about how he expected better from Junior Honors students than he'd gotten on the papers he was about to hand back. In reality I was going over what Gretchen had said, and wondering how I could possibly do anything my father wasn't going to know about.

Mom wasn't really a problem. She was never home when I was during the week anyway, and when we did run into each other it was usually before school and before her second cup of coffee. Our conversations were like:

"Hi, Cassie."

Mumble.

"School okay?"

Mumble, mumble.

"Need anything?"

"Unh-uh."

"Love you."

"Loveyoumore."

"Loved you first."

Sometimes that bugged the heck out of me. I mean, what were we saying? Whatever it was, did we even mean it?

But since I wasn't much of a morning person either, it was usually okay. I would choose those conversations over the ones I had with my father all day long.

Which was exactly the point. I could barely think a thing without him being all over it. That was what was attractive about Gretchen's insistence that her idea I didn't know about yet had to be carried out in secret. I was all for anything that didn't involve him. The man even knew when my period was due. Seriously. Still, just thinking about sneaking around stirred up the Frenemy. Even at that moment she was tying my stomach into a knot.

"Miss Brewster . . ."

I jerked my head up in time to see Mr. Josephson drop my essay on Longfellow on my desk. Face down. Not a good sign. I waited for his coffee-breath-and-Old-Spice aroma to fade down the aisle before I turned it over.

A giant C.

So much for an academic scholarship. I sure hoped that wasn't Gretchen's mysterious solution to my problem.

Mr. Josephson had written something in the margin in blue. He always said he didn't use red to grade our papers because it was demoralizing to get back a piece that looked like it was bleeding to death. I didn't see what difference it made to be critiqued in blue. It just felt like you were being *royally* ripped apart.

"If you put as much energy into *this* pursuit as you do into your other one," he had written, "I might be putting an A on this composition."

I slid the paper into my binder and made a note to myself to throw it away later. I didn't need another reminder that things were slipping away from me. My knee was doing a great job of that already.

"Copies of *The Scarlet Letter* are on the table," Mr. Josephson said.

He always sounded like he was disappointed and barely daring to hope that the next thing he tried with us was going to work. From what he'd told us about *The Scarlet Letter*, I wouldn't put any money on it if I were him.

He nodded his mop of steel-gray hair toward the front table where the paperbacks were stacked. "Sign out a copy and read chapter one. There'll be a vocabulary test on it tomorrow."

"Where's the word list?" Selena said.

"There isn't one, Miss Chen. Just know the meaning of every word in there and you'll be fine. Get a book for Miss Brewster, would you, Miss Chen — and just hand it to her. We don't need you slam-dunking."

Selena and I exchanged eye rolls. Like Mr. Josephson would know a slam dunk if somebody executed one into his file cabinet.

Between the groaning and the semi-chaos of book sign-outs, I managed to sneak a look at my text messages. One was from Kara: *We're taking you to lunch.*

I let myself grin. That would get me through to fourth period, and if the rest of the morning went anything like the way it was starting, I was going to need that.

The other one was from Gretchen: *Call me if you want to meet today.*

I felt my grin fade. Every time I thought about it, I had to fight back the Frenemy with both hands. I wasn't the sneaking-around type — not unless it involved faking out an opposing player on the court. Maybe if I thought of my dad that way ...

No chance. Why did I have to have an attorney for a father?

*

"We're late," Kara said. Whined. Her whine was even more ear-piercing than her squeal.

Hilary glanced at her in the rearview mirror, even as she screamed her beater Nissan into the student parking lot. She looked forward in time to dodge a pile of dirty snow that had been scraped together by the plow. It was a good thing she didn't play defense the way she drove or we wouldn't have gotten within a hundred points of the county title.

"We still have three minutes."

"It takes five to get Cassidy out of the car." Kara snapped quickly to me. "Not that I mind. I'll take a tardy for you, no problem."

"Then why are you freaking out?" M.J. said from the front seat.

"Because it's what she does," I said. "You guys go ahead

38

and get to class so you don't get in trouble. I already have an excuse."

Hilary jerked the car into park and twisted to look at me. "You have P-W this period?"

"Yeah."

"Forget about it. She'd make you get a pass if you were late to your own funeral."

That was true about Mrs. Petrocelli-Ward. In spite of the tattoo on her arm that she had designed herself and enough jewelry for thirty-seven people hanging around her neck, she was a stickler for stuff like being on time. I'd heard her say it about a thousand times since September: *Just because you're an artist doesn't mean you can't be responsible.* I wasn't an artist; I was just taking her class to fulfill my humanities requirement, since the music teachers were all extremely weird and the drama coach was known for having nervous breakdowns in the middle of class. Of course, when I found out that half the people in my fifth period art class were emo Goths and the other half were taggers, I questioned my choice.

"I can get to the office myself," I said. "Seriously, you guys go."

"You sure?" Kara whined.

"Positive."

"We have thirty seconds," M.J. said.

Hilary was already waving to us from across the parking lot.

"*Vámonos*," M.J. said to Kara.

They lit out in pursuit of Hilary, and I followed, planting each crutch gingerly between icy puddles and plops of gray snow. I might as well have been traveling backward. Each tall, lanky figure disappearing inside the doors made me feel farther away.

And then there was the long hall to the main office to navigate. People had tracked in snow and left it to melt into puddles I had to somehow maneuver around so I wouldn't take a dive onto the tile and blow my other knee. By the time I got to the attendance counter, I had broken a sweat under my jacket and would have yanked my knitted cap off my head if I'd had an extra hand. My knee was also throbbing. On Dad's pain scale I was up to about seven and a half. And because whenever things couldn't seem to get worse lately they always did, there was a line at the counter, people complaining that the "road conditions" made them late from lunch. The attendance officer, whose name I didn't know but whose face made me think it could be Winston Churchill, wasn't buying any of that. With seven people in front of me, she nodded, jowls wiggling, for me to take a seat.

There was only one vacant chair, and I wouldn't have sat in it if I could have stood up another second. The kid in the one next to it was one of the taggers in my art class. I wasn't into vandals.

I tried slanting myself away from him, but my left crutch slipped and landed in his lap. I had to say, "Sorry."

He grunted.

I assumed the conversation was over, but then he said, "What are *you* doin' in here?"

"Waiting for a table," I said. "I heard the sushi's really good."

At least I got some benefit from all my years of defending myself with Aaron. The kid — I thought his name might be Rafe — shut up.

For about five seconds. Then he said, "No, for real — what are you doin' in here? What'd you do?"

"I'm here for the same reason everybody else is here," I said. "I need a late pass."

He snickered. It might have been the single most demeaning sound I'd ever heard.

"*What?*" I said.

"Not me."

"Huh?"

"I'm not here for the same reason everybody else is."

"Great. I'm happy for you."

I inspected the line, but it didn't seem to be moving. Mrs. Petrocelli-Ward was going to give me a detention whether I had a late pass or not at this point — if I ever actually made it to fifth period.

"You want to know why I'm here?"

I looked back at Rafe. He was leaning onto his knees, both arms dangling in the sleeves of a fleece-lined denim jacket. He was running a narrow paintbrush back and forth between his fingers, which were brown but not as dark as M.J.'s. I'd never really thought about it before, but he looked sort of Hispanic, but not totally. Cappuccino-colored skin. Thick, wavy dark hair, like something out of an old black-and-white film about juvenile delinquents. Wide forehead that hooded his dark eyes like a built-in disguise. His lips were surprisingly full, as if they belonged on a pouty female model, although I sure wasn't going to point that out to him.

"So do ya?" he said.

"Do I what?"

"Wanna know why I'm here?"

"You stole that paintbrush from the art room?" I said.

He let out a *shhheeee* sound obviously meant to make me feel like an idiot. I squinted at him.

"Look, I don't really care why you're here, okay?"

"I know why *you're* here."

"Right—because I told you."

He shook his head. "You're here because you fell on your—"

"No profanity in here, Diego," said the woman at the counter. I was impressed. He hadn't even cussed yet.

"Come here often?" I said.

Rafe wiggled his eyebrows, which, on closer inspection, were even bushier than mine. "You wanna know why?"

"No."

"We're here for the same reason."

Porcupine quills went up my back, and they weren't from the Frenemy. I squinted harder at Rafe until I almost couldn't see him.

"No," I said. "You're here because you're a loser."

He didn't so much as blink. He just looked at my knee and at my crutches and into my face.

"Yeah," he said. "Like I said—we're here for the same reason."

A door opened and Mr. LaSalle, vice principal in charge of

anything that could get you thrown out of school, jerked his buzz-cut head at Rafe.

"Come on in, Mr. Diego," he said.

Rafe unfolded himself from the chair and moseyed over to the door, shoes swallowed by his pant legs.

We are SO not here for the same reason, I wanted to call after him. But I didn't need to. I knew I wasn't in the loser category. Right?

I glanced up at the Winston Churchill lookalike. She was absorbed in filling out a form like it was a police report. I slid my cell phone out of my jacket pocket and thumbed out a text to Gretchen.

Where should I meet you?

I didn't think I was a loser. But there was no harm in making sure.

*

"Why did we have to come all the way out to Black Forest?" Kara said. "If Gretchen wanted coffee, why didn't you guys just meet at Pike's Perk?"

I didn't want to tell her that Gretchen chose an out-of-the-way place on purpose. And I hated that I didn't want to tell her, because normally I wanted to tell her everything. Kara knew that I thought the bagger at Safeway was cute, and that I still slept with a nightlight on, and that I always diagrammed basketball strategies on the back of the bulletin during the Sunday sermon. This felt like I was keeping something from my own self.

"She says it's off Black Forest Street," I said. "It's supposed to look like something out of *Bonanza* on the outside. Make a right here."

Kara made the turn with her tongue peeking out of the corner of her mouth like she did when she was concentrating. Coach was always telling her to keep it in or she'd bite it off if she got hit.

A severed tongue probably wouldn't keep you out of the postseason tournaments, though. I had to remember why I was doing this.

"What's *Bonanza?*" she said.

"Don't you ever watch TV Land?" I said. "It's an old cowboy show."

"Then that must be it right there."

She swerved off the road and into a parking space in front of a porched building with a single table outside, braving the cold. The car behind us blew its horn and tore off.

Kara squealed. "I forgot to signal!"

"He was following too close," I said.

"No—I'm a moron." She switched off the ignition and dug her hands through her disaster of curls. "I'm just totally stressed. I shouldn't even be driving."

"Now's a great time to tell me that," I said drily.

"I'm sorry! Are you okay? Did you hurt your knee again?"

"I'm fine, Kar." I looked around but I didn't see Gretchen's green Mazda anywhere. She'd said to meet her at 4:30 and it was only 4:20. Coach had let the team go early because nobody was focusing. I had a minute to calm Kara down before I sent her home.

"Are you stressed about practice?" I said.

She nodded, face miserable. "We were horrible. I mean, don't you think we were?"

How was I supposed to answer that? Fortunately I didn't have to, because she gurgled on.

"M.J. can't ever find anybody to pass to, even when we're like 'woo-woo' practically in her face."

True.

"And Hilary's guarding okay, but she missed every single shot."

Also true.

"Nobody ever passes the ball to Emily—especially not Selena. She acts like Em's not even out there."

True again.

"Here's the thing, though," I said. "You're seeing all that, which means you can totally be a leader."

"Me?" Kara's blue eyes widened big as Frisbees. "You mean like you were—are?"

"Hello, yes. Who taught you how to play basketball before you ever tried out for a team?"

She didn't have to answer. She was the one who decided we were going to be friends ten minutes after she came to our middle school church youth group for the first time, back when we were in sixth grade. I probably wouldn't have picked her — she was even ditzier in those days. But once it was clear she wasn't going to leave me alone, I was the one who decided the terms for our becoming BFFs: she was going to have to learn to shoot, dribble, and pass. Personally, I think she would have learned to commit armed robbery if I'd told her to.

It turned out that even though she wasn't the best athlete to ever put on a pair of high-tops, she was coordinated and worked hard, and once she and I got on a team together, she was all about that. Give her a gang of girls and she was happy. Except for right now. Her hands were jittering on the steering wheel like she'd OD'd on caffeine.

"You only have to get through district," I said. "I'll totally work with you before my surgery. And I'll be there for state — probably not playing, but I can help you."

I didn't add that it might be even better than that, depending on what Gretchen had in mind. I snuck another glance at the parking places, but she still wasn't there.

"You should go in," Kara said. "You want me to help you?"

"No. I want you to tell me what else is going on with you."

She didn't even deny that there was something. She just dropped her forehead to the steering wheel. A whine would be next.

"It's not just what's happening on the court," she said. "It's all the other stuff."

"What other stuff?" I said. And why didn't I already know about it? My neck prickled.

"Okay — we asked Selena to go to lunch with us today and she made up this lame excuse about having to take a makeup test."

"How do you know it was an excuse?" I said.

"Hello! How could she have missed a test? She's never absent!"

True. Selena came to school when she had strep throat and a fever of a hundred and one. It must be as hard having a father who was a doctor as it was having one who was a lawyer.

"Besides, in the locker room I asked her how her test went and she goes, 'What test?'"

"Seriously?"

"Yeah. What's that about? You always say we have to have trust off the court or we can't trust each other on it. Right?"

Right. Trust. It took all I had not to blurt out everything about Gretchen and invite Kara to sit in when I talked to her.

"I'm probably blowing the whole thing out of proportion," she said. "I'm just freaked out because you're not out there with us."

"Maybe I will be," I said.

Her eyebrows sprang up. "Really? Are you serious?"

"Maybe," I said. "Look, I can't tell you everything right now, but ... just trust me, okay? It's all gonna be fine." I opened the car door before I could say any more. "I'll call you later. Everything's cool, okay?"

She nodded because she was obviously going to cry if she said a word. I hugged her hard around the neck and pretended to be all involved in getting myself out of the car and up the steps. She waited until I was inside to pull away, and even then it took her forever. I prayed she wouldn't end up in a ditch.

Gretchen wasn't inside either, so I fumbled into a chair at a table and dropped my backpack onto the floor beside me. I unzipped it to stick my hat inside and was about to close it when somebody behind me stuck his arm out almost in my face.

I whirled around, ready to foul the dude if I had to, and I felt like a moron. It was a large dummy, dressed to look like a Native American. Of great wisdom, evidently.

"Sorry, pal," I said. I giggled nervously and turned around to make sure nobody had seen me make an idiot out of myself. The only person in there at the moment was a guy behind the counter, rearranging the flavored syrups on the shelf on the back wall. He didn't even look up. He was probably used to people thinking they were about to be assaulted.

I leaned back and took in the rest of the shop to get my mind off of the anxiety poking me in the chest. It was kind of quaint, actually, with benches made of carved wood and antique-looking knickknacks. Plaques lining the walls said things like "Overworked, Underpaid." My personal favorite was immediately "There Will Be a Five Dollar Fee for Whining." I took it as a sign that I was right not to bring Kara in with me.

Except that it wasn't all that comforting. The Frenemy was starting to freak out now that I was alone, and I did *not* want to be chewing my fingernails up to the elbow when Gretchen arrived. Not that I had any left. My toenails were the next candidates.

So instead, I put my hand on a *Sports Illustrated* from the table, one with Apolo Ohno on the cover. Good grief, how old was the thing? I picked it up and exposed a messed-up-looking leather book somebody'd left underneath it. What was up with that?

It didn't strike me as the kind of thing you had to hide so nobody would know you were reading it. Plenty of other people obviously *had* read it because there were crease marks and initials carved into the cover, all around what appeared to be two letters that were actually engraved: RL.

What was that about? Rude Language? Rockin' Lyrics? Radical Literature?

I looked around, but the guy behind the counter didn't look like he was missing a secret document. Where was Gretchen, anyway? The Frenemy had left me alone for a minute, but the quills were starting to poke again. My knee was also throbbing.

I looked down to lift my foot onto the opposite chair. The leather book was open flat in my lap, and either I was really losing it, or the thing was actually pressing into my thighs.

Not only that, but the words on the page were staring me in the face, like a guard on the court getting all in my business. I almost said, "What?" out loud. Until I read.

So you want me to get you on your feet again? the words said. *Your life's falling apart and you want me to build you up?*

Oh. One of those self-help books. Twenty minutes a day, three times a week, and you'll have firm glutes, strong arms and legs, and a toned, sexy core.

Wrong.

I stared at the word.

Wrong. Different kind of strength altogether. This you can't do on your own. Let me lay out the course for you. Then you can run.

"Run?" I heard myself whisper. "I can't even walk."

"Cassidy—hey!"

I jerked my head up. Gretchen was swivel-hipping her way among the tables, oblivious to the fact that her bag was nearly taking out every antique in her wake. I swept the book off my lap, and it landed in my backpack, but there was no time to fish it out. She was already parking in the chair next to me.

"Thanks for meeting me," she said. "You want something to drink? I love their Smooth-Talkin' Irishman."

I shook my head. "No," I said. "I just want to know what your idea is."

She closed her eyes and let out a long breath. "Good choice," she said. "Let's get started."

CHAPTER FOUR

I didn't take my eyes off of the two miniature Tupperware containers Gretchen put on the table, but I couldn't pick them up yet.

"So what are they again?" I said.

Gretchen put her fingers up to her mouth, but not soon enough to cover a smile. "It's okay, Cassidy—they're not poison." She folded her hands halfway between me and the pills and leaned in. "They're supplements," she said. "You've heard of creatine?"

I shook my head.

"Okay, well, they're similar to that. These will bring your swelling down like that." She pulled a hand out to snap her fingers. "And they'll strengthen the supporting muscles, which should shorten your rehab considerably."

"So it'll happen really fast?" I said.

"That depends on what dosage you take. The higher you go the more side effects you're going to have, but for the short time you're going to be using them, I don't think that's going to be an issue."

I brushed past the word "issue" and locked my eyes back onto the pills. "What kind of side effects?"

"You might be restless at night. Maybe a little cranky during the day."

I had to grunt. "I don't think anybody's going to notice a difference there."

"You look nervous about this," Gretchen said. "It's perfectly safe. I wouldn't be offering it if it weren't."

"That's what I don't get. Why isn't my *doctor* offering it to me?"

"Who's your surgeon? Horton?"

I nodded, and Gretchen rolled her enormous gray eyes. "He's not one to take any risks—"

"Risks?"

She erased that with her hand. "What I mean is that this is experimental. Most doctors stick with traditional treatments. It's the teaching hospitals that are willing to try new things. Besides, surgeons in private practice make their living with a little piece of steel. They couldn't care less about any meds beyond painkillers."

That kind of made sense—as much as anything could right now. The Frenemy had totally dried out my mouth and was pouring sweat from my palms. I hoped I never had to be interrogated by the police; I would probably be the youngest person ever to have a stroke.

"Talk to me," Gretchen said. "I want you to be totally comfortable with this."

I looked up into a face that was so completely focused on me it made me catch at my breath. The only movement was the blink of her thick lashes.

"I've heard a lot of stories about athletes taking supplements," I said. "Some people have gotten really sick."

"Oh, yeah—because they read about them in some magazine ad or let the clerk at the 'health store' sell it to them. I'm a medical professional—*and* your future sister. I'm trying to make you better, not worse."

"I guess I don't see why we have to keep it such a secret," I said. "My dad's going to take one look at me and know I'm hiding something."

"I've been thinking about that, and you know what? Your father doesn't strike me as being that sensitive. Especially when it comes to you."

"Are you serious?"

"It *looks* like he's into your every mood, but essentially he sees what he wants to see, and what he wants to see right now is you dedicating all your energy toward getting back into the game."

"That *is* what I'm doing."

"Yes. Just not for the same reasons." She did the hair thing. "Never mind—it's definitely not my place to be psychoanalyzing your father. I just get my hackles up over the way he treats you sometimes."

"No, go ahead," I said. My own hackles were actually smoothing down, as if she'd just stroked them with her hand. "I want to hear."

She pressed her lips together for a second. "Okay—not that he doesn't care about you and your career, but I sometimes get the impression that you being a basketball star is as much about him as it is about you."

"Ya think? He didn't make it into pro ball so now he wants to live through me making it."

"Right—but it's more than that. He thinks you becoming a WNBA star is going to make him look really good." She pressed her hand to her chest. "That's just my opinion, and my own experience."

"Did you play basketball?" I hoped I didn't sound as doubtful as I felt. Gretchen was only about five-five and way girly for a pair of high-tops.

"Soccer. I was on my way to playing for the University of North Carolina, for Anson Dorrance—he coached Mia Hamm, April Heinrichs, legends of U.S. women's soccer."

"Wow."

"But I blew both my ACLs in high school and tore the meniscus both times. I lost my scholarship. My mother was so bitter because I took away her glory, she wouldn't pay for me to go to college. I got this far totally on my own. If I'd made the Olympic team, she would have been right there with me on the front page of my hometown newspaper, telling everybody how much she sacrificed as a single mother to get me there. She pretty much sees me as a failure."

"You're becoming a doctor!"

"Doctors don't make their mothers famous." Gretchen gave

her head a small shake, as if she were bringing herself back from someplace. "Anyway, I never played soccer again, even for fun. I don't want to see your father take the joy of your sport away from you like my mother did from me."

"I'm really sorry," I said.

"Don't be. Because of that, I can help you. For one thing, you have a chance to do this on your own, without your father taking the credit. And for another—" She picked up one of the containers and jiggled it. "I didn't have this when I was where you are. You have a chance not only to have that knee healed, but to keep the other one from going."

I gripped the seat of my chair with both hands. I had to. For all the Frenemy's pokes and prods and stabs, telling me there was something wrong buried under this, I was close to snatching the container from her and downing the entire contents. There was one more thing I had to know.

"What?" she said. "I can see the wheels turning in your head."

"Is that the only reason you're doing this?" I said. "Because you know what it's like?"

She looked down at the tabletop. "I wish I could say I was that unselfish. I also—look, I love your brother."

I stifled the urge to comment.

"And as much as I hate the way your father is with you, I still love your whole family. Whatever your motives are and however sarcastic you can be with each other, you all do care, and I never had that. Ever."

I was startled to see the gray eyes start to spill over.

"I can do something to help your whole family, and that includes me, since I'm marrying into it. By doing this for you, I can take pressure off your dad, I can see that Aaron gets the house he wants for us, I can ease the tension for your mom, and I can do it without anybody knowing except you."

She gave me the inevitable arm squeeze. "You're going to be my sister-in-law, but I want it to be more than that. Who knows—this could create a bond that'll be there forever." Gretchen pulled her hand away and picked up her purse. "I'm going to get us some coffee. You think about it."

51

"I don't have to," I said. "I'll do it."

The smile she gave me didn't look like she smelled something suspicious. It looked like a smile one sister gave another.

I smiled back.

*

I'd expected the next few days to crawl past while I watched my knee for signs of shrinking, the way you wait for grass to show signs of growing. But they blew by, starting twenty-four hours after Gretchen gave me the supplements.

"You're going to pyramid starting Tuesday," she'd told me, "which means you'll increase the dosage each day for a few weeks, and then we'll decrease and then start over. But as you build the dosage, you'll start to see results. Plus, I'm stacking them, so you're taking two different types, which should speed things up."

She wasn't kidding. By day two I had so much energy I could have hopped from class to class without my crutches. I texted Gretchen, just to make sure this was the "speed" she was talking about, and she texted back, *You're right on track.* I was definitely getting a ton of homework done because I couldn't sleep that much, and I was right on it during basketball practices. It was like I could be all over everybody at once. Too bad I had to do it from the sidelines.

But even that didn't bother me as much, because the swelling was actually starting to go down by Friday, day four. When I texted Gretchen, she texted back: *Score.*

It wasn't that I didn't have my moments of doubt. That afternoon when everybody was dressing out and I was sitting in the gym, waiting for them, I couldn't help staring at my knee. Sure it was shrinking, but what did that really mean? I was still going to have to have surgery. Didn't Gretchen say she lost her scholarship because of her ACL injuries? Was the University of Tennessee seriously going to want a player with the evidence right on her flesh that she didn't know how to land?

"What's your problem today?"

I looked up at Coach, who was standing over me with both

hands on his hips and his head rocked to one side. That was his "I don't want to hear any whining" look. Kara got that one a lot.

I whined anyway. "Is this gonna ruin everything?"

"Only if you let it." Coach put a foot on the bottom bleacher and parked his forearm on his thigh. "Look, if college recruiters stopped recruiting girls who suffered ACL injuries, their pool of talent would dry up."

"Really?"

"I'm not lying to you, Brewster. You can do pull-ups, squat a hundred pounds, bench-press your weight. You have absolutely no fear. You're going to be the same fierce warrior in physical therapy that you are on the court, so quit feeling sorry for yourself." He pretended to kick my calf and stood straight up. "I want you to watch Selena today—see if you can figure out a way to get her to pass more instead of hogging all the shots."

"Okay."

"But you don't have to get in her face."

"I won't," I said.

They weren't out on the court two minutes before I saw exactly why Selena was going for the point instead of passing the ball. She was a lousy passer. I'd never really caught on to that before.

"Don't pass it to where she is, Selena!" I called from the sideline. "Pass it to where she's *gonna* be when the ball gets there!"

She didn't appear to hear me.

"Be ready to change direction, Selena!" I shouted, a little louder. "Don't shoot—fake her out! Come on—it's a game of deception!"

Selena stayed where she was and went for a shot from too far out. It bounded off the backboard. Coach blew his whistle long and hard and waved everybody over to the sideline. They stood in front of us, redoing their ponytails and breathing like freight trains.

Coach drilled his eyes into Selena. "Why did you take that long shot when Kara was open?"

53

"I would have made it if Cassidy hadn't been yelling at me," she said. I think. It was hard to tell since she was barely moving her lips.

"That isn't the point. Didn't you hear what she was saying to you?"

Selena stared at the top of the bleachers. "Was I supposed to be listening to her? I mean, is she the coach or are you?"

"Excuse me," I said. "Coach asked me to watch you because you've turned into a ball hog. It's not all about you, you know."

"Well it has to be about somebody since it's no longer all about you." Selena's eyes were in such tight slits I could barely see them. "I figured I was next up."

Fury raced right up my backbone. I jerked the tip of my crutch in the air and flailed it at her. "It was never all about me!" I screamed at her. "It's not all about any one person, it's about the team."

Selena grabbed the crutch with both hands and pushed it toward me, but I shoved it back. She dropped to the gym floor — and I stood over her. "That's your problem — you're not even thinking about anybody else! What is going *on* with you?"

"With me? Look at you — you're losing it."

"All right, that's enough." Coach Deetz stuck his arm between us, and something crazy in me knocked it away with my crutch. The next thing I knew he and I were nose to nose, and I was sucking in air.

"Sorry, Coach," Selena said from the floor.

I whipped my head around to look down at her. That was clearly not true. I'd never seen cheekbones poke out like that.

"I just won't be coached by her," she said.

"You'll be coached by whoever I tell you to be coached by or you're out of here," Coach said. "We don't have time for girl drama." He turned to me. "And *you*—"

"I'm sorry," I said. "I'm just frustrated."

That was clearly not true either. What I felt leaking out of me went way beyond frustration.

Coach gave me another long look. "All right. You two work

54

out your personal stuff outside the gym. Right now — Selena, I don't want to see you take another shot today, you got that? Every time you get the ball, you pass it." He smoked smoldering eyes over the rest of them. "And I want you passing the ball to Selena every chance you get. Except M.J. If you have defenders on you, Alamo, I want you to practice rising up in traffic and shooting — no fear. You're warriors — turn it loose!"

Heads bobbed at him, but most eyes were on me. Everybody looked confused, like they wanted me to say something. I started to, but Coach blasted the whistle and they retreated to the court.

"I know this is hard for you, Brewster," he said when they were beyond earshot. "But you either lighten up or I'm not letting you back in my gym."

I nodded. But I knew it was going to be hard. I could actually feel the energy racing through my veins with my blood. If I could just slam a basketball against a wall a couple of times, I might be able to calm down.

Instead I propped myself up with my crutches and sought out Selena with my eyes.

"What you have to remember," Coach said, close to my ear, "is that you can't coach heart and you can't coach passion. If it ain't there, it ain't there."

I nodded and pressed my hand to my still-heaving chest. *It ain't there*, I wanted to tell him. *It's here*.

*

By the time M.J., Hilary, Kara, and I got in M.J.'s car after school, my urge to blow up had done a pivot, and I was up for a fit of giggles. None of them were.

We weren't even out of the student parking lot before Hilary was twisting around in the front seat to face me. Even her freckles looked stressed out.

"Okay, so what's with you and Selena?"

"I have no idea," I said. "I was just doing what Coach told me and I guess she couldn't take it."

"He told you to scream in her face?" M.J. said.

"She didn't scream in her face." Kara's eyes shifted. "I mean, not that much."

"It was about to turn into WWE." Hilary got up on her knees so she could look at me full-on over the front seat.

"Put your seat belt on or you're gonna get me pulled over," M.J. said, but Hilary was apparently on a mission.

"You need to be careful, Brewsky. You can totally see how mad she is. She didn't say a word to any of us the whole time in the locker room."

"She was talking to you." M.J. looked at Kara in the rear-view mirror.

I looked at her too. She was squirming in the seat like she needed a restroom.

I nudged her. "What did she say?"

"Nothing."

"You are such a liar!" Hilary said. "Tell us."

"She was just stressing," Kara said. "She didn't mean any of it."

"Any of what?" My need to giggle hysterically had long since disappeared. I didn't even care that Kara's face was draining of all color and that any minute now she was probably going to open the window and throw up.

"She just said she hates it that you act like you're so perfect. And she said that even though she learned a lot from you when she first came on the team, she would never admit it to you because you already have an ego the size of Russia." Kara lowered the window an inch. I could see beads of sweat on her upper lip. "She just needed to vent."

"So what did you say to her?"

Kara blinked at me.

"Did you defend me or what?"

"Of course she did," Hilary said. "You need to chill, Brewsky."

But I didn't take my eyes off of Kara. I could hear her voice spiraling into a whine inside her head.

"I said we were all under a lot of pressure and we probably need to go have pizza together or something."

"And?" Hilary said.

Kara shook her head.

"That's it?" I said.

"What did you expect me to do, Cassidy? Why are you getting all over me? I didn't even do anything."

"No," I said. "You sure didn't."

Hilary turned back around and changed the radio station. Kara stuck the earphones to her iPod into her ears and closed her eyes. M.J. took a different route than usual and dropped me off first.

*

I was on the phone to Kara thirty minutes later, crying and apologizing.

"I don't even know why I said all that stuff," I told her. "Everything's just so weird right now."

"It's totally fine," she said. I could tell she was crying too. "I should have told Selena you don't think you're all that — but I guess I was just trying to keep the team from falling apart."

"Don't worry about that," I said. "I think it's all gonna be okay."

I could say that, because at that moment I was looking at my leg. I could see my kneecap again.

*

Coach wasn't as excited about it as I thought he'd be when I went to his office before school Monday to show him. He said, "Yeah, great," but it was like he was thinking about something else totally. I had no idea what that could be. The team had made it through the district finals that weekend, with me going ballistic from the bench. They were going to state and I was going to be there to help them. What was his deal?

"Are you okay, Coach?" I said.

He shook his head and came around to the front of his desk and sat on the corner. I noticed that the cup of coffee near his thigh didn't have steam coming out of it. He must be preoccupied if he'd let his morning java get cold. Usually he winced when he drank it, like it was burning his taste buds off.

"I got a tip that somebody ... I need to do a drug test on everybody on the team."

Frenemy quills stabbed me right in the heart. Was this about the pills I was taking? No—I wasn't taking drugs. I was taking supplements. Right? I forced myself to speak slowly.

"Somebody's doing drugs?" I said. "Who?"

Coach shrugged. "It was an anonymous tip, but Mr. LaSalle thinks I need to follow up on it. He's having the boys' team take one too."

Even as I shook my head I knew I was doing it harder than I had to. "Somebody's just messing with you, Coach," I said. "Nobody on our team's using—I'd know about it."

"I hate having to do this. It makes the team think I don't trust them."

"Nobody's gonna think that," I said. It came out as a shout—as if it came from somebody who would actually yell at her coach—but I kept on. "Everybody just needs to calm down. If anybody says anything like that about you, I will seriously—I don't believe this!"

I heard my crutch crash into the side of his desk before I even knew I was swinging it. The coffee cup jittered and fell over, splashing its contents across the scatter of papers. I stared at it—but I wanted to throw it against the wall.

When I brought my eyes up, Coach was using a look I'd never seen him give me before. His mouth was halfway open, and he was pulling his chin all the way into his Adam's apple.

"What is going on with you, Brewster?"

"Nothing—"

"That was not 'nothing.' Now talk to me."

"Y'know what, I think I need to just go and get my act together—"

"No. Why don't we just do your drug test now?" he said. "I think I'll do them one by one. There'll be less drama that way." He looked me straight in the eye. "We've got enough of that already."

He had no idea. There was a full-length tragedy going on in my head—with me center stage trying to explain the supplements that showed up in my urine. Maybe they wouldn't. And it shouldn't matter if they weren't illegal, like Gretchen said.

She did say that, didn't she?

Or did I ever ask her?

*

It was a good thing I gave my urine sample then, because Dad picked me up in the middle of third period for my appointment with the surgeon.

"I got you in early," he said. "The way that swelling's gone down, there's no sense putting this off."

For once I agreed with him.

"They didn't believe me when I called in." Dad reached over and squeezed my shoulder. "I told them they don't know Cassidy Brewster."

They still didn't seem to believe it even when Dr. Horton examined my knee for himself.

"I have to say I was skeptical when I saw you were coming in," he said. He adjusted his round glasses and peered at my leg again as if it were going to grow right before his eyes. "But we're there. Let's schedule the surgery."

I so wanted to grab my phone and text Gretchen. This was turning out even better than either of us had expected. Maybe that was because I'd increased the doses of the supplements a little faster than she said to.

"You're still going to want to limit your movement."

I looked up at Dr. Horton. "I'm sorry?"

"You're jiggling your legs. That's going to aggravate the inflammation." He grinned halfway. "You a little hyper?"

"She hasn't been able to get any exercise," Dad said, as if it were Dr. Horton's fault I'd ripped open my ligament.

Dr. Horton flipped through the pages of my chart. "You just seem more restless than you did the other day. I guess you're used to being on the move."

"Twenty-four/seven," I said, hoping the Frenemy wasn't

59

creeping into my voice. Gretchen had used that exact word—
restless—when we talked about the side effects of the supplements. I calmed myself down with the other things she
said—about Dr. Horton not being one to try an experimental
treatment.

"So—how about Thursday?"

"This Thursday?" Dad said. "You can do it that soon?"

"The sooner the better."

"That's great—"

"No," I said.

They both looked at me as if I'd screamed. Maybe I had; I
wasn't sure.

"That's the first night of the Final Four. I have to be there."

Dr. Horton turned to me. "You realize you can't play, even
with the swelling gone—"

"No kidding? You don't understand—I have to be there
to help. Coach is counting on me, the team will fall apart—"

"And so will you if we don't take advantage of this
opportunity—"

"No! Make it Monday."

"All right, stop."

Dad's nostrils were flaring and he had his hand up, but not
to me. He bore down on Dr. Horton. "I don't think you appreciate the importance of this. Cassidy has UT Knoxville looking
at her. Pat Summit."

"I have star athletes in here on a daily basis," Dr. Horton
said. "And I get the majority of them back into their game
in a timely fashion. But that's because they let me be the
doctor."

I almost screamed that I had a doctor who was already better than he was, and she was only a third-year medical student.
But I was too surprised that Dad was actually standing behind
me on this. I chomped down on my lip and waited.

"Friday is the best I can do," Dr. Horton said. "I'm out of
town for two weeks after that. The longer we hold off on physical therapy, the longer it's going to take to—"

"Okay—Friday," I said. I could at least get the team off to

a good start. And they could bring the state trophy into the hospital room and we could celebrate together.

"You okay?" Dr. Horton said.

"She's fine," Dad said.

Yeah. I was fine. The tears running down my face were just another emotion that came out of nowhere.

CHAPTER FIVE

I s it just me," Hilary said, "or does this pizza smell like the inside of my gym locker?"

M.J. sniffed her slice and shook her ponytail. "I think that's you you're smelling."

"It *is* gross, though," Kara said. And then she gave me a nervous look across the cafeteria table. "Not that I'm complaining."

"What would you call it, then?" I said. "If you guys wanted to have lunch off campus, why didn't you just go?" I felt myself squint. "It's not like I can't entertain myself. I blew my ACL, not my personality."

I got the same reaction from them I'd been getting all day. Come to think of it, the last *several* days. Eyes bulged and then darted to some random location. Shields came down over faces. Kara opened her mouth and then closed it — probably because she couldn't find a way to make it okay. What was the deal? I was just speaking the truth.

Hilary put up a freckled hand and rubbed at the air like she was erasing everything we'd said in the last five minutes. "Okay — so what I want to know is, who said somebody was taking drugs? I mean, how humiliating was it to hand a cupful of pee to Coach Deetz?"

"Yes, hello!" Kara looked like she could have kissed Hilary's feet at that moment. "That was, like, so embarrassing."

"Why?" M.J. said. "Everybody's pee looks the same."

"Hopefully."

We all turned to Hilary.

"What if somebody's was different?" she said. "What if somebody *is* using?"

"Don't be stupid!" I said.

"Yikes, Cassidy." Kara's voice dropped like it was toppling off a cliff. She glanced over her shoulder, face going scarlet. "Do you have to tell the entire world?"

"Everyone drop the drama," Hilary said. "Here comes Coach."

"Good," I said. "He's gonna tell us everybody's clean, and we can get focused again. What do you want to bet the anonymous tip was from some other school we're playing, just trying to throw us off?"

Hilary narrowed her eyes at me. "I think it's working."

Before I could demand to know what she meant by *that*, Kara chimed in with, "Hi, Coach!" and dazzled him with one of her "I have to fix this" smiles.

It didn't "fix" him. From the expression on his face, I figured that would have taken a lot more than a Kara smile. His look clearly said somebody had died. I hoped it wasn't me. I hadn't been able to get the vicious circle in my head to stop all morning: What if they found something in my drug test? So what if they did? I hadn't done anything wrong—besides wave my crutch at people and scream.

"You okay, Coach?" M.J. said.

He didn't answer her. In fact, he didn't even seem to know anybody else was at the table, except me.

"We need to talk, Brewster," he said.

My stomach turned inside out, and it wasn't a Frenemy attack. It was genuine fear. Somebody on our team really was using cocaine or smoking marijuana. Nothing else could have made Coach Deetz look that way. Not even somebody taking secret supplements.

I turned to Kara. "Could you—"

"I'll watch your bag," she said.

I grabbed my crutches and followed Coach out of the cafeteria at a double-swing. He didn't look at me until we were around the corner and headed for the gym wing.

"Who was it?" I said.

He gave me a look as blank as paste and shoved open his office door. Okay, it had to be somebody important. Selena?

I stopped breathing. M.J.? Hilary?

My Kara?

Coach went behind his desk and shuffled papers like he was searching for something and then abandoned them to look at me. I was still standing, crutches up in my armpits. Evidently this wasn't going to be the kind of conversation you sat down for.

"Is there anything you want to tell me, Cassidy?" he said.

The fact that he was calling me Cassidy went straight through me. I shook my head. "I don't know who it is, Coach, I swear I don't. If I did, I would've told you, no matter who, even if—"

He put up both hands, eyes closed as if I were spitting instead of speaking.

"I *swear*, Coach—"

"You tested positive for juice, Cassidy."

"Juice?"

"AAS."

"I don't even know what that is."

"Anabolic androgenic steroids."

"*Steroids!*"

My voice went higher than Kara's had ever gone, and I could feel my eyes swelling in their sockets.

"Performance-enhancing drugs," Coach said. "What in the world were you thinking?"

"I wasn't—I mean, I'm not—taking steroids ..."

I let the words trail off as another voice whispered, *They're supplements—experimental, perfectly safe—*

"Don't even try to take me there." Coach's mouth was trembling, as if only sheer force of will was keeping him from opening it and screaming at me.

The way I'd been screaming at everybody else for days.

"They're *steroids*? I thought they were just—to take the swelling down and strengthen the muscles—"

"What do you think steroids *do*? While they're pumping you full of testosterone, making you go off on people—"

"I didn't know they were steroids, Coach. Honest!"

I stopped, because every syllable sounded desperate and defensive and false.

And because he wasn't believing any of it. In place of the trust I'd always seen in his eyes was a look I never thought would be directed at me. It was the purest form of disappointment.

He sank into his chair and jerked a finger in the direction of mine. I would have crawled across the floor if he'd told me to.

"Where did you get it?" he said. He wasn't using any name at all for me now.

"A doctor—sort of," I said.

He threw his head back, hand skimming across his bare scalp.

"Is she going to get in trouble?"

"If I have anything to do with it. But I think you need to be worrying about the trouble *you're* in." He rapped the papers on his desk with his knuckles. "I have to report the results to Mr. LaSalle."

"But I didn't do anything wrong! I didn't know!"

"Do your parents know you're taking it?"

I shook my head.

"Why haven't you told them?"

"Because—for a lot of reasons." None of which even made sense to me right now.

"You thought they were okay, but not okay enough to tell your parents." He lurched back in the chair. "I never thought I'd be having this conversation with one of my players—but especially not you. *Especially* not you."

His voice was thick, his eyes red-rimmed. If he cried, I was done. Somebody really would die, right here in my chair.

"It was stupid!" I said. "I just wanted to be able to help the team—"

"Help the team?" He came forward, almost across the desk. "By screwing with your body? By cheating?"

"I would never do that!"

"Why didn't you come to me?"

"I didn't think—"

"No. You didn't. And now we've got a mess on our hands. A big mess."

I nodded and stared at my knees until they disappeared in a blur of miserable tears. There were so many guilty, self-hating quills firing into me, it was all I could do not to hurl myself from the room. But what good would that do? I couldn't get away from me.

"What do we do?" I said.

"I have no idea what *you're* going to do. An hour ago, I thought I knew you. Now—" He picked up a paper and tossed it away from him. "I do know you, Brewster," he said without looking at me. "I've seen you do the beautiful things that don't show up on the scoreboard. I couldn't be that wrong."

"You're not," I said. "I am that person. I'll prove it to you."

His eyebrows went up.

"I'll just tell the truth," I said. "Which is what I should have done in the first place. Please—just let me tell my parents first, and they'll ..." I closed my eyes. "They'll look at me the same way you're looking at me and I won't be able to stand it."

"They can't get you out of this," Coach said. "I have to report it to Mr. LaSalle. But you're right—you're going to need their support."

Our eyes locked, and for the first time since the office door had closed behind us, I knew we were thinking the same thing. Just exactly how much "support" was I going to get from my father?

"I'll give you twenty-four hours," Coach said. "I want to hear from one of them by this time tomorrow."

I tried to say thank you but the sobs in my throat blocked the way. I flung out my hand and knocked my crutches to the floor.

"I should have known it," Coach said. "You were showing all the classic signs."

"She said I'd just be a little cranky and restless," I said.

He hissed. "No, Brewster, that was 'roid rage. Somebody

66

sold you a bill of goods. I'd like to get my hands on her, and sooner or later somebody's going to have to."

I nodded into the palms I was now smothering my face with. I couldn't go there yet.

"It's almost time for the bell," Coach said.

"I can't go to class like this."

He didn't offer me a pass to get out of Art. Of course not. You didn't bail out students you could no longer trust. I retrieved my crutches and struggled to attach myself to them again. Coach was already at the door, hand on the knob.

"Are you going to get in trouble for this too?" I said.

"I don't know. Like I said, I should have suspected." His eyes settled sadly on me. "But, then, why would I?"

I pushed my way out. I couldn't look at him anymore.

*

Somehow I got myself to the art room and asked Mrs. Petrocelli-Ward for a pass to the nurse. Anybody who knew P-W would have told me I was insane, but I was beyond caring. She looked at me, droopy-eyed, and pulled out her hall-pass pad.

"Are they going to do surgery?" she said as she scribbled.

I squeezed out a yes.

"I've heard it gets worse before it gets better," she said. "But before you know it, it will all be behind you."

With a nod I headed for the door and got out into the hall before the sobs choked out of me again. I had a feeling—a deep-down digging feeling—that this was never going to be behind me.

The nurse didn't even ask me why I was there. She just nodded her bad-perm head and patted my shoulder and offered me a bed in the room behind her office. Nobody else was puking or bleeding or faking that hour, so as soon as she shut the door and disappeared, I pulled my cell phone out of my pocket and texted Gretchen.

They're saying those pills you gave me are steroids. Were they?

Then I spent the rest of fifth period imagining her sitting down with me when I talked to Mom and Dad, explaining the situation until they got it. She was the only one who could convince them that I didn't know what I was taking. And the more I saw it play out in my mind, the surer I was that she could make Mr. LaSalle see it too. And Coach Deetz. All I wanted was to see that trust in his eyes again.

But I knew I wasn't going to see it sixth period, because Gretchen didn't text me back before the bell rang. I dragged myself out into the hall, where Kara was waiting for me, my bag over her shoulder.

"Are you okay?" she said.

Her blue eyes were two huge pools of concern. I was surprised I could even see them, as tear-swollen as mine were. It was pointless to do anything but shake my head.

"Somebody *was* using, huh?" she said. "Ohmigosh. Oh-my-*gosh*."

I stopped her at the corner and put my mouth close to her ear. "It was me, Kara."

Her face went ashen. I propped myself on my crutches and took her face in both hands.

"Just listen to me," I whispered. "Listen really hard."

She whimpered, but she somehow nodded.

I told her everything, in a voice that sounded even to me like it was on fast-forward. I knew my tone was fierce, but I had to get it out before she had a chance to doubt any of it. I might live if Coach Deetz never trusted me again, but not Kara. Without her beside me on this, I couldn't do it.

The bell rang, but neither of us moved until I was done. By then, she was trembling so hard I almost gave her one of my crutches to hold her up.

"It's gonna be okay," I said. "I swear to you — as soon as Gretchen finds out, she's going to make this all right."

"I hope so," Kara said. I could hardly hear her, even though there was barely a paper's width between us.

"Promise me that you won't tell *anybody*," I said.

"Okay."

"I mean it, Kar — not M.J. or Hilary — nobody."

"I promise."

"Swear."

"Cassidy —" Kara's voice snagged against a cry in her throat. "Why don't you believe me? I said I promise."

She looked down at her arm. My hand was clenched around it like the claw of a predatory bird. We both stared as I let go.

"I'm sorry," I said. "I'm just freaked out. I'm sorry."

"It's okay," she said, at least four times, before a door opened in the hall and Coach Deetz scowled out at us.

"You planning to join us?" he said.

"Yes, sir," I said.

But he shook his head. "I was talking to Kara."

She fled, and I waited. I must be dying, I thought, because my life was suddenly standing still.

"What do you want me to do?" I said.

"You can sit in my office," Coach said.

What he didn't say was that he didn't want me around the team. My team.

I wouldn't have wanted me around them either.

I started down the hall, already caving to sobs again, but he stopped me with his voice.

"I want to believe you didn't know what you were doing, Brewster," he said. "But I can't bend the rules—not even for you."

I just nodded and kept on going.

*

I didn't hear from Gretchen all period, and I didn't dare text her again. I was never going to do another sneaky thing as long as I lived. The minute I got in the car with Kara to go home, I dialed Gretchen's number.

"Gretchen Holden," she said breathlessly.

"Did you get my text?" I said.

There was a silence so long I thought she'd hung up. "I'm sorry," she said finally. "I didn't see this was you."

"Did you get it?"

"Yes."

Another stiff silence. The Frenemy attacked me head on.

"I was going to call you—later—when we have time to talk this out," she said. "Right now—"

"Right now you need to tell me you're going to tell my parents I didn't know I was taking steroids!"

"We really need to be face-to-face to do this, Cassidy—"

"No we don't! Just say it, Gretchen. Say you'll tell them you told me they were only supplements."

I could see that Kara was white-knuckling the steering wheel. I motioned for her to pull over so we didn't add vehicular homicide to my growing list of offenses.

"Cassidy," Gretchen said, "we both said we weren't going to tell anybody."

"I didn't! They did a drug test!"

"They don't randomly test for steroid use in high schools. You must have told somebody."

"I didn't—and who cares now? I'm in trouble."

"Not in as much trouble as I would be if you turned me in."

I plastered both hands to the sides of my head so it wouldn't blow off. Kara had her own hands over her mouth. I wouldn't have blamed her if she'd thrown up.

"You'll get a slap on the hand," Gretchen said. "But my whole career would come to an end. Not to mention my relationship with Aaron."

I stared at the phone. Was this the same person who told me she wanted me as a sister? The one who said she knew exactly how I felt?

"Here's what you do," she said. "Tell them you don't know the name of the person who gave them to you. Say it was some guy at a party."

"I don't *go* to parties!"

"And then I'll sit down with you and your mom and dad and convince them you couldn't have possibly known what you were doing."

"Oh—so you'll tell them somebody lied to me and said they were just supplements and that they would just make me a little crabby ... not that they would turn me into a raving lunatic!"

"Would you have taken them if I'd said they were steroids?" Gretchen's voice was icy.

"No!"

"And then you'd still be waiting for your swelling to go down. You wouldn't be scheduled for surgery. You wouldn't have a head start on muscle strength—"

"What good does that do me now? My coach can't even talk to me, my team's gonna think I'm a druggie—"

"I can't do anything about that."

The air went dead again.

"So you're just going to let me go down for it?" I said. "All by myself?"

"I said I'd—"

"No. I don't want you to lie—*again*! I want you to tell the truth!"

"I have a lot more to lose than you," said the woman who wanted a bond with me. "I can't. And it won't do any good for you to do it either, because I'll deny it. At this point, who are they going to believe?"

She threw in an "I'm sorry," in a voice tinged in tears. I hit END CALL so I wouldn't be the one to throw up.

"Oh—my—gosh, Cassidy," Kara whispered. "What are you going to do?"

I shook my head, but I did know. I was going to do the only thing I could do.

"I need Coach Deetz to stick up for me with Mr. LaSalle."

"What about your parents?"

"I'm not telling them yet. I'll go to Coach first thing in the morning." I twisted to face her straight on, knee protesting in pain. "Will you pick me up early—like six thirty?"

"Okay. Anything."

"And will you tell him that the day you took me to meet Gretchen I had no idea what it was about?"

She nodded. Slowly. "That's what you told me—yeah."

I went stiff. "What? Now you don't believe me either?"

"Don't yell at me, Cassidy, okay? I'm already so stressed out over this I can't even think."

71

I let out a hunk of air. "I'm sorry. Take your stress and multiply it by a thousand and you've got mine. What did I say to you that day?"

She squeezed her eyes shut. A tear escaped from the corner of one of them. "You said you couldn't tell me everything right then, but just to trust you — that it was all gonna be cool."

"I couldn't tell you everything because I didn't know. Did I say anything about steroids?"

She shook her head and wiped at the tears with the pads of her fingers.

"That's all you have to say."

"To who?"

"To Coach Deetz, Mr. LaSalle. Whoever."

"Why can't I just say it to your parents?"

I pressed the heel of my hand to my forehead. "I'm not *telling* my parents. Why is this so hard to understand?"

"You got in trouble for keeping stuff from them already," Kara said to the steering wheel. "I don't get why you're doing it again."

"Have you *met* my father? Okay, look — if you don't want to help —"

"I do. It's just — who am I helping?"

"Huh?" I said.

"Am I helping the old Cassidy or the new one?" She started the engine. "'Cause the new one — I don't even think I like her."

We rode home in a silence that screamed that I really was dead. Really.

*

I got through the evening by claiming that I was hurting and needed to do homework. Dad offered me pizza, which I took to my room and tossed in the trash can. Mom came in late, like she always did, and found me pretending to be asleep. She brushed my cheek with cold fingers and said, "It'll be over soon, Cass."

Yeah. That was what I was afraid of. I made another vow to myself that after this, I wasn't ever doing anything I couldn't tell the entire world about. I'd already flushed all the pills down the toilet and drunk enough water to sink the *Titanic* so I could flush them out of me.

I slept a total of about three hours and woke up in a near panic. When I thought about how I was going to have to keep that under control while I talked to Coach Deetz, I panicked even more. I was shaking so hard that when Kara called at 6:15, I could barely open my phone.

"I overslept," she said. "I can't pick you up until—"

"That's okay," I said. It wasn't, but I had to start the self-control now or I wasn't going to make it 'til six twenty. "I'm sorry about yesterday. I keep having to say I'm sorry to you."

"I'll just be glad when this is all done and I have you back," she said. "That's gonna happen, right?"

"Yeah," I said. "Those drugs are evil."

"No doubt," she said, and hung up crying.

I had a feeling she hadn't slept a whole lot more than I had.

Now I had to find a way to get to school before anybody else. There was no way I was asking Dad. Could I call a cab?

Okay. I really was losing it.

I hobbled through the family room, still clueless, and almost dropped my crutches when I found Mom in the kitchen, dressed in sweats, staring into a cup of coffee. She never got up this early.

"You okay?" I said.

"Are you?"

The Frenemy put her pointy fingers around my neck.

"You cried out in your sleep last night," she said. "Was it the pain?"

"I don't know," I said.

Ohmigosh, as Kara would say. Was I ever going to be able to stop lying?

"I feel like your dad has handled all of this," Mom said. "I'm out of the loop, and I'm not happy with that." She ran a hand through her bed head. "What can I do for you, Cass?"

I fought back a new onslaught of tears. "You could take me to school right now," I said. "I have to get there early."

"I'll get my keys," she said.

All the way there, I battled the urge to completely spill it all, tell her everything. She might pull over to the side of the road and put her arms around me and take it all away. She might.

Or she might tell me I had done the stupidest thing a person could do and I was going to have to handle it on my own.

The truth was I didn't know what she would do. She was right. She was out of the loop of my life, and she had been for a long time.

"I'm going to be there Friday," she said when we pulled up to the front of the school.

"Friday?" I said.

"For your surgery. I've already told them at the station. And I'll be with you for as long as you need me to be." She stretched her arm to the back of my seat, like she wanted to touch me and didn't know if she could. I guessed I was out of her loop too. "Between now and then, just—anything you need, Cass. I mean that."

"Okay," I said. And then I clattered out of the car before I could confess everything. I didn't have to, I told myself. I was going to convince Coach Deetz. This was one loop she didn't have to be in.

*

It didn't do me any good to arrive at school at the crack of dawn. I couldn't find Coach Deetz anywhere, and nobody I asked knew where he was. I told the Frenemy—silently—to get off me, that there was nothing to worry about. I still had six hours before he reported to Mr. LaSalle.

My new plan was to ask Mr. Josephson for a pass to go see him as soon as I finished the quiz on the first five chapters of *The Scarlet Letter*. But I wasn't even halfway through the questions when the pass came to *me*.

"You're wanted in the office, Miss Brewster," Mr. J said as he dropped it on my desk.

Somebody said, "Busted." I would have decked him if I

hadn't been almost paralyzed in fear. The hallway grew longer and narrower as I hobbled down it, and yet it wasn't long enough. I was there before I could wrap my mind around any explanation other than that Coach Deetz had broken his promise.

I'd never been so shaken that my teeth chattered, but they were clattering together loud enough for the secretary who showed me into Mr. LaSalle's office to hear them. But they stopped—everything in me stopped—when I passed through the door.

Coach Deetz was there—and Mr. LaSalle and my parents. Mom was still in her sweats, hair still shaped by her pillow. Dad was dressed, but a dot of shaving cream clung to the hairs at the bottom of his left sideburn. Obviously no one had told him.

But they'd told him everything else. It was all firing from his eyes.

"Have a seat, Cassidy," Mr. LaSalle said.

I collapsed into a chair next to Coach Deetz. He looked back at me from his forward fold over his thighs.

How could he even look at me?

"You promised me you would tell your parents," he said.

"You promised you'd give me twenty-four hours," I said, somehow.

"He was doing that." From under his buzz cut, Mr. LaSalle frowned briefly at Coach before he turned back to me. "I got a tip from a concerned student and confronted Coach Deetz. He couldn't deny that he had the results from the drug tests."

Why not? I wanted to say. But I knew. Not everybody was a liar like me. Not even the person who had told Mr. LaSalle. The only other person who knew.

I started to cry.

"All right," my father said. "Who told what to whom isn't the issue here, Cassidy."

I shook my head. I was still sobbing.

"Cass."

My head turned, all by itself. Dad wasn't pointing his face at me. He was searching mine as if for once he hadn't already reached a verdict before I even spoke. Too bad I was hurting too much to appreciate it.

"Coach Deetz says you didn't know you were taking steroids."

I heard Mr. LaSalle grunt.

"Assumed innocent before proven guilty," Dad said. He was giving *him* the pointy face. "Cass—who gave you this stuff?"

"Gretchen," I said. Because now that Kara had betrayed me, nothing else really mattered. Kara was my real sister—and now I could never trust her again. My shoulders shook with the pain.

"Our Gretchen?" Mom said.

"Who's Gretchen?" Mr. LaSalle said.

A discussion went on around me, but I couldn't make out a word. All I could hear was Kara: *"Why can't I just say it to your parents? . . . You got in trouble for keeping stuff from them already. I don't get why you're doing it again . . . This new Cassidy? I don't even think I like her."*

Mr. LaSalle's voice forced its way in. "All of this is beside the point. She took a performance-enhancing drug and she's out."

"What do you mean, she's 'out'?" Dad said.

Mr. LaSalle leveled his chilly gaze at me. "The school policy is clear. It's actually the county policy: Any student found using illegal drugs is banned from participating in the athletic program."

"For how long?" Dad said.

"Permanently."

"Isn't that rather harsh?" my mother said.

"Harsh? It's ridiculous!" Dad stood up and drove his index finger through the air at Mr. LaSalle. "You have a serious problem here, sir. First of all, you ran a medical test on our daughter without our permission. Secondly, you've basically convicted her without any kind of investigation."

Mr. LaSalle waved a sheet of paper at him. "She tested at a ratio of five to one—normal is one to one. That means she was probably taking a dose a hundred times greater than anything used for treating a medical condition. This is all the 'investigation' we need."

"You're going to need more than that in court."

"You want to file a lawsuit, be my guest—"

"Stop it—just *stop*!"

Shock seized the room as I shot to my feet—and then screamed as pain crumpled me to the ground.

"Her knee!" my mom said.

But it wasn't only my knee that cried out for help.

It was my broken heart.

CHAPTER SIX

Thank heaven for anesthesia. It almost blocked out the three most horrible days of my life.

I knew that the rest of Wednesday and all of Thursday happened. I just couldn't remember what was in them. Friday passed in a nightmarish blur of needles and fear and pain. I woke up after the surgery crying. I remember saying, "No drugs! Don't give me any drugs!"

"You won't get through this without pain meds, Cassidy," said a voice in the fog.

"Get away from me, Gretchen! Don't touch me!"

"I don't know who Gretchen is, honey," the voice said. "But I'm glad I'm not her."

I just wished I wasn't me. That feeling grew as I emerged from the stupor and was moved to a tiny room to spend the day. There were no stuffed animals or flowers or giant cards from the team. No DVD of the game I'd missed the night before. My parents were my only visitors, except Pastor Varelli, who assured me God had a plan for my life, and Aaron, who came by to inform me that Gretchen was on suspension from med school, pending an investigation. He didn't say, "Thanks to you," but it was there on the stiff panel of his face. I had messed up again.

"What about the wedding?" I mumbled to him.

"Are you serious?" he said. "There isn't going to be any wedding."

"I know you didn't break up with her over me," I said.

"Well, at least you're smart enough to figure that out. She

called it off. She wants to get as far away from this situation as she possibly can."

I wished I could do the same thing.

He left two minutes later without ever asking me how I was, and I couldn't have told him anyway.

I was in and out of a strange twilight sleep most of the day. Every time I woke up, Dad was pacing around with the cell phone he wasn't supposed to have on in the hospital. Once in a while I'd catch a word— "appeal"— "lawsuit"— and the occasional four-letter one that got a glare from my mother. She didn't say a lot, except to ask me if I wanted ice chips or another pillow.

"I just want to go home," I told her when she offered me a Popsicle.

"I'll see what I can do," she said.

The nurse said we had to wait until Dr. Horton cleared me. He finally sailed into the room about the time the sun was starting to go down behind the Peak, and he was grinning as if he'd given me tickets to Disneyland.

"Everything went great," he said. "I think we've given you the most stable knee possible. After physical therapy, I think you can get back on the court with a minimum risk of future damage."

"I bet you say that to all the girls," I muttered.

"Like I told you before, nine out of ten people have success with this—as long as they follow all our instructions." He folded his arms. "That includes no more 'supplements.'"

"We're clear on that," Mom said. "What do we need to know?"

He said the nurse would give us written instructions, including exercises I needed to do at home before I started physical therapy the next week. I closed my eyes and tried to drift off again. The only plan I had was to change to a school where nobody knew anything about me. I needed no special instructions to do that.

We didn't get home until after dark. All the anesthesia had worn off, and the pain medication they gave me was wimpy in comparison. Every time I went from sitting to standing, the agony rushed to my knee and filled it up until I was sure it was going to explode. Nurse Voice had been right. I wasn't going to get through this without meds.

Mom bustled around like Nurse Fidget, propping up my ankle above my heart and icing my knee down for twenty minutes every hour and telling me about the exercises we were going to start tomorrow. I uh-huh-ed my way through most of that because I didn't have the energy to tell her I had no intention of rehabilitating. I didn't actually say much of anything—until she sat on the edge of my bed when I said I wanted to go to sleep and told me Kara had called. Again. Because she couldn't get me on my cell phone.

"Would you just tell her I can't talk?" I said.

"Why don't you text her?" Mom said. "I'm pretty sure you could've done that under general anesthesia."

She attempted a smile, but it didn't make it all the way to her eyes. They seemed cloudy and sad.

"You two have been friends for a long time," she said. "What did you used to call each other? BFFs?"

"Yeah. When we were ten." I closed my eyes.

"I think you could use a friend right now, Cass. And from what I know of Kara, you could have committed manslaughter and she would still be there for you."

Yeah. Except for the one thing nobody knew: that Kara was the one who had committed manslaughter, and I was her victim.

"I'm really tired," I said.

"I bet you are. Get some sleep. I'll be right outside if you need me."

My eyes came open. "Right outside?"

"I set up a cot in the hall."

"You don't have to do that," I said.

"Yeah, I do," she said.

I was sure that was one of the many reasons why, after she left, I cried myself to sleep.

80

"How's the swelling?" Mom said from the other side of the shower curtain.

I was propped up in the tub, leg sticking out, body soaking like a slab of ribs in barbecue sauce. I couldn't take a shower for another twenty-four hours, and Mom had needed to run the bathwater, help me out of my pajamas, and hoist me onto and off of the toilet. It seemed sort of pointless that she'd drawn the curtain so I could have privacy.

"My ankle's pretty big, I guess." I couldn't see my knee under the bandage they had it swathed in.

"They said that was normal with your bone bleeding where they—okay, sorry. No swelling in the calf, though, right?"

"No."

"You go ahead and marinate as long as you want," she said. "Then we'll get started on your exercises."

I felt myself stiffen. "I don't really feel like it."

"I'm sure you don't. It's probably going to hurt like a mother bear." She gave a nervous little laugh I'd never heard come out of her. "That's why God gave us pain medication."

She left and I lowered myself as far into the water as I could without drowning. I had to try really hard not to consider that as an option.

*

Mom and Dad were both in the family room, which I winced my way through on the way to the kitchen. All I wanted was a glass of water, but Mom immediately started offering me a full menu. Dad, on the other hand, glowered as he pointed me to the couch and piled up the pillows.

"Not behind her knee," Mom said, head already in the refrigerator. "They have to go under her heel."

"That it?" he basically growled when I was settled in.

"Sure," I said.

"Good." He stood over me, hands jammed onto his hips. "Now what's this I hear about you not wanting to do your PT?"

"My what?"

I knew he meant physical therapy. I just didn't want to have this conversation.

"I've said this before, Cass. You've never been one to back away from anything. So what's going on?"

He didn't add, "And this better be good," but it was there, filed tightly between the lines. He wasn't going away. I might as well get this over with.

"I don't see the point in doing physical therapy," I said to my propped-up toes. "I'm never going to play basketball again, so—"

"*Excuse* me—what?"

"I'm through, okay? And I wanted to talk to you and Mom about this. I have to change schools. I can't go back to Austin Bluffs."

"You have *got* to be kidding *me*." Dad bent at the waist, one hand on the back of the couch, the other on the edge next to my leg. The Frenemy erupted into a case of claustrophobia so bad I could feel the sickening sweat on my upper lip.

"You are not changing schools," he said. "And you are not giving up basketball. For the love of the Lord, Cassidy—only five percent of high school athletes even play in college, but you're on your way to a full scholarship, which only *one* percent of athletes get."

"Not now!"

"The Lady Vols have had dozens of players with past injuries—"

"But none of them got caught using steroids, Dad. I'm done! It's over!"

"Not without a fight. You are a Brewster, and that means—"

"I know what it means. It means I have to be perfect twenty-four hours a day, seven days a week—and if I'm not, you'll pick me apart until I am!"

"Trent—what in the world!" Mom cut in.

Dad ignored my mother in the doorway and bore down on me. My heart was slamming so hard I could barely breathe. "We have done nothing but support you in this, Cassidy.

Maybe this is those drugs still messing with your mind because you went off cold turkey ... whatever. You're not giving up—you hear me?"

"What are you going to do? Stand over me like—like this?"

"If I have to—"

"Trent, stop."

He straightened up and glared at my mother this time. I took that opportunity to haul myself off the couch and snatch up my crutches.

"We're not done, Cassidy," my father said.

I didn't answer. I had to focus all my attention on not throwing up from pain and fear before I got to my room. I had never talked to my father like that. I didn't know what he was going to do because I had. And the scariest part was, I didn't care.

One thing I did know: it wasn't the remains of the steroids that made me say all that. I knew, because I waited until I didn't hear him tapping his loafers down the hall toward me before I lurched over to my bulletin board and attacked it.

One arm kept me propped up while I used the other to rip everything off: the MVP awards from tournaments that had exposed me to college recruiters, the certificates saying I'd completed every skills camp in Colorado, the photographs taken in locker rooms and at sleepovers and out on my driveway under the hoop. Kara's smile beamed at me from almost every one of them—and they all came down, rip by sobbing rip, until I stood on one pitiful foot in a pile of my life.

One thought came crashing down on me as I looked at it. This was the first time since I was ten years old that I wasn't on a team. The first time I couldn't wonder, "How can I help Selena improve her shooting?" or "How can I get M.J. to stop panicking when she can't see a receiver?" I didn't even have the right to be at the sideline and cheer on the girls who meant everything to me—who were right now preparing for their third game in the state finals. I couldn't even be there, because in one stupid moment in a coffee shop, I had gone from hero to zero.

With my free hand I reached down and threw the first thing I touched. My bag. Which was unzipped and which spilled its guts all over the floor. Gel pens. Markers. My half-read copy of the stupid *Scarlet Letter*. All the stuff that meant absolutely nothing to me anymore.

I smacked at the whole array with my crutch, and when I did, something leather peeked out from under the mess—the book I'd accidentally but-not-accidentally brought home from the Black Forest Coffee Haus. I would have hammered it now with the rubber tip if it hadn't fallen open flat, looking as if I'd pressed the pages that way myself.

"What?" I said to it.

And then I felt ridiculous, which was only slightly better than feeling like I wanted to beat everybody, including myself, with *both* crutches.

I got myself to the floor, dumped the weapons, and reached for the leather thing. I had really intended to ask Gretchen to return it to the coffee shop. Back when I thought she and I were going to be sisters. Back when I thought she could save my life.

The pages were still pressed open, but not to what I'd read before, something about getting me on my feet. If it had, I might have dumped it again. But this time it said:

If you've found me, you need me. I was left for you for a reason. Read and discover what that is. Before you do, prepare to enter a strange new world.

Why? I liked my old world—the one that existed when I jumped up to make a winning shot and disappeared when I hit the ground.

That one's lost.

It was absolutely what the words said. I blinked. Shook my head. Wondered if Mom had slipped me an extra pain pill. But that was still what it said.

You're not the first person to feel like you've lost it all, it went on. *Interested in some stories on the subject?*

That was it. Mom *had* put a second—or third—Lortab in my smoothie.

Despite the fact that my father eyed every tablet my mother took out of the container so there was no way she was drugging me up, I went with that theory. It let me pretend the thing was talking to me. After all, basically nobody else was.

I hauled myself and the book to my beanbag chair under the window and managed to prop my ankle on some throw pillows. The blinds and curtains were closed against the accusing sunlight, but some of it seeped down over the windowsill and onto the open page.

Yeshua,

I read.

You know who he is?

The name sounded vaguely familiar.

He was catching some serious flak from the church staff for hanging around with lowlifes.

I knew the type. My art class was filled with them.

They basically hung onto every word he said, these people with their rap sheets and their tats and their reputations. Yeshua was getting through to them, so he ate with them, took them to coffee, frequented their hangouts. But the usual teachers and counselors didn't get that. They said he ought to establish some boundaries because there was no changing a loser.

I kind of had to agree with them. What were the chances that guys like Rafe Diego weren't going to end up doing time? I couldn't see Mrs. Petrocelli-Ward having them over to her place on the weekends.

All their yapping finally triggered a story from Yeshua,

the book said.

He told them, "Suppose you were in the wool business and you had a hundred head of prime sheep. Let's say you lost one. Wouldn't you leave the other ninety-nine and go hunt for the one that got away until you found it?"

Oh, for Pete's sake. This was some kind of *Bible.* I knew this story. And the one about the lost coin, and the lost son who got the ring and the fatted calf and the welcome-home bash—

Then you know how it ends. The sheep owner finds the sheep, puts it over his shoulders, and comes back to celebrate with his friends.

Right. Except that even if my knee healed, nobody was going to throw a party and invite me on the basketball team again.

"It is so *over!*" I said. Out loud. Without caring whether my parents heard me. They already knew. Everybody knew.

I put my hands under the book's covers and tried to close it, but it resisted. The harder I pushed, the harder it pushed back.

"*What?*" I said. I could hear the tears in my voice as I looked down at the page.

They all missed the point too. So Yeshua spelled it out for them. He said, "You can count on it: there's more of a celebration at my house over one loser being rescued than there is over the ninety-nine who already get it. I like a celebration."

"Then celebrate this," I said.

With a perfect shot I landed the book in the wastebasket across the room.

*

I didn't know what my mother said to my father to keep him off me the rest of the weekend. It must have been her, because he didn't speak to either one of us for two days.

I was fine with that, at least enough to let Mom talk me into doing the exercises.

"Even if it's not about basketball, Cass," she said on Saturday afternoon, when Dad had stormed out to his office, "you want to be able to walk, don't you?"

Because of that, and the fact that she didn't say anything else about my game, I endured the straight leg raises and the quad sets and the heel slides and the hip abductions and adductions and whatever other kind of ductions, all with the hated tears dribbling down my face.

"I'm so sorry, Cass," Mom kept saying.

That was what made me insist on going back to school on Monday. The bandage was off, and I had an ACE to cover the wound that looked like a grotesque tattoo under my brace. I'd taken a shower. While everything still ached and felt wrong, I had to get away from my mom's sympathy and my dad's chilling silence and my own inner voice that said, "Loser, loser, loser."

Mom finally gave in and drove me to school Monday morning. She wanted to go in with me, but I insisted that she just drop me off at the curb.

"You're stronger than I would be," she said.

No, I didn't say. *I'm just afraid you'll say you're sorry for me again and I'll fall apart.*

I almost did anyway when I swung down the hall on my crutches and felt the stares pummeling me like fists. I never thought I'd be glad to escape into Mr. Josephson's room or be told to read *The Scarlet Letter* silently. I found myself relating to Hester Prynne. I might as well have a big letter on my chest too. A giant A for *Addict*.

"Miss Brewster."

I jumped a little and looked up at Mr. Josephson. "For you," he said.

I stared at the paper he put on my desk. The last time he'd delivered something to me, my life had ended.

"Looks like a schedule change," he said.

"Oh," I said.

I waited until he moved on down the aisle before I unfolded it. A blink later, I wished I had balled it up and done a free throw with it into the trash can.

Change from: Period 6 — Basketball Conditioning, Practice Gym — Deetz

Change to: Period 6 — Study Hall, 109 — Edelstein

"A schedule change now? Dude — it's March."

I looked at the kid next to me, the same one who had informed me I was busted last week when I got the pass to the office. I didn't even know him — people just called him Boz, except Mr. Josephson, who called him Mr. Thacker. He was the first kid who had spoken to me since I entered the building that day, which was the only reason I pushed the schedule change to the edge of my desk so he could see it.

"Dude, that bites," he said.

I attempted a shrug. "I'll get a lot of homework done."

87

"Yeah. Right. Nobody does homework in Loser Hall. You're too busy watchin' your back." Boz bent back his copy of *The Scarlet Letter* and directed his sizeable nose toward it. "Good luck with that."

I didn't even try to answer. I was sure I didn't have a voice now. After all, everything that I used to be just wasn't anymore.

*

It would be a total understatement to say that for the rest of the day I regretted coming back to school.

My team that wasn't my team now was everywhere and I couldn't even look at them. Especially Kara.

My phone buzzed with texts from her:

I'm sorry, Cass.

Can't we talk about this?

I swear I never meant to hurt you.

I sent her only one text: *But you did.*

Then I turned my phone off and left it in my locker. There was no other way I could start over.

At lunch I hid in the nurse's office, although Nurse Bad Perm couldn't resist having a look at my wound and asking me questions until I felt like a science project.

During fifth period art I hid behind a blank easel until P-W found me and told me that most great art arose from pain.

I ought to be able to create a masterpiece, then. I was in absolute agony when I left the arts wing at the end of the period and made my way to Room 109. Most of the pain wasn't coming from my knee.

Room 109 was a math room, bare and tidy and all straight lines. Nobody was there except the woman at the teacher's desk, who I assumed was Ms. Edelstein. Although she was youngish, she definitely wasn't a student. Not with rimless glasses and a too-neat off-blonde haircut and a tweedy blazer over a turtleneck. Most of the other *teachers* didn't even dress like that.

"I guess I'm in here now," I said.

She held out her hand, never taking her eyes from the

paper she was grading. It took me a minute to realize what she wanted.

When I handed her the schedule change, she glanced at it, nodded, and said, "I guess you are."

She still didn't look at me.

"Where do you want me to sit?" I said.

"I don't care. No, wait—all the seats in the back are taken. Any place else is fine."

"Is it true that I won't be able to get any homework done in here?"

She finally tore herself away from the red pencil and let her eyes travel up to my face. They registered surprise behind the glasses, and then flickered to the schedule change.

"Huh," she said. "Oh—I see." She was now studying my crutches. "I guess you can't do much 'conditioning' with those."

"Right," I said.

So she didn't know about me. I'd assumed every member of the faculty had gotten a memo announcing that I was a drug offender. Maybe this wouldn't be so bad after all. Hope rose that I could crawl anonymously to a corner where nothing could remind me that I'd fallen from the heights.

Until I saw Rafe Diego in the doorway. I tried to whip around to avoid eye contact, but he saw me first. His big pouty lips formed a smile that made my stomach turn over. It dropped all the way to my aching knee when he came toward me, bush-brows hooding his eyes. I managed to look away, but that didn't stop him from brushing my arm with his jacket sleeve and whispering into my ear.

"You were wrong," he said. "We *are* both here for the same reason."

"I don't have a rap sheet," I said between my teeth.

"I know. But you're a loser."

He moved away, but I didn't miss his last words:

"Just like me."

CHAPTER SEVEN

I didn't see the banner in the hallway until Tuesday. By then I'd stopped trying to be invisible so people wouldn't point and whisper and had graduated to pretending not to care if they did, which was why I swung right down the main hall after fourth period instead of slithering through the back way to find a place to hide while everybody else ate lunch. I didn't think Nurse Bad Perm was going to let me escape to her office every day anyway.

So I was tooling along, head up, face saying, "You want a piece of me? Bring it"—and suddenly there it was. A banner taller than any member of the basketball team and practically as long as a court, hanging from the wall across from the main office. Two-foot-high letters read:

CONGRATULATIONS, WOMEN WARRIORS
#2 IN THE STATE!!!!!!!!

I knew it already, of course. I wasn't sure if my father had left the Sunday morning paper open to the sports section on purpose—right on the coffee table in the family room, no less—but it had been a whole lot easier to see it there than here.

In smaller letters dancing across the cloth were the names.

Hilary McElhinney   M.J. Martinez   Selena Chen
Kara Van Dyke   Emily Watson

I stopped reading. There were more—the whole team—but all I could see was the blank. The space where *Cassidy Brewster* should have been.

I maneuvered the crutches around and thumped my way on down the hall, but the names called after me.

If you hadn't screwed up, you could have been there for us. We could have been number one. You could have made us the winners.

So what were they now? Losers because they only came in second in the entire huge state of Colorado?

My crutches slowed, and I leaned against the wall outside the cafeteria. People almost unconsciously made a wide path around me so they wouldn't knock me down, but my own thoughts tried to do it for me. *If you always won, what were you when you lost?* Maybe it wasn't a big A I should have on my sweatshirt. Maybe it was a big *L*.

Head down, I stumped into the cafeteria and found a table in a back corner.

*

I tried to avoid thinking the L-word for the rest of the day and Wednesday. It wasn't *that* hard for the first four periods, unless the L-word was actually "lonely." I'd never realized you could feel so alone when you were surrounded by people. I figured out that in high school, Lonely and Loser were pretty much the same thing.

I was probably the loneliest when I saw Kara or M.J. or Hilary in the halls. M.J. waved the first time, but it looked like she was performing a duty. Hilary tried a smile, which was as plastic as Mr. Potato Head's lips. It hurt to feel like they were "trying," like they could tell themselves later that I didn't respond when they reached out to me. Maybe I would have if they hadn't given up after the second day.

Still, I could pretty much deal with it, even during lunch when I parked myself and my crutches at my corner table and pretended to be catching up on *The Scarlet Letter* while I acted like I was eating the lunch Mom had started packing for me. At least Kara, M.J., and Hilary usually went off campus to eat. At least there was that.

But from fifth period on, my Loser status was in my face, mostly in the form of Rafe Diego. I'd barely noticed him in my art class all year long. Now I was suddenly his new career.

When I hobbled up to sharpen my pencil, he was at my elbow, treating me to cigarette breath.

If I held up a sketch to the light to look at it, he leaned his chair back from across the room so he could check it out too. Or so he could try to weird me out.

Even when I wasn't doing anything besides staring at a blank sheet of paper and wondering what ever possessed me to take an art class, I'd get a feeling creepier than the Frenemy and I'd glance around to find him staring at me. It wasn't like the way I used to wish the bagger at Safeway would look at me — back when I had room in my brain to care about stuff like that. This was more like … well, the way a tagger might size up a wall before he breaks out the spray can and starts defacing it.

P-W kept a pretty tight rein on her class — "Artists don't need to be running amok" was one of her pet sayings — so I could sort of ignore him some of the time. Not so in Loser Hall. If Ms. Edelstein even knew we existed after she took the roll, she never showed it. Study hall was evidently like a second prep period for her, and she was always grading a stack of papers that never seemed to get any smaller. I was glad I didn't have her for AP Geometry; it looked like she was working her students to death.

So while she went after it with a red pencil from bell to bell, the four other Loser Hall students sat in a row against the back wall and worked toward their goal, which after the first day I realized was to make the life of the fifth person as miserable as possible for fifty-five minutes. Even though that fifth person wasn't me, since I didn't count myself as an actual member of the class, Boz was right. It was impossible to get any homework done with that going on.

I tried. Maybe Rafe's two evil minions and his girlfriend thought I was actually reading American history and writing up chemistry labs. But mostly, all I did was stare at the same paragraphs about World War II and charts of the elements and wish they would leave that girl alone.

It took about five minutes of the first day to learn that her name was Ruthie. Which wasn't hard, since somebody was saying it every seven seconds.

"So, Ruthie," Rafe would say, out of those lips that to me grew more enormous daily. "You got plans for the weekend? You hookin' up with somebody?"

His girlfriend, the heinous Uma, would punch his arm like she didn't like him teasing Ruthie, although she was obviously eating it up. She definitely showed no signs of coming to the girl's defense. Mostly she just gave the chubby Ruthie looks that clearly said, "You need a makeover, girl—but don't expect me to do it."

Not that she could have pulled off her own look on Ruthie. Uma had the streetwalker thing pretty much down. Seriously, it had to be expensive to look that cheap, not to mention the time involved. She was a tiny, scrawny thing, except for the miracle being performed by her bra, but she had more hair on her head than the entire basketball team put together, every tress curled and cascading down her back in a color not found anywhere but in a package. She was constantly swinging it out of her face like it was this huge inconvenience, which made me want to ask, "So why don't you cut it off if it bugs you so much?"

But I'd already made a vow not to get into a conversation with her. I just watched over the top of my chemistry notebook as Uma strutted past Ruthie in her pencil-heeled boots, standing-room-only leather pants, and tight T-shirts that said things like My PRETENDING to listen should be good enough for you.

If she was even pretending, she wasn't very good at it. Her mouth was always drawn into a little rosebud-looking thing, and her eyes stayed about half-closed most of the time. Of course, that could have been from all the makeup she loaded on.

But Uma wasn't really Ruthie's biggest problem. It was Rafe and his nasty little cronies. There was truly no other way to describe his sidekicks Dumb and Dumber. Their names were actually Tank and Lizard. At least that was what Rafe called them, and their tattoos seemed to confirm it.

Lizard, the skinny one, who wasn't that much bigger than

Uma, had one of a salamander going down his arm, with teeth like a shark and a tongue you'd expect to see on Godzilla.

Tank's was on his large left shoulder. I couldn't see the whole thing—nor did I want to—but the top half of it showed when he took off his jacket and revealed his T-shirt with the cutout sleeves and neck. The oversized gun barrel etched into his skin made me want to say, "For Pete's sake, would you put that jacket back on?" But I didn't. I didn't want a discussion with him any more than I wanted one with Uma, or Lizard. Or Rafe. Besides, they were concentrating all their efforts on Ruthie.

"Roo-*thee*," Lizard would say in a high-pitched voice. "What are you doin'? What are you doin', Roo-*thee*?"

She never answered, which I thought was wise, so the three goons answered for her. Tank would say something stupid, like, "She's lookin' at her navel. No—she's tryin' to find it." More than once I wanted to ask if they'd lost their way and really belonged in middle school. Make that elementary.

Lizard and Tank would go on for a while, and then Rafe would say something that made them look like insult amateurs. Wednesday, when Tank said, "Hey, Ruthie, have you called Jenny Craig yet?"—like he should talk, Mr. "I OD'd on Enchiladas"—Rafe let a big sly smile spread across his face and said, "Leave her alone. She's gestating."

Even Ms. Edelstein looked up.

"*Gestating?*" Lizard said, eyes shifting like his namesake. "What the—what's that?"

"Doesn't that mean pregnant?" Uma said.

Rafe just maintained his sick smile and nodded. For the first time since I'd been in Loser Hall, Ruthie turned around in her desk in front of theirs and looked at them—or somewhere in the direction of their shins.

"I'm not pregnant," she said.

I was surprised by her voice, which was husky and deep and sounded like it belonged to a cheerleader.

"No way she's pregnant, man," Tank said. "What guy would—"

"*You* would," Lizard said. "You're desperate."

"Not *that* desperate."

Their discussion disintegrated into reports on their latest scores, punctuated by Uma pounding on Rafe's arm. He didn't actually say anything. He just sat there looking all satisfied that he'd successfully gotten the humiliation going.

By then Ruthie had turned around and was re-slumping into her seat. Her face hadn't even turned red, although it was hard to tell because it was pretty much covered in angry-looking acne. She had to be mortified. And yet she just went back to reading her thick paperback fantasy novel. Maybe she was looking for a magical way to lose weight so they'd lay off.

It was kind of sad, how heavy she was. Even I thought she was—okay, fat—the first time I saw her hunched into the desk with her head sunken into her shoulders. Limp, unremarkable brown hair strung down both sides of her very round face and onto the sleeves of the oversized (even for her) flannel shirt she always wore with jeans that spilled over floppy tennis shoes.

"Mighty Jabba!" Tank had called her the first day I was in there.

"No," Rafe told him. "The blessed Buddha."

One day on steroids and she might be able to kick them all to the curb.

*

By Wednesday night, I was almost numb. Selena never made eye contact with me in first period. Nobody bothered me at my lunch hideaway. In Loser Hall, Rafe and the others seemed content to concentrate on Ruthie, who basically ignored them like she was in a coma. And my father was working long hours, coming home too late to have dinner with Mom and me.

The first night she had supper set up for the two of us before she left for work, I almost dropped my crutches. Not only was she never home for meals during the week, but she hadn't cooked since she was made head meteorologist. The Brewsters lived on takeout and leftovers from restaurants. Yet there she was, spooning beef stew into bread bowls.

"Wow," I said. "You ... cooked."

"I thought I'd better since I'm the one torturing you twice a day. I don't want you offing me in my sleep."

It was true—the part about her "torturing" me. She got me up every morning at five to supervise my exercises, and she was ready to do it again every afternoon when she brought me home from school. I still didn't see the point in suffering to get my leg more than twelve inches off the bed and practically biting my tongue off to get through prone hangs. I had to admit, though, that it was hurting less and less, and I was even thinking about losing the crutches in a day or two.

But, yeah, homemade beef stew and warm sourdough bread and a table that didn't have my father at it was nice. I kind of wished Mom didn't have to go to work. She was the only person I could go un-numb with and not be bristled by the Frenemy the entire time.

I thought about it Wednesday when I was propped up in bed, examining my knee. There wasn't any feeling around the incision, which had freaked me out when I first took the bandage off, but when Mom called Dr. Horton about it—so I wouldn't totally lose it and need psychiatric care—he said that it was due to "the disruption of a superficial nerve during the operative procedure." He could have just said it was normal and I didn't need to worry about it. Once he assured us that it would resolve over time and probably leave me with only a quarter-sized place with no feeling ever, I was okay with it.

I still poked at it every night, though, just because it was weird. That night it came to me that it was sort of like my life right now. There was a lot of pain everywhere, and yet there was this little place I could go to where I could stay numb, where if I just kept my head down I wouldn't feel the part that had been cut into and reconstructed with a graft from some other part of me that I didn't want to be. *Just stay where it's numb and you'll make it*, I told myself. *You'll make it.*

*

Yeah, well, so much for that plan.

I was numbing out at my private table in the cafeteria

Thursday, actually deep into the last chapter of *The Scarlet Letter*, when I felt a warm presence. It had always been my experience that you could tell when another athlete was close to you—something about their heat or their scent or their energy. It had always come in handy when somebody tried to sneak up on me on the court.

I was right. I looked up to find Selena standing there, the tips of her fingers tucked into the front pockets of a pair of skinny jeans. She seemed taller and leaner than ever, especially with a snug black sweater clinging to hips that barely existed.

"Why are you eating by yourself?" she said.

It might have been a mean question, but I didn't think so. Not from Selena. She did blunt and in-your-face and don't-hold-back, but I'd never thought of her as just plain evil.

"Mind if I sit down?" she said.

I did, but I nodded out of sheer isolation.

"So?" I said.

"Yeah, so, I can't actually stay," she said. "I just wanted to ask you something."

"What?"

"Were you planning to sign up for a club team this summer? I mean, will you be able to play by then?"

I actually hadn't thought about it. Now that I did, a glimmer of hope about the size of a birthday candle flame lit up somewhere.

"I don't know," I said. "I think they said I'd need, like, six months of therapy."

Selena appeared to be doing a mental calculation. "So you couldn't play—not until, say, August."

I felt myself sag. "No, I guess not."

"Okay, well, that answers my question."

"Why?" I said.

Selena folded her hands around her crossed knees. A bracelet with a silver basketball charm dangled from her wrist. "If you were going to sign up I wanted to know which club—so I wouldn't sign up for that one too."

As that registered, I felt my jaw drop.

"I just don't want to play with a druggie," she said. "Not that I have a choice. The parents—including mine—don't want us around you."

"I'm not a 'druggie.' I didn't know what I was taking. Didn't Coach tell you that?"

"Like I can believe anything Coach Deetz says about you. He's totally biased. It was Mr. LaSalle who busted you, not him, right? If somebody hadn't tipped LaSalle off, you never would have gone down for it." She closed her eyes and rubbed at the air with her palm. "Anyway, it doesn't matter. It looks like I never have to play with you again, and I'm okay with that."

She should have gotten up and left then, but she still sat there, legs crossed, looking at me.

"What?" I said.

"I'm just waiting to see if you're going to go into one of your rages. I guess you're not so brave without your steroids, are you?"

"You should back off, Selena."

I turned to see Kara, who had somehow appeared behind me without my best friend antennae going up. She wasn't looking at me anyway. Her blue-blue eyes were on Selena.

"What are you doing?" Kara said to her. "You shouldn't stir something up."

"I was just checking a few things out," Selena said. "I'm gone."

She got up surprisingly fast and padded away in her ballerina flats without a backward glance. If I hadn't known better, I would have thought she was a little afraid of Kara.

"You okay?" Kara said.

I pulled my eyes back to hers, which were now swimming in signature Kara tears.

As I looked into them, I remembered the last time—when she was deciding I wasn't the old Cassidy anymore, and she needed to out the new one. And ruin my life.

"Cassidy," she said. "Can't we talk? I don't even know what I did—"

"No," I said. "What you don't know is that *I* know what you did."

"What are you *talking* about?" Her voice wound up. "All I did was try to help you. I even called—"

"Yeah, I know. And it *didn't* help, okay? All it did was show me that I can't trust you."

"I don't know what else to say to you." She didn't seem to be aware that tears were pouring down her face like rapids.

"You can tell me this," I said.

"What?"

"Did your parents tell you not to associate with me? Yours and M.J.'s and Hilary's?"

"They had a meeting. Selena's father called it—"

I put up my hand. "I get it," I said.

She just shook her head. Her hair got caught in the wet, but she let it stay plastered to her cheeks. "I'm sorry, Cassidy. I really am."

"Me too," I said. "But don't feel bad. You're not the only one. I don't really trust anybody else anymore either."

She was still shaking her head as she ran among the tables for the door. I wished I could have run away too, long and hard and far.

*

So, no, I wasn't numb when I got to fifth period. The Frenemy had completely taken over and it was scaring me. I didn't have basketball anymore to push her away. What if this nauseous, prickling, terrified feeling was going to be in me forever? Was I going to go through the rest of my life with a mouth full of cotton and palms full of sweat? By the time I got to my table in art, I could barely hold on to my crutches.

One of them clattered to the floor when I tried to lean them against the wall, and naturally Rafe was standing only inches away, for no reason that I could think of.

"I don't want to hear it," I said.

"You don't want to hear what?"

"Whatever it is you're going to say. I'll say it for you. I dropped my crutch. I'm a klutz. I'm a loser. There, are we good?"

He let his lips go up on one side, which I assumed was

meant to look sexy or something. "I was just gonna say, 'Let me get that for you.'"

"No, you were not."

"Yeah, I was. See?"

He picked up my crutch and leaned it next to the other one, and did some kind of seductive thing with his eyebrows that made me want to pluck them out, one by one.

"You disgust me," I said.

"That was the idea," he said.

Which it apparently was, because, for the rest of class, he came up with every excuse to get in my space. He chose my sketch to critique when we went around the room, and he pointed out that I would never make it as a graffiti artist. Like that was my career plan. He mimicked my facial expressions when I was critiquing somebody else's piece. And when the bell rang to end class, he was there, handing me my crutches like a butler in a bad sitcom.

"You are *not* walking me to class," I said through my teeth.

"Why not? You're goin' to the same place I am."

He said it just loud enough for Mrs. Petrocelli-Ward to hear. She looked up from a paper she was reading and gave me a curious look.

"You're in a study hall, Cassidy?" she said.

I looked at Rafe and said, "Don't even start."

*

I was still fuming when I got to Room 109. I tried to bury myself in the last chapter of *The Scarlet Letter* again, but even Hester Prynne's issues didn't seem as bad as mine. Besides that, Rafe and the goons were in top form. I could only think that I had gotten Rafe warmed up for Ruthie.

She, too, had her face buried in a book, as usual, and she was twirling a skinny strand of hair around her finger as she read. I was kind of envying her ability to get lost in a fantasy world when Lizard slithered in and headed past her toward his seat. He stopped and backed up and studied her face until she looked up at him.

"Ruthie," he said. "Didn't anybody tell you?"

"Tell me what?" she said.

He actually did seem concerned, so I watched over the top of my book.

"You had pizza for lunch, yeah? You've still got pepperoni on your face — right there — and there — "

I stifled a gasp as he pointed to every acne cyst erupting from Ruthie's skin.

"What are you, stupid, man?" Tank said from the back row. "That ain't pepperoni, that's — "

"Stop. Just, both of you — stop!" I got to my feet, crutchless, and jabbed my finger at Lizard. "You think because somebody has a skin disease she doesn't have feelings? Or ears?"

There was only a momentary stunned silence before Lizard recovered and said, "Ooooh. Scary chick."

"Yeah, watch her. We might be talking 'roid rage."

I turned on Rafe before the last syllable was out of his mouth. "No — we are talking me calling you on the way you treat people."

Uma nodded and gave him a punch and a giggle.

"You too," I said to her. "Why don't you defend her? Because the worse they treat her, the better you feel about yourself? Is that your deal?"

Uma stretched her skinny neck up. "You want to *know* what my deal is?"

"All right, we're done."

There was another shocked silence, because Ms. Edelstein had come out from behind her desk. I personally had never seen her standing up before. She was short and square and had on pumps she could have whacked somebody with, which she looked like she wanted to do about now.

"It's all good, Miss Frankenstein," Rafe said.

"It will be when you zip it."

He looked down at his fly.

"I'm talking about your mouth."

Rafe pulled his finger across his monstrous lips and pretended to drop an imaginary key over the side of his desk. It was the single most disrespectful thing I'd seen him do yet.

"Cassidy."

I turned to see Ms. Edelstein going for the door.

"I want to see you out here."

Me? I'd just stopped a Ruthie crucifixion and she wanted to see *me*?

That couldn't be it, I told myself as I gathered up my crutches and followed her. She was probably going to tell me she would make other arrangements for my sixth period. I would have settled for the dugout on the baseball field if she offered it to me.

When I got out to the hall, she had one hand on her hip and was resting her nose on the other one. Her eyes went from the floor to me.

"I appreciate what you tried to do," she said in a voice that announced she clearly didn't. "But I think you're only bringing more down on Ruthie. She just ignores them and eventually they leave her alone."

They did? When did that ever happen?

"You're a new audience. They're just showing off for you."

"I'm not impressed," I said.

"I can see that." She used her hand for a nose rest again, and then she pulled in air through her nostrils and said, "You've been quiet, and then all of a sudden this outburst. Are you — ?" She shook her head abruptly. "Never mind. Just — let's not stir it with a stick, okay?"

"Okay," I said. But I knew that wasn't what she was talking about at all.

CHAPTER EIGHT

*N*o, lady, I am not still on steroids, I wanted to say. *Isn't that where you were going? Man, if I were—*

If I were, I would be on my way to Mr. LaSalle's office for taking out all of Loser Hall, including her. Off of steroids, all I could say was, "May I go back in now?"

She may have said yes, but all I could hear was the Frenemy screaming, *This is never going to go away! Never!*

The words continued to torment me through the rest of the period, blocking out whatever else the goons had planned for Ruthie. The inner shouting kept up even while Mom was driving me home. I could tell she was giving me looks from the corner of her eye, and I hoped she wouldn't try to talk to me.

Hope didn't do me any good at all. She stopped at a light and tucked her hair behind her ear and played the steering wheel like piano keys before she said, "You have an appointment with Dr. Horton early on Monday morning. Can you afford to miss first period?"

"I have a test on *The Scarlet Letter.*" Which I still hadn't finished reading because every time I tried, somebody was right there to drag out my one mistake yet again and smack me in the face with it.

"I'll see if he can take you later, then," Mom said.

"How about right after lunch?" Yeah. Then maybe we could drag it out for a couple of hours. Maybe even days.

"He's probably going to clear you for physical therapy—"

"Why?"

103

Another strand went behind the other ear. "Are you okay, Cass? Did something happen at school?"

"Yes. No." I ripped off my hat because I was breaking into a Frenemy sweat. "It doesn't matter. I'm just trying to get through it, that's all."

Mom nodded and let it stay quiet until we pulled into the garage. Then she hooked her hair behind both ears and left her hands on the back of her neck.

"You're doing so well with the home exercises," she said. "I hoped you'd changed your thinking about physical therapy."

"You're saying I have to do it."

"I'm saying I think you should try it."

"I just don't get what good it's gonna do when nobody wants me to play basketball for them—or with them. All anybody thinks about when they see me is that I'm the one who took the steroids. Nobody's parents will let them even speak to me. I think teachers are getting *memos* about it now. 'Watch that Brewster kid—she might go into 'roid rage in your class.'"

"What?"

"Never mind." I fumbled for the door handle. "I'll do whatever you and Dad make me do ... like I have a choice. But you oughta just save your money. No—" I got the door open and my good leg out. "Spend it on Aaron, since I messed up his life too."

"Cass—"

"Just let me go finish the stupid *Scarlet Letter*, okay?"

I somehow got to my feet and unsnagged my bag from the door handle and half-hopped, half-staggered into and through the house. When I finally stumbled into my room, I slammed the door so hard my empty bulletin board fell off the wall. Something else slid to the floor too. Off of my desk.

That RL book.

I bristled all the way down my back. I knew I'd thrown it away, which meant somebody had been in my room "tidying up." I was so sick of people trying to "tidy up" my life, I almost picked the book up and smashed it against the wall. But it was already a miracle Mom hadn't called me out for almost splin-

104

tering the door on its hinges, so I settled for hurling RL at the beanbag.

The book fell against the green vinyl and neatly plopped itself open. Then it waited, as if I hadn't just tried to take it out for about the third time.

Okay—for Pete's sake, it wasn't alive. Yet I limped across the floor to it, because I had to see what it had fallen open to. The closer I got, the more powerfully it pulled me in. I was like a magnet in an MRI machine. I dropped into the beanbag and snapped the thing onto my lap.

Are you going to fight me? the words said. *Or do you want my help?*

I'd figured out last time that this had to be some kind of Bible something-or-other—and that Yeshua was obviously another name for Jesus. So if I was fighting it, that meant I was fighting Jesus. Which no doubt I'd been doing even before Pastor Varelli came into my hospital room and told me God had a plan for my life. Right now, I was suddenly too tired to fight anybody. My hissy fits were burning out faster, and not just because of the lack of steroids. They just weren't helping much anymore.

"Okay," I said to the book, "what have you got?" It didn't sound very reverent, talking that way to Jesus, but it was the best I could do.

Here's what I've got. Yeshua told a story about a guy who was a money manager for a rich boss.

I didn't know that much about the world of finance, except that most money managers you heard about these days were basically crooks.

This one definitely was. His rich boss found out that he was running up big personal expenses on his business account: limos, first-class plane tickets, trips to Cancun. So the boss called him in and said, "It's over for you, man. I want you out of here—and if you don't want me to file criminal charges, you'd better give me a complete audit of your books."

I wasn't getting how this was supposed to help me, but I read on. I didn't remember this story from Sunday school, so maybe there was a point I didn't know about.

The manager stepped out of the boss's office and said those familiar words, "I'm toast!"

Yeah. I knew those words.

He was like, "What am I supposed to do now? Managing money is all I know. I can't get a construction job—I'm built like a stick figure. I'll never make it on food stamps ..." And then he came up with a plan.

I slid down so I could prop my ankle on the edge of the bed. I could actually see this guy standing in that hallway, watching his life go down the toilet. I had *so* been there. Only I hadn't come up with a decent plan.

I went back to the book.

The manager figured if he handled things right, people would be so grateful to him that they would take him in when he lost it all and became a homeless person. So here's what he did: He called in each of the people who owed the boss money. He said to the first one, "How much are you in debt?" And the guy said, "It's huge. Like a hundred jugs of olive oil." The manager said, "Okay—here's your bill. Write down fifty." He did the same with all of them—if somebody owed a hundred sacks of wheat, he'd tell them to write down eighty; if it was five head of sheep he'd say make it two.

And this was supposed to help me how?

When the guy's soon-to-be-former-boss found out about it, he was actually impressed.

But the guy was cheating him—

Yes, but he showed that he was shrewd, that he knew how to take care of himself. See, the streetwise people are always paying attention, always looking for a good angle. That's how they survive. It's a different kind of smart.

I knew that kind of "smart." Rafe could get away with calling the teacher Miss Frankenstein, and Tank never got busted in study hall for wearing a sleeveless T-shirt with a skull on it. As for Uma ...

Jesus wanted me to be like that? This wasn't the Bible. I glared down at it, and as always it returned my stare until I read on.

Yeshua said, "I want you to be that kind of smart, only for what's *right. **Let all the stuff you're coming up against get you thinking, let it teach you how to survive, how to get back what you really need so you can totally live.***

"So, wait," I said. "You're saying I could get it back?"

I knew I sounded ridiculous. Who doesn't when they're talking out loud in a room all by themselves? But this book thing actually seemed to be listening to me. And it was the only being that was.

"I know I'm not a loser," I whispered. "I don't care what everybody says—I'm *not*."

I took a breath and waited for the Frenemy to shout back that I was not only a loser, but nuts too. There were no screams in my head. An anxious stirring in my chest, yes, but nothing saying, "No, seriously, you're done."

So I stared into the book and whispered again. "I belong in the game, right? And you're saying I should try to get back in?"

The words that stared back at me were still clear.

"... get back what you really need so you can totally live."

It stopped there. I wanted more, but that was evidently all I was getting for now. So I didn't slam dunk the book this time. I tucked it under the beanbag and limped out to the family room where Mom was setting up for my exercises. It was time for a plan.

"When can I start therapy?" I said.

"Right now," she said, shaking the pillow in her hand.

"No, I mean rehab, like with a professional. No offense to you—"

Mom stopped with a pillow in mid-shake. "None taken. I'm thrilled."

"I'm gonna get it back."

"Of course you are."

"All of it."

Mom tilted her head.

"I *am*."

"Then I think that decision needs to be sealed with some chocolate," she said. "Dark or Swiss?"

107

I never knew before then that chocolate was my mother's solution to just about everything. I even found some in my lunch the next day—a delectable little square of organic sixty-percent cocoa wrapped in gold foil. I was savoring it at my private table when someone dropped heavily into the chair next to me.

"Hi," Ruthie said.

Actually, she kind of huffed it out, as if having gotten across the cafeteria to me was right up there with running a marathon. There was a thin film of perspiration on her forehead, which she wiped off with the back of her hand. For a second I thought she, too, had a tattoo, but it was only some homework assignment, penned across her knuckles in Sharpie.

"Hi," I said.

"I thought I'd sit here," she said. "Y'know, since you don't have anybody to eat with either."

My immediate response was to grope for a way out. *Sorry, I've got to start on* War and Peace*—floss my teeth—brush up on my Swahili.*

And then I felt bad. Really bad. Like how-much-better-am-I-than-Uma bad.

"Sure," I said. Though I still looked around to see if anybody was looking at us. No one was. Somehow that was even more depressing.

"Oh," Ruthie said, "you're having candy too." She pulled a Snickers bar and a bag of M&M's out of a plastic produce bag and dropped them on the table. "You can have all you want. I've got more."

"I'm good, thanks," I said.

She nodded and ripped open the Snickers bar and bit off half of it. She chewed with focus, mouth open, mushed caramel and peanuts oozing from its corners. I could almost hear Kara whining, "Ohmigoshohmigoshohmigosh."

"That must be good," she said.

I was about to tell her that, yes, organic chocolate was good but that I didn't have a bag full to share—but she was pointing to *The Scarlet Letter.*

"You're always reading it," she said.

"I have to for my English class."

"What's it about?"

"What's it *about?*"

She nodded and shoved the other half of the Snickers bar into her mouth.

Oh. My. Gosh.

"Uh, well, yeah, it's about this woman who gets pregnant and has a baby, only she isn't married. Everybody shuns her and they make her wear a big A on her chest."

"Why?"

"It stands for 'adultery.'"

"Is that anything like 'gestating'?"

I looked closer to see if she was kidding. She was licking her fingers. I totally couldn't tell.

"It was supposed to be a shame thing," I said. "So everybody would know she'd broken one of the commandments."

"What about the guy?"

"What guy?"

"The one that got her pregnant. Did he have to wear an A?"

"She wouldn't tell who he was."

"What if she had? Would they make him wear one?"

I stared at her for a second as she tore off the top of the M&M's bag. That was exactly the question I'd wanted to ask since chapter one.

"No," I said. "But he ends up pretty much losing it because he can't stand the guilt."

"What is he, a priest or something?"

"You've totally read this!"

Ruthie shook her head. "But it sounds good. Can I borrow it when you're done? I have to finish reading the one I'm on first. It's not for a class. They're still on *Great Expectations,* which I finished in two days, so I started reading this other book—it's by Tad Williams. Have you ever read anything by him? His series is so good. My cousin had the whole set. Well, she's not really my cousin—she's my cousin's wife. I guess she's like a cousin-in-law. I didn't like his first wife that much because she was, like, an alcoholic, but this one's pretty cool, except I don't get to see her that much because she works full-time at a daycare ..."

I could feel my eyes glazing over as she went on. And on. And on. A small bag of Cheetos came out, got opened, and got eaten without her missing so much as a syllable. I was pretty sure I could have gotten up and left without her even noticing I was no longer there saying "Uh-huh." I was actually considering it when I heard laughter. Loud, pointed laughter. The kind you know is meant especially for you.

Even as I told myself not to look to see where it was coming from, I did. Rafe was lounging against the counter with the condiments on it, ketchup on one side of him, Uma on the other.

"You're gettin' it, Roid," he called to me. "Didn't take you long to see who you gotta hang with now."

He laughed and then stuck a toothpick between his incisors. Uma gave him the usual punch on the arm and shoved him.

"What?" he said. The toothpick came out. "I'm just tryin' to give her a little support. She's one of us now—look at that. And hey, way to go, Ruthie. Nice job."

Uma's shove was harder this time. I suddenly realized she wasn't laughing with him.

"Listen," I said to Ruthie, my face burning like I'd stuck it into a toaster oven. "I've gotta go ... do stuff."

"You should just ignore them," she said. "That's what I do."

"Yeah, and how's that workin' out for ya?"

I caught my breath, because I really hadn't meant to say it out loud. I watched Ruthie pull her head back down into her shoulders, like a turtle retreating into its shell.

"They're not worth it," she said.

By the grace of God the bell rang.

*

And by that same grace Rafe was missing from both art class and Loser Hall. Without him to perform for, Tank and Lizard didn't seem interested in tormenting Ruthie. They zonked out in the back row, leaving Uma to text to her heart's content while Ms. Edelstein graded yet more papers.

At last I could finish that final *S.L.* chapter and be done with Hester Prynne and her little demon child. I still felt bad about hurting Ruthie's feelings, especially when I was so down on everybody else doing it, but at least I had some peace and quiet.

"I brought you this."

I lowered my book and looked across the aisle. Ruthie was holding out her dog-eared paperback.

"I finished it fifth period. We had a sub, which meant we weren't doing anything, so I hurried up and finished it so you could have it. It's not the first in the series but that doesn't matter — you'll still get what's going on because he gives a lot of background, plus you're smart. Anyway, since you're almost done with yours I thought you could read it over the weekend or something —"

"Ruthie, shut up already. Some of us are tryin' to sleep."

She didn't glare at Lizard. She didn't even look at him. She just continued to hold the book out to me.

"Thanks," I said to her and took it from her hand.

She nodded and pulled another thick one out of her backpack. Within moments she was gazing into its pages, lower lip hanging, finger twirling a limp strand of hair. I returned to Hester Prynne, but every few minutes I could feel Ruthie looking at me. And smiling.

*

The melting snow was dripping from the roof when I pulled my bedroom curtains open that afternoon. Sunlight rushed the glass like it had been waiting for me to know it was there. I wasn't exactly ready to greet it like a friend I'd been missing, but I didn't yank down the blinds. After all, I didn't have that many friends left.

Like none, except for Ruthie. Who —

Well, that was the reason I slid the RL book out from under

111

the beanbag. All the way home and all through my exercises I'd been hoping it would give me a little assist. Yeshua—Jesus—had to hang out with loser-types—and so did I. Okay, he did it by choice, or maybe because it was part of his job description—

Whatever. Into the book.

Except that I didn't know where to turn in it. Every other time it had just fallen open when I threw it and I'd started reading from there. I guessed I could give it a toss, but I didn't really want to. And that scared me a little. If I didn't stay angry, did that mean I was giving up?

No freakin' way. This was an inanimate object, even if it was kind of the Bible. It didn't have a will of its own. I was the one with the will. Right?

I tried to open it to a random page but the book smacked itself shut, like that two-year-old down the street I babysat. Once. I tried it again. Same thing.

"Fine," I said, and I picked it up and dropped it into my lap. It splayed open and gave me the look. I swear it did. And I stared back.

Yeshua's follower-friends had a request, the words said.

Yeah, well, I do too. Could you please tell me—

They wanted more faith.

That wasn't my question.

But Yeshua said, "Look, you don't need more faith."

Exactly!

"It's not like you can measure it—you either have it or you don't. If you have the smallest seed of faith—like the poppy seed in your salad dressing—you could say to Pike's Peak, Relocate to Nevada, *and it would do it."*

I huffed out an exasperated sigh. Okay, first of all, I knew plenty of people who were all *about* Jesus-can-do-anything, and I hadn't seen them perform any miracles yet. Pike's Peak was pretty much where it had always been. If this was about me having a faith healing—

Frenemy attack. I shifted in the beanbag and listened to its plastic stuffing beads crunch beneath me. I did not need to go on a guilt trip. I didn't need, "If you would have just a little bit

of faith you would be back on the basketball court right now."
Evidently I didn't have faith. All I had were points of anxiety
driving into my chest. So could we please get on with a plan—

It's not like that.

I flinched, hand still pressed to my collarbone. Wonderful.
Now I was hearing voices, and I didn't have a speck of drugs
in my body. But they were there—those words—in my head.
It's not like that.

And when I looked down at the page, they were there too.

**It's not like that. I'm telling you stories so you'll understand your
own journey.**

Then by all means continue, I wanted to say—bitterly—
between my teeth, my jaw set like a parking brake. And then I
did say it, because the thing apparently read my mind anyway.

**"All right," Yeshua said to them, because they were obviously as
confused as you are, "Let's say you had a personal assistant."**

I wish.

**"And she came in from running your errands and taking care of
your business all day. Would you say, 'Hey, kick your shoes off—
you must be whipped. Put your feet up and I'll fix us both something
to drink and order a pizza.' Would you say that?"**

How much am I paying her?

**"You'd probably say, 'Why don't you get supper going and check
the email. Then I think we'll be done for the day.'"**

I had no idea what a personal assistant was supposed to do,
but that sounded good to me.

**"When she was leaving you would say thank you and see you
tomorrow, but you wouldn't fall all over her every single day and
tell her she was amazing."**

I might give her a Christmas bonus. My dad usually got
one of those. But again, what was I supposed to be getting out
of this?

**"It's the same with you," Yeshua told his follower-friends. "You
work for God. Do the work you've been given to do at this time in
your life, and do it the best you can—but don't expect everybody
to be telling you how wonderful you are for doing your job. It's not
all about you."**

My throat was clogging. I didn't even want everybody telling me I was a shoo-in for the WNBA anymore. I just wanted to be part of the team. Instead, I was spending my time eating lunch with the neediest child in the freshman class while people I once considered beneath me looked on and laughed. What did that have to do with faith? And what did it have to do with me knowing how to deal with the people I'd been thrown in with while I was trying to get my old life back?

No answer, in my head or on the page. Just the sense that I was going to be stared at until I decided to read on.

Yeshua and his follower-friends continued on their road trip to Jerusalem and crossed the border between Galilee and Samaria. It was sort of like entering enemy territory, because there was no love lost between Galileans and Samaritans.

That I knew from the Good Samaritan story. Wait—was this about to tell me that I had to be one and pull Ruthie out of the gutter she lived in?

Different Samaritan story,
the book said.

As Yeshua and his group entered the village limits, ten guys approached them, all suffering from leprosy. If you've ever seen pictures of lepers, you know their disease isn't pretty, and it's painful. People were terrified of it and wouldn't come near a victim. Lepers were completely isolated—like it was somehow their own fault they'd been afflicted—so they didn't even have the comfort of loved ones to ease their suffering.

No Mother Teresa back then.

Right. So these ten guys kept their distance from Yeshua and his friends, and they had to yell to say, "Yeshua—Master—have mercy on us!"

I thought that was a little weird. "Have mercy on us"? Not, "Please get this nasty stuff out of our bodies and heal us"?

Exactly. Yeshua gave them a long stare, and then he said, "Go to the priests. Let them look at you."

I thought they weren't allowed to be near anybody.

Right again. Those seemed like strange instructions, but the ten guys headed for the synagogue.

I probably would have too. When you're desperate, you'll try anything, cling to any hope. Was that what I was doing?

On the way, like before they even got to the priests, all ten of the lepers realized they'd been healed. Their skin was completely clean.

Once again I whispered, "I wish."

One of them turned right around and literally ran back to Yeshua, who could probably hear him from a quarter mile away because he was yelling, "Thank you! Thank you, God!" And when he reached Yeshua he threw himself at his feet. He couldn't find enough ways to express how grateful he was.

I pulled my eyes from the page and stared at my knee. It wasn't exactly a miracle healing — not after reconstructive surgery and exercises that made me want to pull my mother's lips right off her face with my bare hands. But at least I could walk. Maybe I'd even play again in six months.

And yet there was still the question: For whom?

I went back to the page. There had to be an answer in here somewhere. How did these lepers, whose legs were probably falling *off*, get the miracle? Was there more?

There was. Yeshua said, "Didn't I heal ten people? Where are the other nine whose lives I just gave back to them?" Nobody seemed to know. Yeshua said, "Huh. No one could come back and give the credit and the praise to God except you. Interesting. You're a Samaritan. You're supposed to hate us Galileans, and yet here you are."

There was that guilt trip I said I didn't want to go on.

Then Yeshua said to the guy, who was still on his knees in front of him and showed no sign of moving, "Get up, my friend. Go on with your life. Your faith has not only healed you, it has saved you."

I tried to turn the page, but it wouldn't budge.

"That's it?" I said — out loud, because there was no reason not to.

It's enough. For now.

Yeah, enough to mess with my head even more. Being angry and frustrated and scared wasn't plenty? Now I had to feel guilty too?

That you can do something about.

I closed my eyes. It was the voice again, in my head, and it was more urgent this time — like Coach humming instructions in my ear before I went back into the game. Only somehow not.

"What?" I whispered back to it.

Say thank you.

Thank you?

Say thank you.

The questions elbowed their way in. I didn't ask any of them, because the book was once again pressing into my lap. I stared at it, long and hard, and read through all it said —

You don't need more faith ... only the smallest seed ... understand your own journey ... do the work ... it's not all about you. Be saved.

I closed my eyes, and the words arranged themselves behind my lids. Like steps in a plan. Steps I had no idea how to follow. Except to say —

"Okay. Thank you."

I didn't expect anything to happen, and it didn't. Not unless I counted the whispered voice saying, *You're welcome.*

CHAPTER NINE

O kay, so maybe the RL book did have it going on — unlike Ruthie's fantasy novel, which I tried to read over the weekend to pass the time, and which I couldn't follow because I didn't have a fantasy brain. I was pretty sure RL was right, that I could get my life back, because I took one look at my physical therapist and knew God had sent him to heal me.

Seriously. When Mom and I walked into the Sports Medical Center the next Friday and my therapist came into the little curtained cubicle to meet us, I could feel the Frenemy quills falling out of my spine.

It helped that he was cute. No, "cute" didn't work for a guy in his thirties. And not "striking" either. He was "attractive" in that buff, trim, toned kind of way. He wasn't any taller than I was — a lot of men actually weren't — and he didn't look like an exercise snob or even a jock. He just looked like he did stuff and liked it.

"I'm Ben Dillon," he said, first to me. His hand was warm when I shook it, and he smothered both of ours in his other one as he connected with his eyes. Smoky eyes. Gray with some flecks of gold.

I had to blink to keep from staring.

"And you're Cassidy."

"Oh, yeah." I actually giggled. I saw Mom cover up a smile with her hand. Good start. Next thing I knew I'd be drooling.

He smiled too, big and open. Not like "another one has a crush on me." When he let go of my hand and turned to Mom, I checked him out from the back. His light brown hair was cut close to his head, but I could tell it was curly. And he had great shoulders. I forced myself not to look any further down than that.

Besides, it wasn't just his general fineness that made me sure he was the one who was going to get me back on the court—and everywhere else I needed to be. It was the way he listened to Mom and the way he asked her if she would mind letting us get to know each other without her there, without making it sound like "get out." It was how he pulled a stool up next to the examining table I was sitting on and then put all his smoky-eyed attention on me. And it was right there in the first question he asked me:

"So, where do you see yourself six months from now?"

My mind stuttered for a second. Was he seriously asking me for the answer I'd been practicing for days? Could it actually be this perfect?

"I'm going to be playing basketball again," I said.

"Good."

"No—not just good. Great. I'm going to come back stronger than I was before I got hurt." I could feel my face coloring up. "I hope this doesn't sound conceited, but I was one of the top players on my team, and I want to be even better when I go back out on the court."

Ben hooked his heels on the rungs of the stool and let his hands fall lazily between his knees. "You were *the* top player," he said. "At least, that's what I heard."

A small quill poked me. What else had he "heard"?

"Is there more?" he said.

I jerked.

"Any other goals besides slam-dunkin' your way to Old Dominion?"

"Not Old Dominion. UT Knoxville."

"There you go. Anything else?"

"You mean like the WNBA? The Olympic team?"

He grinned. "That all goes without saying, doesn't it?"

"Yeah," I said.

"What about personal goals?"

"Those *are* my personal goals. Basketball's my whole life."

Tears had crept into my voice. I blinked hard so they wouldn't make it into my eyes. Ben just nodded and waited.

"It's not just about me, either," I said. "My team needs me. We could *win* the state title next year. We are—were—good together. I'm going to get that back too."

I didn't add that I had no idea how I was going to pull off that part, especially Kara, or that I knew he couldn't help me there. I wasn't even sure why I'd said it, except that his *way* just drew it out of me. So I said even more.

"I would go through pain every single day if it meant I could be with them again. I miss them."

"That's right, the season's over, isn't it? You don't see them much now?"

I just shook my head.

Ben's eyes drooped. "That can be the toughest part, not having the support. How 'bout your folks? Your mom seems to be there for you."

"She is," I said. "Don't even ask about my dad."

He gave me a half grin. "Okay, not today. So, you mind if I ask you a couple more questions?"

"Do I mind?" I said.

"Yeah." He shrugged. "You're basically in control here. You get to decide how hard you work, which instructions you want to follow, how much you're willing to tell me. Nobody can make you do anything."

"Are you serious?"

He let his head drop back, and he laughed. It was a deep, gurgly sound that made me want to laugh too, and I probably would have if I hadn't been trying so hard to keep up with all the things I hadn't expected.

"I'm serious as a heart attack, Boss. You call the shots. I'm just here to show you what they are."

"Okay," I said. "Ask me anything you want."

He propped one ankle over the other knee. "Okay, first off, what's your diet like?"

"My diet? I'm not on one."

"Everybody has a diet. It's just how you eat."

"Um ... I don't really have breakfast. My mom packs my lunch but it's usually too much. We eat dinner. I'm just not that hungry."

Ben nodded. "Okay, well, you weigh one twenty, which for a girl who's five foot ten is like eighty-five pounds for a girl who's five foot two."

"Is that too much? I can cut back more — I'll do whatever I have to."

"No, it's not too much. It's borderline malnourished. Did you lose weight on purpose?"

"No — it was just from playing so much, I guess."

"You're not playing right now, and you're going to need your strength for what we're going to be doing in here. I'll give you a nutrition plan and you can work with that."

"I guess you could give it to my mom."

Ben swiveled the stool so he could look at me — because I was trying to get my eyes away from his. "You're in charge, Boss. You might want to take control of your own eating."

"Okay," I said.

"You up for another question?"

"Sure."

"How fatigued were you before you got hurt?"

"It was the fourth quarter," I said slowly, "and we'd been playing really hard. I didn't feel that tired but I was probably running on adrenaline."

"I'm not talking tired," Ben said. "Fatigued — not just when you were playing or practicing, but in general. Did you have to drag yourself out of bed in the morning? Feel like you could've taken a nap anywhere, anytime?"

"Well, yeah." It had never occurred to me to call that anything other than being an athlete.

"Did you stop having periods?"

"You mean, like, am I ... gestating?"

Ben laughed. "No. They just stopped happening."

Although that was one thing I did *not* want to discuss with a member of the male gender, I nodded. It was hard to be embarrassed around him.

"How long ago?"

"Um, since December. Should I have told somebody?" Like, who was I going to tell? Coach Deetz?

"We're not going to do 'should have.'" Ben's eyes were serious. "But I will tell you what I think we're dealing with, besides your knee. It's called the female athlete triad."

"I haven't ever heard of that."

"Unfortunately the people who need to know about it don't. It's becoming common in really hardcore girl jocks like yourself."

"Is it a disease?" I said. A weird picture of the ten lepers came into my mind.

"No, it's more like a syndrome of things." Ben held up three fingers. "Underweight, menstruation stops, fatigue. All of which leads to bone loss like older women get when they go into menopause." He nodded grimly. "It happens to the best female adolescent players, the ones with the passion and the heart, because you're pushed beyond your limits. I think all of that was warning you before you got hurt—"

"So it was my fault?"

"No, no." He pressed his hands on my table. "You had no way of knowing what was happening—and anyway, that just set you up for your injury. When you come down from a layup, you put about fourteen times your body weight on your feet, and when you landed off balance—"

"Perturbation," I said. "Which *was* my fault."

My voice had tears in it again.

Ben put up both hands. "*None* of this was your fault. I'm not going to play the blame game, but if there's any responsibility to be taken for it, it's directed toward coaches and sports therapists for our failure to train girls how to run and cut and land—because you naturally do those things differently than boys do." His grin came back. "Females jump funky and land worse, which is why girls tear their ACL eight times more often than boys do—and you can't take the rap for that. It's part of what I'm going to teach you once we get your range of motion back and get your muscles strong."

"You can do that?" I said. Pleaded.

"*You* can do that."

I sat up straight on the table and squared my shoulders. "I totally can. I don't care how much it hurts."

"Can I stop you there?" Ben's eyes were solemn again. "I think you probably have a high pain threshold, and that's great, but don't endure pain because you think you have something to prove. We're not out to show the world how tough you are."

"But I am," I said. "I have to be ..."

"Have to be what? Invincible? Because nobody's that. Strong? Yeah, I'll go there with you. But there will be some things you can't do the first twenty times you try them."

I didn't agree with that, but I kept my mouth firmly closed.

"Here's the thing," he went on. "We want to get you to stop thinking of pain and fatigue and depriving yourself of food as 'normal' for an athlete. True athletes are healthy and they're balanced." He stopped and rubbed the tops of his thighs. "So what do you say — you ready to get to work?"

Somehow I felt like we'd done about a whole day's work already, but I straightened my back again and said, "Well, ye-ah."

He hopped off the stool. "Then let's do it."

Ben kept telling me stuff as he led me out to the open area where people in all kinds of braces and elastic bandages were twisting and wincing in what looked like medieval instruments of torture to me. So much for not showing how tough you were.

"We're going to start out working on your range of motion," he said. "Doc Horton says your wound is basically healed, so now we can break down the scar tissue and get you back some muscle tone."

"How do we do that?" I said.

He turned to me and gave me the biggest grin yet. "We work our tails off."

He wasn't kidding.

We did quad sets that made what Mom and I had done feel like lying on the beach. He didn't settle for leg raises that only got my foot twelve inches off the table. That was for wimps, he said. Did I want to leave before I got it to eighteen inches?

No way.

When he did the moving-my-kneecap-around thing, I accused him of being a sadist.

"You need to let me know when it's too much," he said.

Like I was going to do that. Besides, he talked the entire time, which took my mind off of how hard it was. Not painful, just hard, like suicide sprints or those calf-killing runs Coach used to make us do up and down the bleachers. Ben's talking also kept my mind away from the words "used to."

"The human knee is a wondrous thing," he said as he rocked my patella from side to side. "It's the most athletic part of your body, and the most vulnerable."

"Why would God make it that way?" I said.

He gave me a quick glance and for a second I was afraid he might be an atheist or something.

But he said, "I'm sure He has His reasons. He always does."

When we'd moved to dangling my legs over the side and immediately put Mom's and my act to shame there, he said, "So—I always ask team players this because it fascinates me. Why is winning so important?"

I laughed in spite of the "discomfort" in my knee bend. "See, I think that's a weird question. I think the question should be, 'Why doesn't *everybody* want to win?'"

"Don't they? Let's change legs. Put the other foot behind the other ankle—there you go."

"No. I've played with girls, like on club teams, who act like they don't care if they win, and I don't get that. Why would you want to put yourself out there without wanting to be the best?"

Ben put his hand out. "See if you can get your foot to here. Talk to me about that—about being the best."

"I don't know. Okay, I do. I don't want people looking at me and saying, 'She could be great if she'd try harder.'"

"I doubt anybody would ever say that about you."

He hadn't met my father. No. But they said a lot of other things. I swallowed hard.

"Too much?"

"No."

"I'm serious now. You don't want to be so sore after the first day that you can't come back Tuesday."

"Not tomorrow?"

He grinned. "You want to work on Saturday?"

"I want to work every day. I know I only get you two days a week, but couldn't I still come in and work on my own?"

"You want to be here six days a week, you can do that. We open at six."

"Then I'll come in before school."

He didn't look that impressed, but he didn't say no. He patted my shoulder and got me to my feet.

"Let's do a little gait training—teach you how to walk on that knee again."

That took all my concentration, and his. We didn't talk about anything else until he got me back on the table and wrapped my knee in ice. Then it was like we'd never *stopped* talking.

"So let's get back to the winning thing," he said. "See, I'm more of a recreational athlete myself. Hiking, rock climbing, surfing when I get to the beach. I just do it for the fun of it, so I don't totally get the concept of 'winning'—not the way you do."

"Okay," I said. "What's the opposite of 'winner'?"

"I guess that would be 'loser'?"

"Right. And I don't want to think of myself as a loser. When I lose, it's like I don't even want to be in my own skin. I feel like a stranger to myself, and I've never been that good with strangers."

I looked at him with what I was sure was the same surprise he had in his eyes. I hadn't intended to say all that.

"So what you're saying is that when you don't win, you're not you."

"Well," I said. "Yeah."

How could that not make sense?

"Okay, Boss. I'm going to write down some exercises for you to do when you come in on your own. There will always be somebody around in case you need help." Ben grinned for the first time in a while. "And it's okay to ask for help. That doesn't make you a loser. Actually—" He drew me in with his smoky eyes. "Nothing does."

*

Mom was talking to another woman when I walked into the waiting room—what Ben called the "Hangout Area." She broke into a smile when she saw me.

"No crutches?" she said.

"Nope."

"I told you they were good here," the other woman said.

Mom tucked her arm through mine as we went for the door.

"You know what this means," she said.

"Yeah," I said. "Chocolate."

There was a Pike's Perk Coffee and Tea House across the street, and I insisted on walking over there—although I was totally ready to sit down at a table by the stone fireplace while Mom ordered us both Perk's famous white hot chocolate. The place was packed with college students with laptops, who had crowded chairs around tables so they could complain and laugh and try to see who could be the most cynical. We'd done that on a high-school scale—Kara and Hilary and M.J. and me, and sometimes Selena—and we always tried to get one of the leather couches to do it. The Frenemy tried to get her quills into me, but I shook her away. I was going to have a team again. One thing at a time.

"You did want whipped cream, right?" Mom said. She put two frothy-looking cups on the table.

"Did you already talk to Ben?" I said.

"About . . . ?"

"He says I have to gain weight. Well, I don't *have* to. It's up to me—that's actually what he said."

"Really. Tell me some more."

I filled her in on everything, including the part about me being allowed to come in every day if I wanted to.

"I can take you and then get you to school," she said. "That'll still give me time to get to work."

"Well, yeah, you don't go in until five."

"Actually, I'm changing my schedule," she said. "I'm doing the noon show and the late news."

"Why?" I said.

"Because we're in this thing together." She looked into her mug. "I know Ben says you're in the driver's seat, but you're still going to need support. Is that okay with you?"

"Yeah, Mom. But I don't expect you to mess up your career because of this."

"It's all about priorities, Cass," she said.

She tucked her hair behind her ears, which I was figuring out meant she was about to say something I might not want to hear. I was seeing a lot of those ears these days.

"You saw that lady I was talking to over at the Center?"

I nodded.

"She said to me, 'Well, at least your daughter's rehabbing in the off-season,' and I thought, you know what, there *is* no 'off-season.' If you weren't hurt right now, you'd be practicing for All-State, and then there would be at least one summer skills camp, and then preseason conditioning before the whole thing started all over again." She ran her fingers behind her ears even though her hair was already tightly tucked. "And I thought, 'No one's body can take that year round.'"

"They say you have to do that if you want to make it."

"Who is 'they'?"

I took a long sip out of my hot chocolate. She waited.

"Dad," I said.

Mom leaned back and looked like she was staring at the model airplane that hung from the middle of the ceiling. I was fairly certain she wasn't seeing it. It occurred to me as I watched her have a conversation with herself that nobody had stopped by our table and said, "Aren't you the weather lady?" Maybe that was because she didn't look like the polished-up meteorologist right now. She looked like somebody's worried mother.

"Well," she said, pulling her eyes back to me. "I really like Ben's approach—letting you make decisions about your treatment. I'll only intervene if I think you're hurting yourself. Sound like a plan?"

"Yeah," I said. I spooned off the whipped cream and looked at it before I closed my lips over it. I wondered if she realized that was probably the longest conversation the two of us had ever had.

*

I was glad it was Friday and I didn't have to do homework, because I was so wiped out I went to bed without even checking in with RL. And for once I didn't lie there thinking about Kara and Coach Deetz—or Rafe and Ruthie—until the Frenemy got a stranglehold on me. I whispered my nightly *thank you* and checked out about the same time my head connected with the pillow.

But I woke up with a jerk sometime later to the sound of voices from the other side of the wall. They were coming from my parents' room, and they had an edge to them that cut right through the Sheetrock.

"What part of this seems like a good idea to you?" my father said.

"All of it," Mom said.

I started to pull my slobbered-on pillow over my head. If they were arguing about her taking a pay cut or something, I didn't want to hear about it. I didn't need any more guilt.

"You honestly think she's capable of making decisions about her body?" Dad gave a harsh laugh. "Why? Because she's made such good choices already?"

"It was an honest mistake—"

"Do you really believe that?"

I shoved the pillow aside and sat straight up.

"Yes, I believe that. Are you saying you don't?"

"I did at first."

There were sounds of shoes being dropped and hangers being scraped.

"What does that mean?" Mom said.

"She had to have some idea that what Gretchen gave her was steroids. She's an athlete, Lisa—she hears the stories. I know Deetz has talked to them about that stuff—or maybe he hasn't. I'm not that keen on him right now either."

"What do you mean, 'either'?"

I could imagine the cold look in my father's eyes because I could hear it in his voice. "I thought she was exceptional. Now—"

"Now what?"

"I've taken a step back."

"Yes. I've noticed. Have you even spoken to her this last week? Asked her how she's doing?"

"I know how she's doing. You've got that handled. Look, she's holed up in her room by the time I get home." The closet door banged. "Make up your mind, Lisa. Do you want me to leave her alone to 'make her own decisions' or treat her like she's 'special' the way you're doing?"

"I'm treating her like my daughter."

"Well, your daughter refuses to listen to me—"

"You know what? It was listening to you that got her into this situation in the first place. I wouldn't have blamed her for taking steroids if she *had* known what they were."

The air went dead. I stared at the wall like I might be able to see through it if I tried hard enough. Although I didn't have to see to know everything on my father's face had come to a point.

"I love how you always bring this stuff up when I'm ready to go to bed," he said. Snarled.

"When else do I see you, Trent? It's like you've totally dropped out of our family life."

"I haven't 'dropped out.' I'm dealing with things."

"How is that helping Cassidy?"

"Oh, now you *want* me to help her. A minute ago it was my help that messed her up to begin with. Look, I told you I'm dealing with it, so just—just back off."

I wondered miserably if stomping out of the room and slamming the door was my mother's way of backing off. When the footsteps paused outside my door, I squeezed my eyes shut and pretended to be asleep.

CHAPTER TEN

My parents' fight definitely had the potential to collapse my plan to get everything back. Who wouldn't be taken out at the knees by her father thinking she took steroids on purpose and saying she couldn't be trusted to make decisions — and implying that because of her, he had things to 'deal with'?

But I kept thinking about what Ben said. He was the professional, right? And I thought about my mom. Okay, so she was only *now* getting to know me, but at least she didn't carry on like a Doberman pinscher while she was doing it.

And there was RL. I read the same pages over and over, because that was all it would let me see — and I had the part I needed memorized.

Get up, my friend. Go on with your life. Your faith has not only healed you, it has saved you.

It said I only needed faith the size of a spot in my poppy-seed dressing. I had that much, didn't I? I went to church — at least I did before I got hurt. Kara and I used to go to youth group — except when we had practice or a game or a tournament or I was at camp. I prayed before games. I used to. And I tried to be a good Christian — you know, by trying to help people. Right?

And now I had the plan. I decided it was a God plan, and I was going for it with everything I used to put into basketball. As long as I could stay away from words like "used to" and "loser," as long as I could hear Yeshua saying, "Get up, my friend," I could keep the Frenemy from paralyzing me.

And it was happening. I worked out at the Center on Saturday, Monday, and Tuesday at six in the morning while

Mom sat in the Hangout Area with her coffee and her laptop and her hair tucked behind her ears. My range of motion was improving by more than a degree a day. Ben was going to be impressed.

In school my plan to make straight A's was gaining momentum, except in Mr. Josephson's class, where the best I could get so far was a B+. Boz said I was doing good to get that, but I wasn't settling. I'd do better somehow.

I had faith.

Although it shrank below poppy-seed size a couple of times. Like when I turned a corner in the hall and literally ran into Coach Deetz. We stood there with the word *awkward* echoing between us until he said, "How you doin', Cassidy?" If he had called me *Brewster*, maybe I would have said something besides, "I'm fine." I might have said, "Please forgive me?"

I didn't. I had to wait until I was worth forgiving.

The other time was when I saw Kara and Hilary and M.J. in the cafeteria, picking greasy pepperoni from their pizza slices instead of being off campus in a cozy booth. They were whispering like they were in a world of their own. I missed being in it. I wanted to go to them and tell them to save me a place — that somehow I would be acceptable again.

Only I still didn't know how I was going to forgive Kara ... at least not enough to fill the hole that gaped between us.

But then Ruthie would appear at what was now obviously "our" table and start telling me the plot of some novel or the life story of her third cousin twice removed, and I'd have to pretend to listen to her while my heart broke.

Tuesday, though, I was psyched up for my session with Ben. I just had to get through fifth and sixth periods, and maybe that wouldn't be so bad, since Rafe seemed to have disappeared. Actually, I heard Uma say something about him being suspended, but I tried not to ever actually hear Uma, so I didn't know how long he was going to be out. I hoped it was a long sentence.

No such luck. When I walked into fifth period he was standing inside the door like a Walmart greeter.

"Roid!" he said. "Dude—somebody stole your crutches."

"Was it you?" I said. "Is that why they put you under house arrest?"

"No, man, I was called as an expert witness."

"Expert at what?"

He wiggled his eyebrows.

"Is that supposed to tell me something?" I said.

The bell rang. Maybe God was listening to me after all.

I settled in and half listened to P-W and half daydreamed about showing Ben how much progress I'd made. I snapped to full attention when I heard her say my name.

"—and Rafe Diego."

"Hey, Roid—it's you and me, babe."

I stared—stupidly, I was sure—at Mrs. Petrocelli-Ward, who continued to pair up names while she handed out sheets of paper. I snatched up the one she put in front of me, and as I read it, my stomach tied itself into a square knot.

You and your partner, it said, *will collaborate on a project in which you will visually represent a significant movement in art history. You may choose—*

"Before we go over the instructions," P-W said, "I want to make it clear that a piece of this magnitude is going to require time outside of class, so I will keep the art room open before school—"

I'll be at the Center.

"During lunch—"

I'd rather eat with Ruthie.

"And after school."

I'd rather be shot.

P-W stopped next to my table, bracelets clanging. "This project is worth fifty percent of your grade for this quarter."

She must have heard my low groan above the jangling of her jewelry, because she said, "Art takes time. And we are not spray-painting hoodlums here, people. We are artists."

"Man, that's cold," Rafe said.

He glared from under the hood of his forehead and slid down to his tailbone in his chair. He took my plan to make straight A's down with him.

But there was no way I was letting it happen. As soon as Mrs. Petrocelli-Ward finished going over the endless list of requirements and told us to get with our assigned partners, I practically leaped over three tables to get to her, bum knee and all.

Before I could even let out the words "Can I please talk to you?" she had a jangling hand up.

"I know what you're going to ask me, Cassidy, and the answer is no. I put people together for a reason."

"To torture us?" I said. I stuck up my own hand. "I'm sorry. It's just that I really want to make an A in this class and I don't see how that's going to happen with—"

I swept my gaze over to Rafe, who was watching me under the hood. When I caught his eye, the brows wiggled.

Ugh.

"Can I please just work on my own?" I said. "I'll do twice as much as you expect."

P-W toyed with her necklace with paint-stained fingers. "Interesting," she said. "My understanding was that you were a team player."

Why didn't she just slap me?

"I am if I have a team," I said.

"I've given you one," she said. "Go with it."

I looked at Rafe again. He had his chair rocked back on two legs, wearing a smarmy smirk he could have borrowed from a mug shot.

If that was my "team," I might as well forfeit the game.

*

But I couldn't give up. There was even more at stake now, because it became obvious to me, as I pretended to study the instruction sheet for what was left of fifth period and then made my way to sixth, that Mrs. Petrocelli-Ward assumed what everybody else assumed about me. Why else would she set me up to fail?

I wasn't having it. Time to supplement the plan.

The minute Rafe swaggered into Loser Hall, I was on him.

I planted myself in the desk in front of his and turned sideways so I could look him straight in the eye.

"We have to do this project together," I said. "Trust me, I tried to get out of it, but P-W won't budge, so here's the deal. We just do Cubism because it doesn't take that much to draw a bunch of boxes. I'll do all the background research. I don't care if I have to do *most* of the work, but I'm not bombing on this project."

I had to take a deep breath, during which Rafe folded his arms and looked at me. No eyebrows wiggling. No smart-mouth retorts. I took it as a yes.

"Rafe-man, you gonna let her diss you like that?" Lizard said.

Tank grunted—a most attractive sound. "You're whipped, man. You see that, Uma?"

"You could take some lessons from this woman," Lizard said to her. He was by now sitting on the back of his desk chair, feet on the seat. I could almost hear the scratching of Ms. Edelstein's red pencil across the calculus papers.

Uma let go of the knot she had her lips in. "What's 'cubism'?"

"Doesn't matter," Rafe said. "We're not doin' it."

"We have to do *something*," I said. "It was the only thing I could think of."

"You ever think about askin' me?" Rafe bounced the heel of his hand off his forehead. "Gee, what a concept."

"Like you would *so* come up with something."

"I did."

"What?"

"Graffiti art."

My eyes rolled completely up into my head. "You are *not* serious. You want to do the history of *tagging*? We might as well just take the F right now."

"Fine with me."

Tank punched Rafe on the shoulder like he'd just scored two points. He kind of had.

"Okay, look," I said. "We have to find a 'movement,' not some gang thing—"

"First of all, I'm not a tagger. Second of all, what I do is art. And third of all, true billboard liberation is not a 'gang thing.'" Rafe twitched his fingers in quotation marks, but the light in his eyes wasn't sarcastic. "It's a statement against the culture."

"It's a crime!"

"It's the reverse side of a culture that is itself criminal."

The words sounded like he was reading them out of a book, but even that was enough to make me stumble over the ones lining up in my mind.

"Pierre Klossowski," he said. "1871."

I shook my head.

"French painter. Gustave Courbet. He saw vandalism as an artistic expression of contempt and creativity." Rafe shrugged. "We trace 'the history of graffiti art'—or we take the F."

"Oooo—"

"Shut up, Lizard," Rafe said. But his eyes were on me.

"So what are we going to do?" I said. "Find a railroad car and spray paint it?"

"Knock yourself out. I don't do that."

I tightened my ponytail with a yank. "Okay, since you've got the whole thing mapped out—"

"We do a legal wall."

"A legal wall."

"Yeah. A wall where it isn't a 'crime' to make your art."

"And we're going to find that where?"

"We're not gonna find it. We're gonna make it. Out of something."

"So we do that. And what? We tell P-W we made a wall?"

"No, Honors English. Then we paint on it, showing, like, how the movement's progressed. Only we do it in graffiti art."

"Oh," I said. And then I said nothing. Because it actually was a pretty good idea.

Except for the part where we were going to have to work on it together outside of class. Where was I going to feel safe meeting Rafe any place besides school? It wasn't even that safe in here—

I stumbled over my thoughts again, but they were still there when I turned to Rafe.

"Okay, say P-W approves our idea."

Rafe was back to working his eyebrows. "She will."

"We're gonna have to work on it on our own time, and most of mine's booked. So"—I leaned in and lowered my voice—"what if I ask Ms. Edelstein if we can work on it in here—you know, planning it out and stuff. I'll—"

"Hey, Miss Frankenstein," he said over my head.

"Hey, Rafe," she droned back. She didn't even look up.

"Can me and the Roid work on our art project in here?"

"As long as you don't spill anything."

I stared at her and then at Rafe. "How is it that one minute you can sound like an art professor, and the next minute you're talking like you never saw a grammar book?"

"I never have."

"I believe that."

I got up to go back to my seat for some paper, but something snagged at me. It was the look on Uma's face.

She'd drawn everything tight: rosebud mouth, made-up eyes ... even her cheeks were sucked in like she was pulling the juice out of something. It was obviously me she had in mind.

Problem? I wanted to say. But I didn't. She wrapped both arms around Rafe's right bicep, and I got the message.

Don't worry about it, honey, I thought as I turned away. *He is so not my type.*

*

My "type," if I even had one, was Ben. Not Ben as a guy, obviously. Ben as the coolest physical therapist that ever lived. Not like I'd ever had one before, but the point was, he was fabulous.

In the first place, his entire face opened into a smile when he measured my range of motion and when I weighed in at 122.

"Your discipline is off the charts, Boss," he said, eyes sparkling their flecks of gold. "You're this intense in everything you do, aren't ya?"

"I have to be," I said.

"Which is why I'm going to say this." His face went serious. "Anything in the extreme has the potential to be damaging. Remember how you got here."

"Am I doing it wrong?" I said.

"You're doing it great. It's just something we're going to work on."

"I'm working on as much as I can!"

Ben cocked his head in that way he had. "You want to tell me about that?"

"No."

"Whenever you're ready. Okay, let's—"

"I'm already trying to get my grades up and my knee working and my faith stronger. I haven't even *started* on getting my friends back. And now you're saying I have to work on not working so hard?" I put up both hands and tried to rub it all out. "I'm sorry. I'll get it. I just have to …"

"You just have to what?" Ben sat on the table beside me and swung his legs.

"I just have to figure out how that fits into my plan," I said.

It sounded lame, now that it was out there, but Ben didn't laugh. He nodded at me like I'd actually said something that made sense.

"A plan is a good thing to have," he said. "You mentioned God the other day, and you said just now you're trying to bulk up your faith some."

"Yeah. Am I not supposed to talk about religion in here?"

He grinned. "If that were the case, they'd kick me out. Here's the thing, though, about faith—" He pressed a hand to his chest. "As I understand it. You can't grow it yourself. You can feed it, you can exercise it, but you can't actually 'make' it stronger." He tapped my knee. "It's like what you're doing here. You can put in the work, but you aren't the one building the muscles and getting your joint operating."

"But if I didn't do the work, it wouldn't happen."

"Exactly."

"Exactly what?"

"You pray—you study the Word—you live it—and

God builds up your faith." He made a grimace face. "Am I preaching?"

I shook my head. It wasn't like any preaching I'd ever heard, anyway. This I could actually understand. He was talking like—

"I don't try to figure it all out," Ben said. "When I'm in trouble, I just say, 'Please, God.' And when He shows up, I just say, 'Thank you.'"

Yeah. He was talking like RL.

*

During the hour of mini squats and mini lunges—neither of which felt very "mini" to me—and "small" step-ups and "easy" leg presses on one of those torture machines, I was definitely saying, "Please, please, please!" And when we stopped, I said a major "Thank you."

"Oh, you need chocolate," Mom said when I dragged myself into the Hangout Area.

"Ya think?" I said.

We got our table at Pike's Perk, and I was shoveling in the whipped cream when Mom looked past me to the doorway, an odd expression on her face—like she was surprised, but not necessarily in a good way.

"What?" I said. "Is Dad here?"

"No. It's your brother."

"Maybe he won't see us," I whispered.

Mom gave a half laugh. "Too late."

She obviously hadn't invited him, but from the way she was tucking her hair, I was pretty sure she had let it slip to him or Dad that we had come here last week after therapy. I also got that from the way Aaron marched right over to the table and sat himself down.

"Hey, guy," Mom said as she reached over to rub his arm.

"Hey." He gave her a quick peck on the cheek that made me glad we had never been affectionate with each other. I wondered if as a mother you had to love your kid even if you couldn't stand him. If so, I was never going to gestate.

137

Aaron peered into my cup. "Now that looks healthy."

"Doctor's orders," I said, and I gave my hot chocolate a loud slurp.

"They keeping you busy at school?" Mom said. "You haven't been by the house in—"

Two and a half weeks. Thank you, God.

"I was just there last week," Aaron said. "Nobody was home."

"I changed my work schedule," Mom said.

"Let me guess—Cassidy needs to be taken to physical therapy. And school. And drug rehab."

"Aaron, stop it."

Both of us looked at Mom. Hopefully my face didn't match my brother's, but if it did, my eyes were popping from my head.

"Stop," she said again. "You're better than that."

That I couldn't agree with, but I was still too stunned to say anything. She was actually reprimanding her precious firstborn Aaron? All right, Mom.

"Sorry," he said to her, not me. "I'm a little bitter."

Mom nodded. "I know. Losing Gretchen was huge. But seriously, you don't need to take it out on your sister. You want a coffee?"

Okay, who was this woman and what had she done with my mother?

Aaron shook his head and looked at a Danish that we hadn't started on yet.

"Go ahead," Mom said.

That was fine with me. I'd lost my appetite when he sat down. What was he *doing* there if I was the reason for him being "bitter"?

"I just want to know something," he said. He was looking at me.

"What?" I said.

"Did you ask Gretchen for the drugs or did she offer them to you?"

"I already said it about five thousand times. *She* approached *me*, and she didn't tell me—"

"That's what you said when you got caught, but seriously, now that you're 'clean and sober,' are you still sticking to that story?"

"Aaron—" Mom said.

But I shook my head at her. "It's okay. I'm getting used to people calling me a liar."

"Hey," Aaron said. "I can completely see why you'd want to put the best spin possible on this for yourself."

"Why?" I said. "Because that's what you would do?"

"I'm not like you—at all."

Thank you, Lord, for that, I started to say. But then I stopped. *Thank you.* RL said it. Ben said it. *Just say thank you.*

Why that made sense now, of course, I had no idea. My relationship with my brother was not one of the things I was working on. What would be the point? But it came out of my mouth anyway.

"Thank you," I said.

Aaron blinked. "For what?"

"I don't know. For whatever it is you're trying to do, I guess."

Oh my gosh, what was I doing?

"What I'm trying to *do*," he said, "is get my life back."

"Wow," I said. There was no sarcasm biting through my voice. "That's exactly what I'm trying to do. How's that going for you?"

"Cass—"

"No, I'm not being smart, Mom. I totally know what it's like to feel like you've lost everything."

"Except in my case, I didn't do anything to cause it." Aaron's voice wasn't biting either. "I'm just trying to get to the truth."

"I'm *telling* you the truth. I know—it hurts, right? Trust me, I feel that every time I tell the truth to myself."

Something flickered in Aaron's pale blue eyes. But only for a second, before they came to a point and he turned into our father again.

"If you think we're going to bond over this, forget about it," he said. He looked at Mom, who was looking hard right back at him. "You're enabling her, Mom. That never works. She's still playing the victim, because that's what addicts do." He stood up and tapped his knuckles on the table. "I hope you're keeping up those random drug tests, because I guarantee you, once a user, always a user."

He wasn't two steps away from the table before I was saying, "Mom, I'm not—"

"I know, Cass," she said. Her eyes followed him sadly to the door. "I know."

I pushed my hot chocolate away, but the Frenemy wouldn't be moved. Her guilt quills stabbed me straight in the heart. Helping me was ruining what Mom had left with Dad, and now Aaron.

I had to wonder how many more relationships I was going to mess up before I made it back.

That wasn't part of the plan.

a re you reading that book over again?" Ruthie said Thursday at lunch.

I turned the opened *Scarlet Letter* onto its face on the table and glared at its spine. "I think I'm going to be reading it for the rest of my life."

I'd thought I was done with it when we took the multiple choice test and I got an A-. But then Mr. Josephson assigned a paper on it, which was guaranteed to send my average plummeting again. He had a problem with the way I wrote.

I want to hear your voice, he'd written on my last essay.

I was sure that didn't mean he wanted me to come up to his desk and scream, *What do you want from me?*

"Do you know that guy?" Ruthie said.

She was pointing behind me, but I didn't have a chance to turn around before Boz, from my English class, pulled out the chair next to me.

"Do you mind if I sit here?" he said.

"Um, no," I said. I looked at Ruthie. "Do you mind?"

Her eyes widened. "Me?"

"Yeah. Do you care if Boz sits with us?"

She shook her head and lowered it, so that the strings of hair covered her face like a grass skirt. The latest fantasy novel came out of her bag.

Boz stared at her for about a half a second and then nodded at *The Scarlet Letter*.

"Working on your paper?" he said.

"Trying to. I don't know what I'm doing." I watched him

pull his copy out of his back pocket. "You probably have yours finished already."

"I've got a rough draft done. But, then, I basically have no life."

He blinked, rapidly, and pulled down an eyelid with his fingers.

"Something in your eye?" I said.

"Yeah. My contacts. It's only my second day wearing them."

"Oh, yeah," I said. "You usually wear glasses, huh?" I hadn't noticed the change, but now, come to think of it, he did look less geeky today. Not having glasses on definitely made his nose look smaller.

Ugh. I hated it when I thought shallow stuff like that.

"Need help thinking of a topic?"

"I'm sorry?"

"For your paper. You said you don't know what you're doing yet. I could brainstorm with you."

"Oh." I stared at the book, still facedown on the table like it was ashamed of itself. "Well—we're supposed to relate it to our own life somehow, right? And I just don't exactly see myself in Hester Prynne."

"You could write about gestation."

I whipped my head around to Ruthie. She was peeking out from behind the fairies and humanized dragonflies.

"That's what the book's about, right?"

"It's not what *I'm* about!"

"No, not like you're pregnant."

"Hello!"

"But the girl in the book's taking all the blame. You could write about one time when you had to take all the blame and it wasn't fair. Like my brother's girlfriend." Ruthie put the book down and pushed her hair out of her face. "She has like four sisters—okay, maybe five. There was, let's see, Jenna, Jodie, Jade, Joanna—"

"Ruthie," I said, "do you have to go all the way back to Genesis every time you tell a story?"

Boz laughed. I was surprised at how deep the sound was, like a radio announcer or something.

"Sorry." Ruthie started to duck behind the fairies.

"No—tell it," I said. "Just, like, skip ahead to Revelation."

She looked puzzled, but Boz laughed again.

"What did your brother's girlfriend take the blame for? The short version."

"But see, it doesn't make sense if I don't tell you the whole thing. You have to know about her sisters because they're the ones who got away with murder—I mean, for real."

"They killed somebody?" I said.

"Almost. See, when Josie was little … okay, so there *were* five sisters—"

"What's the protagonist's name?" Boz said.

"The what?"

"The protagonist. The main character."

Ruthie's eyebrows crumpled.

"Your brother's girlfriend," I said.

"Oh. Jeannette. Isn't that pretty? I mean, it's old-fashioned, but it's pretty."

"Kind of like Ruth," Boz said. "I mean, that's kind of old but cool, right?"

Ruthie smiled. I saw for the first time that her eyes were green. How had I missed that before? Probably because I was always watching her mouth.

She took off again on the harangue about poor victimized Jeannette, and I got lost about halfway through. Boz, on the other hand, seemed captivated.

"So, let me get this straight," he said when Ruthie finally brought it to a close. "What you're saying is—"

"Oh my gosh, Boz," I said. "We don't need a recap!"

He laughed again, and so did Ruthie, although I was sure she had no idea why—except that at the moment nobody was telling her she was fat or ugly or dumb or had a Pizza Hut Supreme for a face. I was no closer to a topic for my paper, but I was farther away from the glaring mood I'd been in when I sat down.

*

It actually made me want to brainstorm for an idea, though, which I couldn't do in sixth period because Rafe and I were working on our art project. Well, *I* was working, writing down all the stuff he already knew about Norman Mailer being the protector of graffiti and the city of New York getting all over him because he compared "vandals" to Giotto and Rauschenberg (famous artists, Rafe told me when I asked—like I should have *known*), and they had to cover the subway walls with Teflon paint and make hardware stores keep spray paint under lock and key.

Yeah, through all that, I took notes like a crazy woman while Rafe lounged against the back wall at his desk, one arm around Uma, the other hand pushing a toothpick in and out of his dental work. It didn't help my concentration that Uma gave me the death stare the entire time. I really was going to have to get her alone and tell her I wasn't after her man.

On second thought, maybe I could just send her a text.

*

Right after I did my afternoon exercises, I took the smoothie my mom made me to my room, making a silent vow not to come out until I had a topic and an outline for my *Scarlet Letter* essay.

I stopped inside the doorway. The hair on the back of my neck stood up, but it wasn't the Frenemy. It was the creepy-weird feeling that somebody had been in there. Again?

I heard Mom coming down the hall and I stuck my head out.

"You don't have to clean my room, Mom," I said. "I can do it."

She laughed. "You're giving me way too much credit, Cass. I haven't cleaned anything in this house for about two weeks. Not that it doesn't need it—"

"No, seriously. You haven't been in here tidying?"

"Since when have I ever 'tidied'? That's your father's MO." Her face clouded. "And, no, I'm sure he hasn't been in there. He's never here when one of us isn't."

That was true. He was usually off "dealing with things."

"Is something wrong, Cass?" Mom said.

"No, I'm just being weird," I said. "I'm gonna do some homework."

It had to be that I was spending way too much time alone in there and I was getting paranoid or something. With resolution I took my bag straight to the beanbag chair and sank into it. Maybe a little RL would calm me down. It usually did.

But when I reached my hand under the beanbag, my fingers only touched carpet. There was no gnarled-up leather book, there or in any of the other six places I looked—frantically— like a cop with a search warrant. By the time I'd pulled everything out from under the bed, I was dripping sweat and my heart was slamming.

"Is this what you're looking for?"

My head jerked up. Aaron stood in my doorway, my RL book in his hand. I didn't even know where to start.

I chose getting up off the floor first, while Aaron slapped the book onto my desk. Hard.

"You came in here and *took* that?" I said.

"It didn't meet me at the front door."

"You had no right to even come into my room."

"Yeah, well, you know something, Cassidy? I'm not real concerned about anybody's 'rights'—especially not yours."

His eyes glittered with something way past his usual disdain. Fine. I was sure mine were glittering too.

"I'm going to get to the truth," he said.

"What truth? You were looking for *drugs?*"

"Not even you are that stupid." He picked up RL and dropped it again. "I saw the journal—thought maybe you wrote something in a journal."

"That's not a journal."

"Yeah. I should have known—you never were the contemplative type. Matter of fact, you never were one to think at all." His face went hatchet narrow. "If you were, I wouldn't be in the position I'm in right now."

"Look—I'm sorry your girlfriend broke up with you—"

"My fiancée."

"Whatever—but—"

"No, not 'whatever.'"

Aaron shoved RL aside and leaned on my desk with both hands, so that his face was barely a foot from mine. We hadn't been that close to each other since the last family photo. Only then, I'd seen total disdain. Now I was seeing almost hate.

"We were getting married. Now we're not. Because of you."

"Why is that my fault? What if she'd offered me the stuff, and I didn't take it and I told you—wouldn't she still be wrong?"

"If she really did offer it to you." He picked up RL and shook it at me. "That's what I thought I might find out in here."

I grabbed for the book but he pulled it out of my reach.

"I told you what happened," I said. "Now give me—"

"I think you're lying. Gretchen and I had a good thing—and then out of nowhere she risks her whole career and gives you steroids? I don't think so. No, see, what I think is that she did give you supplements and you got the steroids from someplace else and blamed her."

I felt my mouth drop open. "Why would I *do* that?"

"Because you thought she'd cover for you. But I know Gretchen. She has more integrity than this whole family put together." Aaron breathed hard through his nose. "She had to separate herself from us—from me—so she could clear her name. If she doesn't, I might never get her back."

I opened my mouth to tell him that made absolutely no sense. But I closed it. Because my brother had tears in his eyes, and somehow, in some way I'd never meant to, I had put them there.

"You know what?" I said instead. "I'm not having this conversation with you."

"Why? Because you're afraid you'll let something slip?"

"No, because I don't like who I turn into when I'm around you. I just don't want to be this—this cynical, I-can-say-worse-things-to-you-than-you-say-to-me person. You're never going to believe me because you don't want to believe me, so please, will you just leave me alone?"

146

It looked like Aaron's eyebrow went up in spite of itself. "Did you just say 'please' to me?"

"No," I said. "I meant that for God."

"Oh, so now you've got religion too. At least you can't take anybody down with that."

"Please go," I said.

"Going," he said. He opened his hand and let RL drop to the desktop.

When I was sure the front door had closed, I sank myself into the crunch of my beanbag and pressed RL onto my lap the way it had pressed itself there before. I ran my fingers across the battered cover and traced them through every set of carved-in initials and dug-in doodles and into every dent and crack worn there by the others who had found its wisdom. Aaron obviously wasn't one of them.

After I creased down every page and examined it for traces of my brother, I decided he hadn't tainted it in some way. It freaked me out that if he hadn't brought it back himself, I might never have known what happened to it. And it freaked me out that it freaked me out. I actually depended on this thing—I trusted it, I needed its voice. And that was more than I could say for most of the other voices in my life.

Something poked at me, and again, it wasn't the Frenemy. It was more like a nudge, like somebody telling me there was something way off about the thought I'd just had.

What? What other voice was actually changing anything?

Okay, maybe Mom's.

And yeah, Ben's.

And freakin' Ruthie's—who was about as bright as the dome light in Mom's car, and yet she didn't talk to me like I was somebody who could have been. I guess you could throw Boz in there too, for that matter.

I looked down at RL. The thing was, if I hadn't listened to this book, I would never have heard any of them.

I pressed the covers together and then let it fall open. It chose a new page that yanked me into itself like we only had ten seconds left in the quarter. I dug into the chair and read.

Yeshua told his follower-friends another story. They were getting close to the end of their road trip, and he needed them to hear this. He said, "There was a city judge who couldn't have cared less about whether there was a God or not. As for people, he didn't have too much time for their problems either."

Nice guy. Mr. LaSalle came to mind.

"In the city, there was a widow. She was supposed to get some public assistance, which she totally needed because her husband had left her with zilch, but she wasn't receiving her checks, her food stamps, her free health care, nothing. She kept going before the judge—we're talking weekly, and then daily, saying, I need help here. My rights are being violated! This judge kept putting her off, thinking she'd eventually give up and go away. He had important people to deal with—rich, influential types who could get him reelected. This woman could do absolutely nothing for him, and frankly he saw her as a nuisance."

Jerk.

You got that right. Yeshua went on to say that, yeah, she was a nuisance, even though she had a good case. She about drove the judge nuts, until he finally said to himself, "Y'know, I don't give a flip what God thinks, and I sure don't care about anybody else's opinion, but, man, I better see that this woman gets what she's supposed to get or I am going to end up on tranquilizers."

I stifled a snort. I'd sort of felt that way with Ruthie.

That evidently wasn't the end of the story, because the book got heavy in my lap.

Then Yeshua said, "Did you hear what that judge, jerk that he was, said to the widow?"

Yeah.

"How can you think God won't come in and help you if you keep asking? Even if nobody else pays any attention to you—even if you've lost all credibility—God will be there for you."

But what about when I tried to tell Mr. LaSalle and Coach—even my own brother and father—that I didn't know I was taking steroids and they didn't believe me? Where was God then?

Yeshua said, "How much of that kind of nagging, begging, I-won't-give-up kind of faith am I seeing here?"

I felt a little sick. He was seeing none.

I hadn't nagged or begged. I'd pitched a fit and formed a plan. But I hadn't prayed.

You said thank you.

I didn't even flinch at the sound of the voice. I only said, "So what do I do now?"

There was a silence as deep as my empty place. And then I heard *Say please.*

Just say please.

*

For the rest of Thursday evening and the whole next day, I had a strange off-and-on sensation. It happened while I was covering a piece of posterboard with ideas for my paper, and again when I was in the shower, and several times when I was just moving with the mob through the hallways between classes. Suddenly, I was just hit by the realization, again, that voices that didn't know each other had said the same words, and it somehow changed everything.

It didn't *really* change anything. I still wasn't part of the basketball community. I still couldn't sit at lunch with the girls I'd sweated and giggled and gone through puberty with. My teachers still looked at me when they didn't think I knew, like they were checking for the steroid-use symptoms they'd gotten on a memo.

But everything was different in some way I couldn't identify. The closest I'd ever come to that feeling was the first time I realized I had a crush on a boy. And the first time Coach Deetz confided in me. And the day I suffered a concussion and Kara cried and said, "Cassie, please don't ever die. I couldn't live without you." It was like spring happening inside my body.

I just hoped it wouldn't go away like all of that had. Maybe if I took better care of it, it wouldn't.

*

Boz joined Ruthie and me for lunch again Friday, and Ruthie shared her Cheetos with him.

"These have to be the single worst thing you can ingest," he said as he licked the orange stuff off of his palm.

"They have cheese in them," Ruthie said. "That's good for you, isn't it?"

I shook my head. "If there is anything even remotely resembling actual cheese in those things ..."

They both looked at me, orange curls poised between their thumbs and fingers.

"What?" Boz said.

I couldn't finish. Ruthie was there with her pretty sage-green eyes that nobody noticed because all they could see was the acne and the torso that couldn't be stuffed into a mini T-shirt. And she was smiling, like she was pretty sure I wasn't one more person who was going to tell her what she already thought about herself.

And I wasn't.

"Okay, you guys," I said. "What do you think about this idea for my paper?"

"Give it," Boz said.

"This might be totally lame, but what if I write, like, a modern-day version of *The Scarlet Letter*—you know, not as long—"

"Right, I get you," Boz said.

"Only it's my story instead of Hester Prynne's." I looked at Ruthie. "Sort of like you said."

"I did?"

"That whole thing about Jeannette," Boz said.

"*Which* we heard already," I said quickly. "So it wouldn't be exactly an essay, but Mr. Josephson said he wanted to hear my voice. I don't know—is it lame?"

"No," Boz said, blinking rapidly in his contacts. "It's amazing."

"Okay," I said, "I'm gonna write a couple of paragraphs right now and see if I can do it."

"You can totally do it," Ruthie said.

"And you know this how?"

"I just do."

The feeling swept through me again, and I decided she might.

*

I got the story started while Boz and Ruthie shared the rest of the Cheetos and their love for *The Lord of the Rings*, which I personally could never get into. When we got to sixth period, I scooted my desk next to Ruthie's, holding what I'd done so far.

"Can I read this to you before the bell rings?" I said.

"You want to read it to *me?*" she said.

"You've got your head in a story twenty-four hours a day. You ought to know what makes one good by now."

She smiled, a soft smile, and in the midst of the bumps that made her life such a misery, I saw two deep dimples. Ruthie was actually cute.

"Okay, but read it slow," she said. "I read good when I do it myself, but when somebody reads out loud I'm sometimes like, 'What? What did you just say?' It's like bad audio memory or something. My brother has it too, and one of my cousins …"

Annoying. But cute.

I read what I'd written, and apparently Ruthie's audio memory was having a good day, because when I was done, she repeated "the good parts" back to me, almost word for word.

"So you think it's okay?" I said.

"I think it's wonderful! You *could* describe the coffee shop more, though. But maybe that's just me. I like a lot of description."

"Good point."

I was making a note of that as the bell rang and Rafe sauntered in, which meant it was time to shift gears and be an artist instead of an author. Sheesh. I got up to pull my desk back into place and discovered Ms. Edelstein watching me. The fact that she'd lifted her face from the never-ending stack of papers was surprise enough. But the look in her eyes startled me. It was like she'd never seen me before.

"Um, could we move some desks back?" I said, as long as I had her attention, "so Rafe and I can unroll our paper and start mapping out our—"

"Sure, go ahead," she said, and went back to the stack. But the look stayed with me for a while.

151

*

The map of our project turned out way better than I expected. Rafe drew most of it, and fast. His hand moved across our big paper in swift, broad strokes, and it occurred to me that you probably had to make art fast when you were trying to stay ahead of the police.

"Where do you actually do your tagging?" I said to him as we worked.

He rocked back on his knees and gave me a disgusted look.

"What?" I said.

"For a smart chick you're, like, dense sometimes."

"Really."

"The 'tag' is the signature a graffiti artist uses to sign his work. It's not the art itself."

"Oh," I said. "So what's your tag?"

"I'll tag this when we're done," he said. The eyebrows kicked in. "You'll see it then."

"Can't wait," I said. It occurred to me that every time he wiggled his brows, I rolled my eyes. We must have looked like the Marx Brothers or something.

I sat back and surveyed our handiwork. "Okay, so we've got the cave pictographs here, the stuff from the catacombs here, the prostitution ads from Ephesus here—"

"Say what?"

I looked up at Lizard, who was stretched across three of the desks we'd pushed back.

"They think the really beautiful graffiti art they found on the walls from ancient Ephesus were ads for prostitutes."

"You mean, like hos?"

"Language," Ms. Edelstein said in a bored voice.

"Sorry," Lizard said.

Rafe tilted his chin at me. "Where's my main man going?"

"Who was he, like a mobster?" Tank said. He propped himself on the edge of Ruthie's desk.

"No, man, he's a guerilla artist," Rafe said. "Cult artistic figure."

"Or just a criminal," I said. "Depends on who you talk to. Y'know what—we should put him right in the middle because he kind of represents the fine line between a political statement and a crime. Then we can put all the pop culture–hip-hop-underground stuff on the other side of that."

Rafe pulled his mondo lips into a smile. "Dang, Roid, that's good. I'm on it."

"When are you going to build the legal wall?"

All of us, Ms. Edelstein included, looked at Ruthie.

"I was just wondering," she said, and pulled her book in front of her face.

"That's actually a good question," I said, before Lizard and Tank could go after her. Tank had already snatched her book from her hand and was leafing through it like he was looking for dirty passages.

"We haven't figured out how we're doin' that yet," Rafe said.

I didn't remind him that "we" weren't supposed to figure that out—"he" was.

"Refrigerator boxes," Tank said.

"Huh?" several of us said in unison.

"You could put a bunch of 'em side by side and paint on 'em."

"Sweet," Rafe said.

"Where are we gonna get, like, four refrigerator boxes?" I said.

"My old man."

Our heads swiveled to Lizard.

"He delivers refrigerators and washing machines and—stuff." He glanced warily at Ms. Edelstein. "For Home Depot."

I looked at Rafe. "So we could paint one box at a time and then connect them all, right?"

"Hey, Miss Frankenstein," he said, still looking back at me.

"Hey, Rafe."

"Can we set refrigerator boxes up in here?"

"Absolutely not."

"Dude."

"But you can collapse one at a time and work on them on the floor like you're doing now." She adjusted her glasses.

"Like I said, just don't spill anything, and be out of here by four o'clock. That's when I leave."

"Hey, Miss Frankenstein."

"Hey, Rafe."

"You rock. You wanna go out sometime?"

"No, Rafe, I do not."

I grinned. At least Ms. Edelstein and I had that in common.

"Psst—Rafe-man," Lizard said. He rolled toward Rafe. "What's wrong with your woman?"

I glanced back at Uma, who, come to think of it, hadn't said a word all period. She had stayed in her usual seat, and I'd thought I smelled nail polish at one point. Right now she was apparently casting an evil spell on somebody with her eyes.

Me.

"PMS," Rafe said.

I squinted at him. "Y'know, just because a female is ticked off about something doesn't mean it's hormonal. She might just have something to be ticked off about."

"Like what?"

"Like, I don't know, she's dating you?"

"Ooooo!" Lizard said.

"You scored, Roid," Tank said.

I looked back at Uma. I hadn't scored any points with her.

*

Lizard was true to his word—amazingly—and he showed up sixth period on Monday with a refrigerator box, already nicely collapsed, with the assurance that it could be unfolded back into a big cube when we were ready.

I'd brought in newspapers that Ruthie helped me spread out on the floor, and Rafe produced a set of paintbrushes that definitely hadn't come from among the motley bunch Mrs. Petrocelli-Ward had us using.

"Those look like some serious brushes," I said.

"I'm a serious artist," he said. No eyebrows wiggled.

I didn't roll my eyes.

The painting was a lot more fun than I thought it was going

to be. Of course, how hard was it to do caveman drawings? But Rafe said it couldn't look like some lowlife street kid did it, so I followed what he was doing and it actually looked—well, like professional cave artists had painted it.

Lizard, Tank, and Ruthie were our art critics, although we ignored most of what Lizard and Tank said. Ruthie was actually more like a cheerleader. As for Uma, she watched from the back, looking like she wanted to go after the whole thing with a can of black spray paint.

I got a little carried away with the sienna at one point and ended up with more on me than on the "cave wall." I got a pass to the restroom and was in there washing it off my elbows when Uma's face appeared in the mirror. Our eyes collided in the glass.

"Hi, Uma," I said.

"It's not gonna happen," she said.

"I'm sorry, what?"

"You and Rafe. It's not gonna happen."

My laugh bounced off the tiled walls and the metal sides of the stalls.

"I don't see how this is funny," she said.

"You've gotta be kidding me. In the first place, he's yours."

"Yes. He is."

"Okay, and in the second place, I don't want him. I mean, that might be hard for you to see because you're into him, but seriously—can you even *see* us together?"

"No," she said, although she'd obviously envisioned that exact thing, or we wouldn't be having this conversation. I should probably come up with a third reason fast. Please.

"And besides, you're always here when we're working together," I said, "and trust me, this is the only place we're ever going to *be* together, so you don't have anything to worry about."

"Oh, I know I don't." She was giving me the tight face. The one where I was sure her cheeks were going to meet in the middle of her head. "You're the one who has something to worry about if you don't watch yourself."

"Note to self," I said. "Watch me."

Uma gave me one last tight-faced look and rocked her almost nonexistent hips out of the restroom. If there had been a door to slam, she might have dislocated a wall with it.

I turned back to the sink and let all the air come out of me.

"Are you okay, Cassidy?"

My head jerked up. The face I saw in the mirror this time was Kara's.

"I wasn't eavesdropping on purpose," she said. "I was about to come out of the stall when I heard you and that girl talking." She darted her blue eyes nervously toward the exit. "Who *was* that?"

"Just a girl in Lo—in study hall."

"Oh." Kara gave the exit another wary glance. "Was it just me, or was she, like, threatening you?"

I leaned against the sink. Of course Kara wouldn't know what a threat sounded like. And she wouldn't know who Uma was, or Rafe Diego, or Ruthie. They had all come into my life since she had gone out of it.

"It's fine," I said. "She's just insecure. I've got it handled."

"Cassie—"

"It's fine," I said. "Really."

She nodded her head of curlier-than-curly blonde hair. She'd had it cut. It made her look older, more sophisticated, like some part of her had moved on.

"Well, okay," she said. "I'll see you, then."

"Yeah," I said. I left out the part where she couldn't "see me" because her parents wouldn't let her and because I couldn't trust her.

She left and I stayed, looking in the mirror, until I was sure she wasn't coming back.

CHAPTER TWELVE

I thought I'd had about all the surprises one person could expect to have in a single day until my father tapped on my door that night, just as I was opening RL.

"Come in," I said—calmly—even though the Frenemy was stirring from sleep somewhere deep in my backbone. It was the first time I'd heard from her all day.

Dad came in and looked around like he expected that I would've completely redecorated. I took that opportunity to slide RL back under the beanbag. I had no doubt my brother had already shared his version of our little scene with Dad, and I didn't want a reenactment of it.

But my father didn't seem to be in search of evidence. He just leaned on the edge of my desk and folded his arms. We were about to go into lecture mode, without the car. No wonder he looked like something didn't fit him.

"How's therapy going?" he said.

"Great. Ben—that's my therapist—he says I'm doing great." Could I sound any lamer?

"How long before you can play again, does he say?"

"Uh, six months, minimum. I'm thinking about a club team."

He dismissed that with his hand. "A club team won't get you a scholarship. I've been working this from another angle."

I gripped the sides of the beanbag, just to make sure I wasn't being taken back in time by some invisible hand.

"Don't schedule any therapy for April fifteenth. That's three weeks from now."

"What happens on April fifteenth?"

"Your appeal."

"I'm sorry?"

"There's a school district appeals board that meets once a month. We already missed it for March, but I wasn't ready anyway."

"I don't understand—"

The trench between his eyebrows deepened. "I'm trying to tell you. They hear appeals on disputes individuals have with a school administration. We've filed against LaSalle. I'm going to get this thing overturned—this ruling about you not being able to play."

"Are you serious?" I said. "I'm sorry—I know you are. This is just . . ." I shrugged my shoulders up to my earlobes. "Thank you, Dad."

"It's what I do. I'm staying out of the therapy issue. Apparently your mother has that handled." He pulled away from the desk and looked down at me. "I'm sticking my neck out on this, Cass."

I was still trying to figure out how to respond to that when he closed the door behind him.

*

It was good news. It was *great* news. Too bad I couldn't share it with Ben, since he didn't know about the steroids, and I didn't ever want him to. At first I thought that was why I had to fend off the nudges of the Frenemy. But once I was there with him on Tuesday, I knew it was something else.

"What's this I'm seeing?" he said when we were having our usual how-was-your-week conversation.

"What?" I said.

"This." Ben hugged his arms around himself so his shoulders almost met at his chest.

"Am I doing that?"

"Ever since you came in the door."

I looked down at my legs, swinging over the side of the table. "My dad is talking to me again. He wants to help me."

"I take it he didn't before."

I shook my head.

"So is this a bad thing?"

"No," I said. "Only I feel like I'm going backward."

"Back to where?"

I couldn't give him an answer right away, but Ben's eyes waited, like it was only a matter of time before I'd come up with the right one.

"Okay, it's like I'm back to stuff I used to do. Like I feel like I should ask you if we can step up my therapy—you know, give me more reps or more weight, and let me come in twice a day instead of once."

"Not happening."

"And I'm glad, because I don't really want to do that, but it's like I *should* want to."

"Didn't we decide there weren't going to be any 'shoulds'?"

"Yes! Only now ..."

"What's different now?"

"It's like my father's in here," I said, waving my hand across the workout area. "And he wasn't before. And I don't want him here."

"Then he's banned," Ben said.

"So you don't think I need to work harder?"

"Is that what your dad said you needed to do?"

"He didn't *say* it, but it was like it was there. That's the way it always was."

Ben nodded. "Well, I gotta tell you, you already do a little more than I ask you to, every time. You're my poster girl for ACL recovery, and we've only been working together for what, ten days?"

"Eleven," I said.

"But who's counting, right?" He grinned. "Look, Boss, my only concern right now is that you don't reinjure yourself by doing too much with that knee. I don't want you to be a girl who used to play a sport she loved. But if you take off running, that graft is going to fail and you'll be right back where you started." He looked at me closely with his gray-and-gold eyes. "And we've already decided we're not going backward, right?"

159

"Right," I said.

"So—you want to take another step forward?"

"Yes!"

"Then why are you sitting there, girl? Let's do this thing."

*

By Friday, Rafe and I had done all the pieces of the wall. When he put the final brushstroke on the last box, Ruthie whipped out a bag of Three Musketeers miniatures and went around to all of us, distributing them.

"We should celebrate," she said.

I was ready to smack any one of them if they gave her the slightest bit of grief, but evidently chocolate could sweeten anybody up. I made a mental note to ask Mom if she'd tried it on my father.

"Now we have to put it all together," I said to Rafe.

"Hey, Miss Frankenstein."

"Absolutely not." Ms. Edelstein pointed the red pencil at him without looking up. "It's too big. Where are they now?"

"The other boxes?" I said. "They're collapsed in my garage." When each one was dry, Mom and I had transported it in the back of her Jeep. "Portable graffiti," she called it.

"Sounds like a no-brainer to me," Ms. Edelstein said.

Then I must not have a brain, because I didn't see where she was going. Not until Rafe wiggled his eyebrows at me.

"You're saying we should set it up at *my* house and finish it?" I said.

"I bet you got a real nice place, Roid."

I gave him the customary eye roll, but it actually made sense. And my house was definitely safe—as in, I could throw him out when I couldn't stand him anymore.

"What about tomorrow, then?" I said.

"Ooooo—ren-dez-vous."

The second Lizard said it, I turned to Uma, who was, as usual, in the back of the room with ice cubes for eyes.

"You should come too," I said to her. "Seriously."

Tank looked at Lizard. "Dude, if we're gonna party—"

160

"We're not," I said.

I could just see a meeting of the local graffiti artists' union taking place in my family room. There wasn't enough chocolate in the world to make that work.

"I'm just inviting Uma," I said.

"I won't be there."

She frosted the room so fast I shivered. Her eyes pointed at Rafe.

"Guess you won't either, dude," Lizard said.

Rafe let his own eyes smolder under the hood for a moment before he turned to me.

"What time?" he said.

I didn't look back at Uma again. I didn't want to have my eyeballs frozen.

*

Ruthie hadn't said a word through any of it. But when Rafe and the entourage left and Ms. Edelstein stepped out to go to the Coke machine, she came out from behind the fairies, her eyes round as nickels.

"Did you see the way Uma was looking at you?"

"Yeah. She wants to slit my throat."

"Totally. She's scary."

"She thinks I'm after Rafe," I said.

"You mean like as a boyfriend?" Ruthie actually shuddered.

"I guess if you like somebody, you can't see why everybody else wouldn't like him too."

"Love is blind," she said.

She was so serious I forced myself not to laugh.

"I hope she doesn't call you out," she went on. "That happened to my cousin—"

"What do you mean, 'call me out'? You mean, like, challenge me to fight her?"

Ruthie's nod was solemn, but I did laugh this time.

"In the first place, I'm like three times bigger than she is, and in the second place, I don't do junk like that."

"I know," Ruthie said. "You're way too nice."

161

I almost laughed again, except that her eyes were so sincere she could have sold used cars.

"You think I'm *nice?*" I said.

"You're, like, the nicest person I know."

"You must not know that many people."

"I don't know *any* people like you," she said.

All I could do was stare at her while a lump formed in my throat. If she knew how many times I'd wanted to press her mute button ...

"What are you gonna do about Uma?" she said.

I swallowed. "What do you think I should do?"

She looked down at the novel she still had her finger in, marking her place, and I thought for a second she was going to consult it for an answer. But she lifted her chin and said, "You should just be you."

*

Rafe was alone when he pulled up to my house at noon the next day in an ancient pickup truck. I didn't know whether to be relieved or start worrying about another face-to-face with Uma in the restroom.

"He's more attractive than I expected him to be," Mom said as we watched him swagger up the driveway with enough attitude for about five of his kind.

"Attractive?" I said. "Mom, are you *serious?*"

"Well, yes. In a bad boy kind of way. You know, the dark, haunted look and all that."

"Okay, Mom, stop — please."

She laughed and headed toward the hall. "You two have fun."

The doorbell was ringing by then. When I let Rafe in, I found myself checking for signs of a "dark, haunted look."

"What's up, Roid?" he said. "Do I have lettuce in my teeth?"

Okay, so much for that.

We went out to the garage, which Mom's Jeep had vacated. Dad, of course, had gone to the office, which was good because I wasn't sure he would have moved the Inquisition Mobile out to make room for my art project.

I stopped in the doorway and shook off a few quills. It hadn't occurred to me until then that the only time the Frenemy was showing up lately was when I thought about my father. Ruthie wouldn't think those thoughts were "nice."

Huh. Maybe they weren't even me.

"Good space," Rafe said.

I pulled my focus back to him and stepped down into the garage. He was moving around in it, gazing up at the ceiling and measuring the walls with his gaze. I would have thought he was casing it for grand theft auto if there hadn't been something softer than the usual gonna-getcha glint in his eyes.

"You could make some major art in here," he said.

"Does my father waxing his car count?"

"You could do big pieces."

From the way he spread his arms toward the wall, I was pretty sure he wasn't seeing the gardening tools that hung from it.

"Who knew it was an art studio?" I said. "All this time I thought it was just a garage."

"Everything could be an art studio when you don't have one."

"Is that why you make art on freeway overpasses?" I said.

He didn't look at me. He just said, "Something like that." And then he shrugged, and the glint came back and he said, "Are we gonna do this or what?"

Yeah. I felt like I'd just spit on somebody.

*

It took us two hours to set up the four boxes and paint the tie-ins so that together they looked like one big wall. It would only have taken me about twenty minutes doing it alone, but where Rafe had worked in broad, sweeping strokes before, he was now the ultimate perfectionist, stepping back to squint at it and then going in to touch up some microscopic detail I would have missed completely.

"Why am I not seeing all this little stuff?" I said — and then immediately braced myself for one of his zingers.

But he just kept shading the nose on a gargoylesque face until I thought he hadn't heard me. Then he said, "You would if you practiced."

"No, really. I could practice until I'm ninety-two and never be able to do what you do. I mean, look at this. It's a masterpiece."

"Somebody else's masterpiece."

"Huh?"

"All I did was put together copies of other people's stuff."

"But it's still amazing!"

He stepped back from the "wall" again and stood beside me.

"How'd you get to be an amazing basketball player?"

I stared at him. He was perfectly serious.

"How did you even know I was a basketball player?"

"What am I, deaf? Who goes to that school and doesn't know that?"

"I guess I just thought you didn't pay attention to stuff like that."

"I pay attention to everything." The eyebrows wiggled, but only slightly. "So how did it happen?" he said. "How'd you get to be so good?"

I hadn't really talked about it in so long I had to hunt for the thoughts behind all the others.

"I guess part of it's a gift," I said. "Does that sound conceited?"

"So what if it does?"

"Okay—well, then it's just hard work and good coaching and doing it over and over."

"Right. So it's the same with me and art."

I shook my head, sort of sadly. "I don't think so. I don't think I could learn to paint the way you do."

"I bet I could learn to play basketball the way you do."

A laugh exploded from me.

"What?" he said. "I played sports when I was a little kid."

"Everybody did."

"You could teach me."

"Teach you what?"

"How to be a basketball star."

I laughed again, hands over my mouth. Although his eyes were sparkling deep under their hoods, the eyebrows were perfectly still.

"You're serious, aren't you?" I said.

"Why not? I can be more than one thing."

"Well, yeah —"

"So — you've got a hoop out there. You got a ball?"

"Do I have a ball. . . . Do you have a tattoo? Of course I have a ball."

"So. Bring it on."

*

It would have been surreal enough showing Rafe Diego how to do a layup in my driveway. But add to that the fact that the last time I'd held a basketball in my hands was seconds before my life crashed around me, and it was like I was in one of those paintings where pocket watches drip over the sides of tables.

And yet the minute I rested the ball in my palms, everything came into a focus so sharp I could hardly blink. That ball belonged there.

"Coach me," Rafe said.

He had his jacket off and his sleeves rolled up, which was the closest we were going to come to him *looking* like a basketball player that day. I didn't even try to imagine him in shorts and high-tops, because I knew I'd be deafened by my own guffaws if I did.

"We aren't going to do a bunch of running," I said. "Because one, I'm not allowed to, and two, you don't have on tennis shoes. I'll just sit here and teach you how to shoot."

Which was going to be hard without actually showing him — and I didn't even want to face Ben on Tuesday with the news that I'd been practicing free throws.

Rafe was standing there with the ball on his hip, giving me a game face. I did laugh then.

"If you're trying to look like a jock ..." I said.

"What?"

"Okay, it's sort of working. But lose the toothpick."

He did.

"All right, so put the ball in your right hand and rest it on your fingertips—not your palm."

I demonstrated with one ball and he mimicked me with the other, just about perfectly.

"Now turn like you're going to shoot—yeah, only keep your elbow at an *L*—that's it. Now shoot it up and snap your wrist."

The ball stayed in my hand, but Rafe's ball left his and dipped just short of the hoop.

"That actually wasn't bad."

"It sucked. I'm doing it again."

"Just remember, the ball should go off your fingertips." Like a part of yourself is dancing right from your fingers. Oh, man—how I missed that feeling.

Rafe's ball bounced off the hoop.

"All right—closer that time!"

"I don't want close. I want it in there."

"Okay, so we'll add the guide hand. Use your other hand to direct the ball, but don't let it shoot. That comes from your other hand."

Rafe nodded and did everything I told him. The ball dropped in without so much as brushing the metal.

"Two points!" I said.

Rafe wiggled his eyebrows at me. "Get back, Michael Jordan," he said, and tried to dribble the ball between his legs. It of course bounced off down the lawn, straight for my mother's car, which was pulling up in front of the house. I didn't even know she'd left.

"This looks like artists at work," she said as she emerged from the driver's seat with two Pike's Perk bags. "Lisa Brewster. You must be Rafe."

I cringed, with several possible Rafe-versus-a-parent scenarios playing in my mind. But Rafe put out his hand to shake hers.

"LeBron James, ma'am. You may have heard of me. I'm with the Cleveland Cavaliers."

"I hope you're not in training," she said. "I don't know if these burritos are on your diet."

"I can make an exception. Let me carry those for you."

Oh, bro-ther.

*

Rafe and I ate burritos with Baja salsa in the garage while we admired our wall. The more it dried, the better it looked. I already hated the thought of taking it apart after Monday.

"Hey," I said. "You haven't tagged it yet."

He chewed thoughtfully for a minute and then shook his head.

"Why not? You said you were going to before."

"Changed my mind. It's not my original work."

"Bummer," I said. "I've been waiting to see your tag."

"I'll show it to you. You done eating?"

"Uh, *yeah.*"

"Then come on. I'll take you to it."

I hesitated, waiting for the warning quills, or at least a saving sarcastic sentence. But nothing came except the words "Let me just tell my mom where I'm going." I stopped on the steps. "Where *am* I going?"

"Old Man Stutz's."

*

The sky had been so bright that day we'd been outside without coats all afternoon. But as I stood gazing at the wall, I zipped my jacket and turned my collar up around my neck. The air was turning colder as the sun started to go down behind the Peak, but that wasn't the only reason I was chilled. There was something about what I was looking at—like it had been done by somebody who knew what it was like to be out in the cold.

I pulled one hand out of my pocket and swept my arm across the expanse of the wall that separated the old man's yard from Interstate 25. It was at least fifty yards from the back of his house, blocked from view by a line of overgrown fir trees my father would have had dug out of there so they wouldn't kill his lawn. Old Man Stutz didn't have a lawn. We stood in gravelly dirt to look at Rafe's art.

"You did this whole thing?" I said.

"Yeah. Took me two months of painting every night."

"You did it at night?"

"I had to at first so the old man wouldn't see what I was doing. Then after he caught me and he made me finish it for him, it was like I could only paint in the dark." Rafe shrugged. "It's the only way I ever did it."

"He made you finish it?"

"Yeah. He said he didn't want some half—well, half-done piece of art in his backyard. He set up lights and paid for the paint and brought me coffee until I got it done."

"It's beautiful," I said. And it truly was—but also painful. I couldn't tell exactly what was going on, because the twisting, writhing people he'd painted were all tangled up in fists that came out of nowhere and shouting mouths that were disconnected from faces and words that seemed to have lives of their own. Words like *No* and *Hate*. And *Loser*.

It would have made me want to turn away, except that at the far end, there was a space filled with nothing but blue—a sky-washed blue like the color of my mother's eyes. Along its edge, letters flowed down as if they were being poured from an unseen pitcher somewhere in the sky.

"What does that mean?" I said.

"It's my tag," Rafe said.

"What does it say?"

"It says, 'The Angel Raphael.'"

I felt him stiffen beside me, like he was expecting me to say what I would have said an hour before—before I saw who he was, painted on a legal wall.

A blue light suddenly flickered from the road beyond the old man's house, and Rafe jumped like a ninja in one of those old cartoons I used to watch. Except the look in his eyes wasn't comical.

"We gotta go," he said.

"What's wrong?"

"I just don't want to be here," he said.

Rafe grabbed my arm and pulled me away from the wall.

"Rafe, I can't run."

He nodded, and then he threw his head under my shoulder and hauled me up onto his back. I squealed, but I let him run with me like a firefighter performing a rescue. He was barely breathing hard when he deposited me in the front seat of the truck and took off from his parking place behind the house. I didn't see any more blinking blue lights.

"Did we just run from the *cops?*" I said.

"Nah. They were just driving by. I didn't want to talk to them, that's all."

I didn't ask if there was a warrant out for his arrest. I didn't want the answer to be yes. But Rafe kept glancing at me, as if he wanted me to say *something.* Maybe anything.

"I'm sorry I didn't get to meet Old Man Stutz," I said.

"He's not home. He's in the hospital." Rafe's eyes went to the rearview mirror. "I guess the cops are keeping an eye on the place. Which they don't need to do, because I'm not gonna let anything happen to it."

"He must be amazing, y'know, for you to care about him so much."

Rafe let his mouth relax into a smile. "He's actually a pain in the butt most of the time."

"Then why—"

"Because he's one of only two people who ever said I was an artist."

"And the other one's P-W," I said.

"No," he said. "The other one's you."

It got hard to breathe. It got even harder when we turned into my driveway and I saw my father standing on the front walk. Arms crossed. Face pointed. Smoke all but shooting out of his ears. I would have known that body language from a hundred yards.

"That your old man?" Rafe said.

"Yeah. Listen, just drop me off and go, okay?"

"Why? Are you busted?"

"I have *no* idea."

"Stay in the car. I'll take you someplace."

I stopped, fingers on the door handle, and stared at him. "It's fine," I said. "I just don't want you to be involved."

The hood I'd hardly seen all day came down over Rafe's eyes.

"I get it," he said.

"No, you don't — " I said.

But my father was already rapping his knuckles on the window, and I could see his pointedness reflected in Rafe's face as he looked past me at Dad.

"I'll see you Monday," I said.

I was barely out of the car and Rafe was backing it out of the driveway. Only my father's voice kept me from going after him. It went through me like an ice pick.

"You have a decision to make, Cassidy."

I turned slowly from the sight of Rafe's disappearing taillights.

"You are either going to have a career in basketball, or you're going to run around with lowlife losers. Before I put myself on the line for you before an appeals board, I need to know which it's going to be, because it can't be both."

"He's not a loser," I said.

Dad narrowed his eyes at me until they were no more than tiny points. "Then I guess that answers my question, doesn't it?"

He turned from me and disappeared into the house. His words didn't echo in my head as I watched him go. Rafe's did.

I can be more than one thing, he'd said.

For the first time since I was ten years old, I wanted that to be true.

CHAPTER THIRTEEN

"W ell?" Ms. Edelstein said.

Six heads, mine included, came up from cell phones and fantasy novels, and, in my case, the rough draft of my *Scarlet Letter* paper. Ms. Edelstein was leaning on the front of her desk, her ungraded equations behind her.

"Whatever it was," Lizard said. "I didn't do it."

"I didn't say you did anything. I want to know how our art project went over this afternoon."

I glanced back at Rafe, but he was sitting under his hood, like he'd been doing for two periods now. He came out long enough during fifth to help me make the presentation, but he didn't so much as wiggle his eyebrows when people said things like, "I don't even want to present ours now after that." I couldn't blame them. It really was the best one. Even P-W couldn't come up with a single thing to critique us on. Except when she said—

"I think you might have glorified vandalism somewhat."

"We weren't trying to do that," I said. "We just wanted to show that it's art and it makes a valuable statement."

"I'd just rather see that statement made someplace besides the freeways I have to drive on."

I glanced at Rafe, who was watching me with still, dark eyes.

"Rafe doesn't make his art on illegal walls," I said. "Just so you know."

He started to smile at that point, I knew. But then it was like a memory tripped him and he had to go take care of that. The hood had slammed down and it had been there ever since.

"We got an A-plus," I said to Ms. Edelstein. "Our wall's on display in that enclosed courtyard in the art wing."

"It's up now?"

I nodded.

"All right, then," Ms. Edelstein said. "We're going on a field trip."

It was like being back in kindergarten, all of us moving single file out of the math hall and across to the art wing, whispering because Ms. Edelstein told us to keep it down. Once we got there, though, everybody stood speechless before our creation.

Except, of course, Ruthie, who murmured to me, "It's even better than I thought it was going to be."

"I want a picture of everybody in front of it," Ms. Edelstein said. She pulled her cell phone out of her pocket and blinked at us—because we were all just looking at her, slack-jawed. "Hello—am I speaking Lithuanian?"

It was like they were waiting for me, so I stepped in front, and of course Lizard and Tank weren't going to miss an opportunity to ham it up. Rafe stood somberly on the other side of them, and Ruthie crowded behind me. I was pretty sure being photographed wasn't her favorite thing. Only Uma opted out, and Ms. Edelstein didn't coax her. I avoided looking at the girl, although I didn't see how she could still be mad at me. Rafe wasn't even speaking to me.

"Now just Rafe and Cassidy," Ms. Edelstein said.

"Ooooooh-oooh!" Lizard said.

"I think we would all appreciate it if you would grow up, Lizard," she said as she motioned everyone else off. "Come on, you two, off to the side there."

She kept gesturing until we were standing with our shoulders touching. All I could think about was being hiked over those shoulders and carried—

"Why you gotta make such a big deal out of this, Miss Frankenstein?" Rafe said.

"Because." She snapped the picture and held up her hand for us to give her one more. When she lowered the cell phone, she said, "I just want it on record that something beautiful came out of this class. All right, let's get back. I have work to do."

Rafe moved away from me and headed for the door.

When the rest of us turned into the math hall again, I heard a coarse whisper behind me.

"Hey, Roid."

I had never been glad to hear those words before. Still, I eyed the hall ahead of me for Uma. She'd already slipped into Room 109, so I stopped and turned.

But it wasn't Rafe behind me. It was Tank.

"What's goin' on with Rafe?" he said.

"How would I know?" I said. "He's not talking to me. And why would he? The art project's over. There's no reason for him to talk to me anymore."

Even I heard the sadness in my voice. It wasn't lost on Tank either.

"But you still *want* him to talk to you."

"Why are you asking *me* this? He's *your* 'homeboy' or whatever."

"Because he's not talkin' to me neither. And Uma's mobilizin' for somethin', and that's never a good thing." Tank shrugged his weapon-tattooed shoulder. "If I can tell her you and Rafe had a fight or somethin', she'll probably back off and I won't have to deal with it."

"Why do you have to?" I said. "Why can't you just leave it alone?"

"I don't have a choice. She's my sister."

"Oh." Really?

"If she gets messed up in something, my old man blames me."

I had to roll my eyes. "Do all fathers go to some school to learn how to be jerks?"

"Huh?"

"Look, tell Uma whatever you want, but there is nothing going on between Rafe and me, and there never was."

Tank looked at me for so long I almost snapped my fingers in front of his face.

173

"You're still lyin'," he said at long last. "But I'll tell her. You just gotta stop lookin' at Rafe like that."

"Like what?"

He pointed into my face. "Like that."

*

I did better than that. I didn't look at Rafe at all.

It was stupid anyway.

We'd had one afternoon when he didn't call me Roid and try to gross me out with his eyebrows. We had a couple of decent conversations.

Like you don't have every day.

And he carried me. On his shoulders.

So I got a peek at the light under his hood—no big deal.

Okay, it could have been a big deal. But the minute he thought I didn't want Dad to see who I was with, it was over. He got the wrong idea. He shut down.

I didn't need it.

What I needed was to focus on getting back in the game. And maybe my Tuesday session with Ben would make that easier.

But when I took off my brace in the dressing room, what I saw sent me out into the workout area screaming for him.

He caught me halfway across the floor. "Whoa, whoa, whoa, Boss. What's going on?"

"Look at my knee, Ben! It looks like a grapefruit!"

I wasn't exaggerating. My knee was almost swollen back to its presurgery size. And so were the Frenemy quills in my spine. My whole body shook as Ben ushered me into a cubicle and hiked me up onto the table.

"What's happening?" I said.

"We're going to find out. Just try to calm down—"

"Tell me I'm not going to need another operation. Please—"

"I doubt that very seriously. Come on now, breathe with me—deep breaths."

My first few were ragged, but I somehow pulled back from

the edge of hyperventilation. Ben felt around my knee and moved my leg and watched my face.

"Any more pain than you've been having?"

"No."

"That's a good sign. Have you done anything differently with it over the last couple of days?" He coaxed me with a grin. "You haven't been out playing pick-up games or anything?"

I hooked my eyes into his.

"Boss?" he said. "Talk to me."

I shook my head. "I showed this guy how to do a layup, but only with my hands. I was sitting down. I didn't even shoot—"

"Okay. Anything else? Did you try to run on it?" He looked at me closely. "I'm not going to yell at you. I just need to know."

"I didn't run. I told him I couldn't. So he picked me up and put me over his shoulder and carried me to his truck."

Ben didn't ask me who or why or what on earth I was thinking. He actually looked almost relieved.

"And when he set you down?"

I closed my eyes. "He didn't put me down hard. Honest."

"Cassidy. Look at me."

I did. He was tilting his head at me.

"I believe you," he said.

I burst into tears. Big, embarrassing sobs that I couldn't have stopped if I'd tried. Which I didn't.

Ben squeezed my shoulder and told me to lie down. His hands wrapped around my leg above my knee and pressed gently while I cried. And cried.

"This is called a milk massage," he said. "It's going to help move the swelling down and out."

"Did I mess it up?"

"No, you just set yourself back a little bit. I think you might have twisted it funky when you were in a position you're not usually in. Like hanging over somebody's shoulder." He grinned. "Did you at least enjoy the ride?"

I felt my face crumple again.

"I'm hitting all kinds of nerves today, aren't I?" Ben kept massaging. "Anything you want to say about those?"

"I want to say thank you," I basically blubbered out.

"For?"

"For believing me."

"Why wouldn't I?" He let his hands go still. "Because of the steroid thing?"

"You *knew*?" I cried even harder. "Is it in my medical records for every doctor I ever go to my entire life to see?"

"No, Boss." Ben drew the curtain closed and pulled his stool up to the table. "I don't know if it's in your records or not. I found out from your father."

A sob caught in my chest, and only by the grace of God did it not explode.

"He called me right after we started working together. He asked me to keep an eye out for signs that you were using again."

"You're not gonna see any!"

"I know that. I knew the minute he told me."

The sob let go and I cried some more. "I can't believe he did that. I make one mistake and it's like I'm some junkie who can't ever be trusted again."

"I don't think it's so much that." Ben went back to the milk massage. "I got the sense—and I could be wrong about this—but I got the sense that he's more afraid somebody else is going to take advantage of you the way the med student did."

I pressed the heels of my hands to my eyes. "Did he mention that she was my brother's fiancée—now ex-fiancée?"

"Ouch. No, he didn't share that with me."

"I'm scared."

"Of what, Boss?"

"That this is never going to be over. I'm trying so hard, but ... I'm scared."

Ben pulled an ice pack out of the freezer and settled it around my knee.

"I think people suffer more over what *might* happen than over what definitely *will* happen," he said. "So let me tell you what I know is *going* to happen."

176

"Okay," I said.

"You're going to continue to work hard, and work right, and give yourself the best chance."

I blinked. "That's it?"

"That's all I know. Look, Boss, I can't guarantee that if you do everything you're supposed to do and then some, you won't get hurt again, and I can't promise you'll go all the way to the WNBA."

"This isn't helping me that much," I said.

Ben gave me a soft grin. "Look at how far you've come in a short time. You came in here shattered in more ways than one, and yet between you, me, God, and whoever else is out there helping you, you're coming back together." He glanced at my knee. "With a few minor setbacks."

"Maybe I just shouldn't do anything but work out until I'm all healed."

"No," Ben said gently. "Maybe you should have a life. If you only focus on this, your knee will heal, but I don't know about the rest of you."

I tried to let that sink in, but the Frenemy was blocking the way. I was suddenly sick of her.

"Can you not tell my dad about this?" I said, nodding at the ice pack.

"I don't have conversations with your father. Enough said on that?"

I nodded.

"Listen, Boss, let me just say this one more thing and then we'll put your brace back on and get you out of here so you can rest."

"Okay."

"We don't know exactly how this is all going to turn out. There are too many unexpected things that could happen. That's just life."

"I hate that," I said.

"You can't predict any of it, but you can practice for it."

"I can practice for what I don't know is going to happen?"

"Do you ever read the Bible?"

I was startled—and yet I thought right away of RL.

"Yeah—sort of. I mean, it's a long story. But yeah."

"Okay, that's how you practice. Jesus tells stories of hard situations, and then he shows us how to work with them. It's like your coach making you practice free throws, in case you get fouled. Or rebounds, in case you don't make the shot."

There was that feeling again, where voices that had never met were practically talking in unison. The Frenemy collected her quills and slipped away.

"So what do you say, Boss?" Ben said. "Shall we accept the unknown and focus on what we can do to get ready for it?"

"How do we do that exactly?"

"We keep our minds on the process. Not what you did wrong last time or whether you can do perfectly next time, but *how* you're going to do what needs to be done. It's all about saying 'what can I think about to make this better in this moment?'"

"And 'please,'" I said. "And 'thank you.'"

Ben grinned. "Now you're talkin', Boss. Now you're talkin'."

*

Even through white hot chocolate at Pike's Perk with Mom, I was itching to get home to RL. Although while we were splitting one of their homemade brownies—which Mom said would be a sin to resist—she did tell me that Dad was going ahead with the appeal. Apparently he'd decided what my decision was going to be.

Even after we got home there was my *Scarlet Letter* final draft to finish, and supper before Mom left for the late news. The moon was already up and glimmering through my window when I finally made it to my beanbag. I hoped RL would let me look back at the stories I'd read so far.

It did.

And this time, I tried to think of them as "practices."

There's more of a celebration at my house over one loser being rescued than there is over the ninety-nine who already get it. I like a celebration.

178

He was talking sheep and coins. I was thinking Ruthie passing out Three Musketeers miniatures, and Ms. Edelstein taking us on a "field trip."

Let all the stuff you're coming up against get you thinking, let it teach you how to survive, how to get back what you really need so you can live.

I'd thought that was all about basketball before. And Coach and Kara and the team and a scholarship ... But what about being up against my brother, and my father? What about surviving a potential catfight with Uma? What about getting back those moments with Rafe when I felt like there might be more to him—and me?

I'm telling you stories so you'll understand your own journey.

Wow. Wasn't that what Ben said?

Do the work you've been given to do. Do it the best you can—

Ben said that too.

But don't expect everybody to be telling you how wonderful you are for doing your job. It's not all about you.

It used to be. With Coach. With the team. With my father. Even Aaron, because *I* was the one who messed everything up. And now? Now it was Rafe and me and the whole Loser Hall doing an art project. Boz and Ruthie helping me write my paper. Mom and I turning into allies.

And then—

How can you think God won't come in and help you if you keep asking? Even if nobody else pays any attention to you—even if you've lost all credibility—God will be there for you.

Say please. Say thank you.

I couldn't say either one at the moment because my breath had been sucked away. When lights flashed through the window behind me, I thought for an insane second it was God sending me a message. Closer inspection revealed it was a vehicle in the driveway. Not Dad's Escalade.

Rafe's truck.

Forcing myself not to try to run, I got to the front door as fast as I could and let myself out. Rafe still had the motor running when I got in, which was good because it was early-

April-Colorado-cold, and I was barefoot and in flannel sleep pants and a sweatshirt. And that wasn't the only reason I was trembling.

"Hey, Roid," Rafe said.

"Hey," I said.

"Is your old man home?"

"Not yet. He doesn't usually get home 'til after nine. Look, Rafe, about that—when I told you to go the other day, it wasn't because—"

"Did you get busted?"

"I'm sorry?"

"When you showed up with me. Did he bust you?"

"No. Well—okay, sort of, but that wasn't why I told you to—"

"What did he do to you?"

"Nothing. He actually didn't even yell. He just—pointed." Rafe pulled his chin in.

"It's just this thing he does," I said. "It doesn't matter."

"But it was because of me."

"Only because you're not a basketball. He and I are just—not getting along."

He nodded, as if he completely understood that, even though I wasn't even sure I did.

"You looked like you got kicked under a bus today or some-thin'," he said. "If he busted you, I was gonna tell him you weren't doin' anything—y'know, with the 'loser kid.'"

I didn't even know which piece of that to pick up first. I went with, "You were going to *talk* to him?"

"What would you expect me to do, punch him in the face?"

"No! Although, there are times when you could be my guest."

"I hear that."

The hood came down and he glowered at the steering wheel. I took in a breath.

"Did you have a fight with *your* dad? Is that why you were all in a funk today?"

Rafe shook his head.

"Then you were thinking I was afraid for my dad to see you. I hope now you—"

"The old man died."

"Mr. Stutz?" I said.

He nodded. I'd never seen anybody swallow with that much pain.

"Rafe, I am so sorry. I really am."

"I don't know what's gonna happen now."

"To your wall?"

"No. To me."

"I don't—"

I stopped, because Rafe was staring over my shoulder toward the street, eyes glinting.

"What?" I whispered.

"Car coming."

"Is it an SUV?"

"No. Dude!"

He shot his hand up to his eyes as lights blasted over his face. Just as quickly they were gone, and the car peeled off with a squeal.

"What was *that*?" I said.

"Just somebody being an—" He wiped at his lips with his hand like something tasted off. "You better go in before your old man gets home."

"Are you gonna be okay?" I said.

"I'm always okay," he said.

I nodded. But I knew it was the biggest lie I'd ever heard.

*

I never thought I would *want* to turn in an English paper to Mr. Josephson. Or that I would look forward to lunch with Boz and Ruthie so I could read them my copy. Or that I'd get a will-he-be-there-oh-I-hope-he's-there squirmation in my stomach when I walked into art class.

He was, of course, and he called me Roid and was basically as obnoxious as ever, despite the grief I could see lurking in his eyes. We started to talk about it again on the way to Loser

Hall, but Uma met us outside the door. My stomach then did worse than squirm. How had I forgotten about her for the last hour? And how had I not asked him whether they were still together?

Not that I wanted *us* to be together. But us even being friends was going to be a problem if *they* were together. What was it Tank had told me? If Uma was "mobilizin'" for something, that was never a good thing. Her sucked-in face told me he was absolutely right.

Please, please, please, somebody's voice said in my head. I was pretty sure it was mine.

"Hey, Uma," I said. "We should talk. Would you tell Ms. Edelstein we're in the restroom?" I said to Rafe.

Coach Deetz always said that if you had the element of surprise on your side, even for a second, you should take advantage of it. I started talking on the way to the bathroom while Uma struggled to get her eyes back into their sockets.

"Y'know what? I was wrong before," I said. "I can totally see how you'd like Rafe. He's so funny and talented and all that. You are way lucky to be going out with him."

I led the way into the restroom with her practically running to keep up with me. Even with a brace on my leg, I could take one step to her ten.

"And I think I'm lucky to be his friend. I mean, here at school, working on projects and stuff. It's not like we're gonna hang out anyplace else—"

"Oh, really?"

Uma jumped in front of me, barely missing a collision with the sink, and tilted her head back so that, in theory at least, she could get in my face. She wasn't icy today. There were invisible flames coming out of her nose.

"If you're not going to hang outside of school, what were you doing sitting in his truck at your house last night?"

"How did you—was that you flashing your lights in his face?"

"No. It was somebody I sent."

Like that let her off the hook.

"You had him *followed?*"

"I didn't have to have him followed. I knew where he was going."

"So he told you he was coming over. He didn't tell *me*—"

"No, I just knew. Do you think I'm stupid?"

No, not stupid. Insane maybe.

"Well, so what, Uma?" I said. "He was upset about Mr. Stutz dying, and—"

"Who's Mr. Stutz?"

"The old man who—"

"Just shut up and listen to me."

I did, only because shock paralyzed my lips. She was pushing me against the sink with her chest—and I could feel the heat coming out of her eyes.

"You think because you're, like, the Savior of Study Hall, you can 'save' Rafe. But I've got that handled. You either back off, or I will kick. Your. Tail. Am I clear?"

She didn't wait for an answer. She nearly threw out a hip getting out of there, and she hadn't cleared the exit when a stall door opened and Kara stepped out.

"What *is* it with you?" I said. "Do you just hide in here waiting for me to have it out with Uma?"

I turned to the sink and leaned on it. I was shaking, hard.

"Never mind," I said. "I really don't want to fight with you too."

"I don't want to fight either." Kara came to stand next to me. I could almost hear the curls popping out of her bun. "But if you don't stop getting involved with losers like her, you are totally going to ruin your reputation."

I gripped the porcelain. "What reputation?"

"It's not totally over. Coach told me your dad's appealing."

Did my father ever work anymore? Or did he spend all his time sharing my business with people?

"But if you're all changed," Kara said, "it's not gonna—"

"I *have* changed," I said. "So I guess I should say thank you for that."

Her blue eyes sprang open. "Me? Why?"

Because you're the one who called Mr. LaSalle, I almost said. And would have said, just a few weeks before. But now—

"I need to get to class," I said instead.

I started to leave, but something struck me that I had to ask.

"Why are you all the way down here using this restroom during basketball?" I said.

"We're just doing weights now," she said.

"There's a bathroom in the locker room." My chest seized. "Kara—are you down here spying on me?"

"No!" She put both hands up to her curl-covered temples. "I just have to get away sometimes."

"From what?"

"From Selena. She's all up in my business all the time, telling me what to do to make All-State. She's, like, scary now."

I wanted to cave. I wanted to sit up on the sinks with her and swing our legs and vent. I almost did. And then she said—

"She just thinks she knows everything and that it all revolves around her. I hate it—it's like she's trying to take your place."

Kara jerked on a faucet and plunged her hands under the running water and seemed unaware that she had just slapped me with a truth I already knew.

"Kind of makes you think about who the losers really are, doesn't it?" I said.

Before any tears could come, I made my way out of the restroom.

CHaPTeR FOURTEEN

When I got back to 109, the only people there were Ms. Edelstein, Ruthie, and Uma, who was sitting with her cell phone, her back to us.

"Where is everybody?" I whispered to Ruthie.

"They were all called to the office," Ms. Edelstein said. She looked up at me, pencil poised. "Do you know what's going on?"

I heard Uma stop texting behind me.

"No," I said. "Do you think they're in trouble?"

"That would be my guess. But they were doing so well." Ms. Edelstein adjusted her glasses. "I guess it takes more than one art project to turn somebody around."

When she'd returned to her papers, Ruthie shielded us with her copy of *The Mists of Avalon*. "Rafe looked surprised when they called him out," she whispered. "I don't think he knows what's going on either."

I thought about asking Uma—but then, I'd thought about trying to reason with her once, and that hadn't gotten me far. All I could do was wait.

And say please, please, please.

*

Since my fall from basketball grace, Friday nights had become long and boring, but that one was absolutely endless. By the time Mom left for work and Dad came home and grunted a few things and barricaded himself behind his computer in the study, I had almost paced a path in my bedroom carpet and worn a hole in my brain asking it questions.

Why hadn't I ever given Rafe my cell phone number?

Why had I bothered to stay in the restroom with Kara when I could have been there when Rafe got called out? Wouldn't I have been able to tell something from his expression? Ruthie said he'd looked surprised, so he was probably innocent of whatever trouble it was, right?

Or what if he wasn't in trouble? What if it was about what was going to happen to him now that Old Man Stutz had died?

But what did that have to do with Tank and Lizard? Yikes, were they *all* related? No, that couldn't be. And who was that pulling into the driveway?

I got to my window and peered out, hoping it was Rafe, and hoping, since my father was home, that it wasn't Rafe.

It wasn't. It was a beater Nissan. M.J.? My heart almost simultaneously rose and sank, and then rose again when a petite person in stilettos jumped out of the passenger seat and headed for the front porch. It was Uma.

Okay. How to handle it. Jesus hadn't given me any practice for this kind of situation in the pages of RL. I was going to have to wing it.

I went first to the study door and tapped on it.

"A girl from one of my classes is here, Dad," I said through it. "I'm going to sit outside with her."

"Fine," he said in his best why-are-you-bothering-me-with-this-information tone.

That done, I made it to the front door, grabbing my jacket on the way, just as Uma rang the doorbell and pressed her forehead against the narrow panel of glass in the door.

I barely had it all the way open when she said, "I need to talk to you."

There was neither fire nor ice in her face. She actually looked scared—makeup collected in black smudges under her eyes, lips naked, skin pinched and pale. I started to nod her toward the bench when I saw how hard she was shaking.

"You should come in," I said.

She only hesitated for a few seconds before she waved to the person in the car. The banged-up Nissan was backing out of the driveway before I could even lead Uma through the house and into the kitchen. Even though Dad had shown no interest in what I was doing, I still wanted us as far away from the study as we could get.

Uma stopped in front of the refrigerator and grabbed my arm. "Did you hear what happened?" she said.

"I don't know — what's going on?"

"They're saying Rafe pushed some guy down the side of an overpass last night."

"*What?*" I covered my mouth with my hand and pulled Uma to the table in the far corner. "Who is saying that?"

"The police — and somebody else — something to do with that house where he goes."

For once I wished for a Ruthie-style telling. "Start from the beginning," I said.

"I don't even know what the beginning is! Rafe used to hang out with some guy at this house — he didn't ever talk to me about it — and Tank told me the guy died and these people who knew the old guy want to get Rafe in trouble because he's getting money or something —"

"Uma," I said. "Breathe."

"I don't have time! Anyway, I guess some kid fell off an overpass when he was painting. He probably slid down that sloped part and broke his leg and his arm and got knocked out — that happens all the time. Only, when he was unconscious, those people told the cops they saw Rafe push him, and Rafe wasn't even there!"

"What about the kid? Didn't he tell them the truth when he woke up?"

"He said he didn't know what happened. You have to help Rafe!"

"How can I do that —"

"Rafe was *here* when it all went down."

"You mean it happened while he and I were sitting out there in the car?"

"Yes! You have to talk to the police."

"What about your spy?"

"What?"

"Whoever you sent over to see if Rafe was here. He shined his lights right in Rafe's face—he had to have seen him."

"That was my brother."

"Tank?"

She nodded. Tears were now making mascara tracks down her cheeks. "He told them when they called him out today, but they didn't believe him. They said he wasn't an incredible witness."

I knew she meant *credible*, but I didn't correct her. I had to think—which was hard to do with my heart pounding in my ears.

"What makes you think they'll believe me, then?" I said.

For an instant, the old Uma disdain returned. "Are you serious? You're all white bread–honors classes jock. And you wouldn't have a reason to lie. I haven't even told anybody Rafe broke up with me because of you, so nobody knows you would have a motive to cover up for him."

I closed my eyes to keep anything else from coming into my head. It was so full, and spinning so fast, I actually felt nauseous.

"Please, Roid," she said. "I don't even know your real name—but you have to help. I don't even care if Rafe gets together with you, I just don't want him to go to jail. He's the only guy I ever loved."

She plastered her tiny hands over her face and rocked back and forth in the chair. Dad had to be hearing her wail. I put my arms around her and pushed her face into my chest to muffle the sobs.

"Okay," I said. "I'll talk to the police. But I have to wait 'til my mom comes home, and that'll be around midnight."

"You can wait 'til morning," she said. "His dad's bailing him out—and then he'll probably beat the—"

"So where do I go? I don't even know how this works."

"I'll call you," she said. "What's your number?"

I gave it to her, head still spinning. She keyed it in and then hit another button and murmured into her phone for whoever to come and get her.

"I just had to know if you'd do it," she said to me as I went with her to the front door. "Or I wasn't gonna sleep tonight. You will talk to the cops, right?"

"Absolutely," I said.

After the door clicked shut, I was the one pressing my face to the glass, watching her teeter down the walkway in her impossible heels. I wondered if *I* was going to sleep tonight.

"Absolutely *not*, Cassidy."

I turned around so fast my knee protested inside its brace.

"Are you out of your mind?" Dad said. "You're not going to the police and giving that thug an alibi."

The point of him was so sharp I could feel it driving into my heart. I put my hand to my chest to physically push it away. "He's not a 'thug,' Dad."

"You know what—no, we're not even going to have a discussion about this. Not you, not your mother, not your new 'friend.' No more Cassidy-makes-her-own-decisions." He held up his index finger. "Next week I am taking you before the appeals board, and you are getting back on the basketball team. And I am personally going to oversee your therapy. And there will be no more sneaking around with dead-end kids who are trying to drag you into nowhere with them."

"Nobody dragged me anywhere!"

"No? What about this kid?"

"Rafe?"

"Was he the one who gave you the drugs?"

"No, Dad. I didn't even know him them!"

My father jerked away, took a step, and jerked back. The finger came at me this time, so hard I shrank back to keep from being stabbed. "I should never have stepped out of this whole issue in the first place. You were doing fine until I stopped being involved. I'm here now, and you *will* get your heart back in it and get on track."

He lowered his finger and strode off toward the hall.

"You can't control my heart."

He stopped and turned back to me, his face like a hatchet.

"I'm sorry, Dad," I said. "But you can't decide what I care about."

"You don't know what you care about, Cassidy." His voice

suddenly dropped, and he took a step toward me. I could see him controlling his face. "I'm not going to let you throw it all away over something you've grabbed onto because you think you've lost what you really love. We'll get it back, Cass. I miss it, don't you?"

I closed my eyes so I wouldn't see the manipulation in his.

"Stay out of this mess," he said. "You might get the kid out of it this time, but there's always going to be a next time for somebody like that. You can't save him. Focus on the one thing you can save. Focus on you."

For once I was happy that, just like always, he had the last word. Because none of mine were fit to be heard.

*

Five weeks ago, I wouldn't have believed this could be happening to me. Even if it had, five weeks ago I wouldn't be considering disobeying my father. Maybe I wouldn't have, even though he was wrong to say that I didn't know what I cared about. Five weeks ago, I cared about what he told me to care about.

But now I couldn't think any of that. I could only go straight to my room and fall into my beanbag chair and say, "Please. Please. Please," and wait for RL to press itself into me.

The book opened the moment I placed it in my lap, and the words seemed to rise up to meet me, as if they were afraid I would miss them.

Yeshua was noticing that a lot of people—a lot of them—were pretty pleased with their sweet selves, thinking they were all that in a moral sense, and acting all superior to your basic person who wasn't getting any kudos for excellence, if you get what I mean.

I got exactly what it meant, and as desperate as I was for RL to get on with it, I knew better than to try to push forward. It was like there was something I needed to know in every word.

Yeshua said to them, "All right, there were two guys who went to church to pray. One was Mr. Man, Mr. Check Me Out I'm Godly. The other one was your At-Risk Kid. Straight out of Loser Hall."

I blinked. Those last five words weren't on the page, but I'd definitely heard them in my head, like they were coming through earphones.

Mr. Man stood there in the pew with his hands in the air and his face looking all churchy and his eyes closed, and he said, "Thank you, God, that I am not a lowlife loser, that I don't give in to peer pressure, that I don't cuss or drink or see R-rated movies. Thank you that unlike some people"—*his eyes opened into slits and slanted toward the At-Risk Kid*—*"I go to church and read my Bible and drop money into the collection plate."*

In a way that was Dad. My gut clenched. In an even worse way that used to be me.

Meanwhile, in the back of the sanctuary, our at-risk-headed-for-juvie guy was on his knees, face smothered in his hands because he didn't even want God to see him. He mumbled between his fingers and his tears, "God, I don't even deserve a minute of your time, but I'm desperate and I know you're the only one who can save me from myself. Please."

I held on hard to the book. That was sort of me now. I *had* said something like that. But the way this person did? Like I believed God was the only one who could help? Like there was no help without him? And what if I did? Was that going to change Dad's mind? He was Mr. Man ...

RL pressed against my lap. I dug my eyes back into the page.

Yeshua said, "This guy was the one who left the church with God—not Mr. Man. If you walk around thinking you and I are like this"—*he crossed his fingers*—*"because you say all the right things and look good, you are going to trip over yourself and you won't be able to get up. But if you will just be who you are—hurting and needing me and knowing it—you are going to become so much more than you ever dreamed you could be."*

I pulled the book to my chest and had the very sure sensation that it was hugging me.

"Okay, God," I whispered. "I don't deserve your help, but I'm asking for it anyway because you're the only one who can tell me what to do. Please tell me what to do."

*

I woke up the next morning knowing that I knew the answer. It was too early to hear from Uma, but that was okay because

I had things to do first. I needed to talk to Mom and then I knew—I hoped—she and I would go to Dad and tell him I was going to the police. The Frenemy tried to elbow her way in when I thought about what might happen—that Dad would say to forget about the appeal, that he and Mom would have a huge fight, that Kara was right and what little reputation Uma seemed to think I had left would be gone.

Then I remembered what Ben said, that I couldn't predict what would happen, but I could practice for it. I could ask, "What can I think about to make this better in this moment?" And an RL-sounding voice would somehow give me the answer.

I'd been hearing it all night.

Which was not to say that I wasn't still whispering, "Please, please, please," all the way out to the kitchen. Where I found a note from Mom saying:

Cass,
    There is a major spring snowstorm coming in and I probably have to be on the air most of the day. I'm sorry you have to be alone. Dad had to go to Denver and I'm afraid he might get stuck there for a while due to weather. I'll call you. I love you.
    Mom

She'd added a PS:

There's plenty of chocolate in our usual stash places.

It was going to take more than chocolate to make *this* moment better. I read the note again and crumpled it in my hand. I couldn't call her while she was on the air. Not unless I did it during commercials.

I clicked on the kitchen TV and waited for her face to flicker onto the screen. She was looking right at me, talking about air pressure and wind chill and bringing your pets inside the house so they wouldn't freeze to death.

"I don't care about that!" I said to her beautiful, reassuring face. "I need you!"

I checked the garage, but both cars were gone. Not that it would have done me any good to talk to Dad alone anyway. Okay, I had to think what to do before Uma called.

And then my cell phone rang, and it was her.

"Roid?" she said when I answered. She sounded even more hysterical than she had the night before.

"I'm not ready to go to the police yet, Uma," I said. "My parents aren't home—"

"No! Not the police! You have to talk to Rafe!"

Her panic got hold of my stomach. "I don't understand."

"His father bailed him out last night, and then he took him home and messed him up—"

"His dad hit him?"

"Yes! So Rafe took off and now he's saying he's going to skip bail and run away, and if he does that ... you have to go to him and you have to make him stay. He'll listen to you!"

"I don't have a car, Uma, and—"

"I'll send somebody to get you."

"Where is he?" I said.

But she had already hung up.

"Dear *God!*" I said, out loud, to my empty home. "*Please show me what to do.*"

And then I got my clothes on and brushed my hair into a ponytail and waited by the front door.

*

The car that pulled into my driveway was so covered in snow I couldn't even tell what color it was, but I knew it was a vehicle I hadn't seen before. And it definitely wasn't one I would have expected Lizard to be driving.

"Is this your grandfather's or something?" I said when I climbed into the front seat. What kid our age drove a land yacht with leather seats?

"I borrowed it," Lizard said.

"Can you even see over the steering wheel?" I looked nervously through the windshield, where the snow was smacking

193

into the glass faster than the windshield wipers could slap it away. "Can you even see, period?"

"It's all good," Lizard said.

But now that I really listened to him, he didn't sound like anything was good. I'd never seen his face puckered like it was right then, as if he were barely holding something back.

"You okay?" I said.

"No, man. Somethin' bad is goin' down. You're the only one can stop it."

"It's not like I have this power over Rafe," I said. "You and Tank are his friends—you could probably talk him out of running better than I can."

"No, see, you don't get it. Rafe talks *us* out of doing stupid stuff. It'd be like him tryin' to tell his old man what to do."

"Is he hurt bad? From when his dad hit him?"

"Not any worse than usual, but it's gonna *be* worse if his dad finds him before you go to the police and get him off."

"Then why don't we go to the police first?"

"Because his dad might find him by that time." Lizard pulled his eyes from the driving snow to give me a look I could only describe as helpless.

"You don't think Rafe's gone already, do you?" I said.

"No," he said, "'cause we already told him you were comin'. He said he'd wait."

"Where is he?"

Lizard turned the wheel and the car slid into what was probably a driveway under the snow.

"He's here," he said.

He pointed a shaky finger at Old Man Stutz's house.

"How is he here?" I said. "I thought Mr. Stutz died. You guys didn't break—"

"Rafe always came here when his old man messed him up. He still has the key the old man gave him, in case Stutz wasn't home when he came."

I fought off panic. Just because Rafe had a key didn't mean it was legal for him to be in there. I had to get him out before this got any worse than it already was.

Rafe looked small sitting in a huge recliner in the corner of a room as big and empty as a cavern. Even my rubber-soled boots were loud as I walked across the rugless floor toward him. There were no drapes at the windows, only blinds, and the walls were bare. They obviously hadn't always been, because large rectangles looked cleaner than the spaces around them.

"Hey," I said when I was close enough for my voice not to echo in the void.

"They already took all his stuff."

"I'm sorry?" I said. I sat on an ottoman that was oddly placed without its chair, right next to the recliner.

"They already came in and got his Navajo rug and all his art. They even took the curtains. They were made out of cloth the Utes wove by hand."

I started to ask him *who* had made off with Old Man Stutz's belongings, but we didn't have time for that. I was already imagining blue lights flashing through the blizzard.

"We shouldn't be here," I said. "Why don't we—why don't we go to my house?"

Rafe's eyes came out from under their heavy, grieving hood. "You gotta be kiddin' me. Your father's not gonna—"

"He's not home," I said. "We'll go to the police first, and then we'll go to my house—"

"Yeah? And then what? They decide I didn't do it and then they send me back to my old man."

Rafe leaned forward into what little light there was in the room, slanting through the blinds. I gasped out loud. His left eye was swollen shut and his wonderful lip was split and twisted.

"I'm not goin' back," he said.

"Okay," I said. And then again, "Okay." Nothing was, in truth, okay, but I had to say something while I swallowed back the nausea that was creeping up my throat. "Okay, we'll go to the police and get you cleared, and we'll tell them your dad's abusing you, and they'll find you—"

"What? A foster home?"

Rafe scooted to the edge of the recliner, where I could see the fresh scrapes on his knuckles. His father evidently wasn't the only one who'd gotten his licks in. I felt sicker.

"See, you don't know about the system," he said. "Foster 'parents' are worse than your real parents. And if it doesn't work out with them, they put you in the state home, which is this far"—he held his thumb and forefinger a quarter inch apart—"from bein' in juvie. I might as well go to jail, and I'm not goin' there, either, because I didn't do anything wrong."

"I know," I said. "I'd know it even if I hadn't been with you while that kid was falling off the freeway. I'll tell the police that—and *then* we'll figure out what happens next."

Rafe shook his head. "I know what happens next."

"Nobody can predict that," I said. "All we can do is whatever's going to make it better in this moment. And in this moment, we need to get out of here."

He didn't move. He was, in fact, so still that I realized he was paralyzed down to his soul.

"Come on," I whispered to him. "I'll be with you the whole time. We're here for the same reason, remember? The two losers?"

He stood up and reached for his coat from the back of the recliner, while I held my breath. He nodded at the ottoman where I was perched.

"I used to sit there when I talked to the old man," he said. "He was, like, deaf as a brick, so I had to get close to him—"

Rafe's voice broke. I stood up and his arm came around my shoulders. I could feel a shudder going through him.

"I'll come with you," he said. "Under two conditions."

"One."

"If it starts meltin' down, you get as far away from me as you can. I mean it—you're not going down for my stuff."

"Two."

"You stop calling yourself a loser." He pulled my face against his neck and whispered, "You never were."

"Rafe—dude!"

196

Lizard bolted into the room, eyes wild.

"We're comin'," Rafe said. "Only we're not takin' the old man's car. We're callin' Tank—"

"No, man—you gotta run. It's the cops!"

*

The only place I had ever seen a human being move with that kind of practiced precision was on a professional basketball court.

Rafe had the light off and Lizard out the side door to create a distraction and me at the back door before I even had a chance to panic. That only kicked in when he said, "We have to make a run for the wall."

"I'm sorry, Rafe," I said. "I can't run, remember?"

"I know."

"You go and I'll stay here and explain to the police—"

"Do you women never know when to shut up?" he said.

And then I was over his shoulder and we were sliding across the back deck like a pair of figure skaters. Rafe stopped short of the edge and tightened his hold on me before he jumped into the drifts below. He was already running again when I heard an engine roar.

"Is that the police?" I cried.

"No." Rafe swore under his breath. "That was Lizard takin' off in the old man's car."

That must have been Lizard's choice of a "distraction." No wonder Rafe was always telling him not to do stupid stuff. Even when he was warned, the moron didn't listen. It struck me that Lizard was taking a huge chance so Rafe could get away. Had I ever even had friends like that?

"Rafe, stop!" I said. "I'm slowing you down."

If he heard me over the now howling wind, he didn't show it. His steps got longer and faster, and the wall got closer and closer. What we were going to do when we got there, I had no idea.

"There's scaffolding down there at the end." His words came out in heavy breaths, and with them thick puffs of frost.

"That's how I reached the high parts. I'm gonna carry you up there, and then I'll—"

"Police! Stop!"

The voice was so loud it had to be coming through a bullhorn.

"Do it, Rafe!" I said. "Stop!"

"No!"

"Please—it's only gonna be worse. I'll tell them—please!"

I felt him slow, and I felt him turn so that he faced the direction of the bullhorn. My head dangled down his back, but I just kept saying, "It's okay. It'll be okay."

"Put the girl down!" the officer screamed through the bullhorn.

Rafe bent his knees, and I knew he was trying to lower me gently.

"Put her down!"

"I am!"

"Do it!"

Someone lunged across the snow and Rafe lost his hold on me. I tumbled face-first into the snow and twisted to get my face free. Pain seared across my knee.

"All right—on your feet!"

I blinked into the icy pellets that stung at my face. An angry face came toward me, still shouting, "On your feet!"

"I can't!" I shouted back. "I can't!"

Because the horrible, wretched truth was—I couldn't move my knee.

CHAPTER FIFTEEN

The ambulance ride was the worst part.

Next to the part where I lay in the ER wrapped in a heated blanket while a doctor said he thought I might have blown my graft, he couldn't be sure, and that I'd need an MRI to confirm it.

And even that was nothing compared to the part when the police officer came in as I was constructing a wall to hold back the tears, to say they'd arrested Julio Jimenez—who I assumed was Lizard—for auto theft, and Raphael Diego for breaking and entering, and that if I told him where they could find DeLeon Shermann, they wouldn't charge me as an accessory to all of the above.

I was trying to convince him that I didn't even know *who* DeLeon Shermann was, much less *where* he was, when the curtain scraped back and my mother flew into the cubicle and knocked Officer Whatever His Name Was out of the way to get to me.

The wall came down.

"I'm sorry, Mom!" I sobbed into her neck. "I was just trying to get Rafe to go with me to the police so I could tell them he was at our house when that kid fell off the freeway so he couldn't have pushed him off, and he was trying to get me out of that house so I wouldn't get in trouble, only he shouldn't be in trouble, because Mr. Stutz gave him a key—"

"Okay, Cass, it's okay. I'm concerned about *you*. The doctor—"

"Wait," the officer said.

Mom pulled away from me just enough to be able to say over my head, "Do you have to do this now?"

"If you don't want her arrested, yes, I suggest we do it now."

It was my turn to pull away. I shrugged the blanket off my shoulders and pushed aside my tears with the backs of my hands.

"It's the truth," I said. "All of it. And I would have told you before but you didn't give me a chance."

"Are you willing to make a formal statement of everything you just told—your mom, is it?"

"Does that mean you'll let him go? Raphael?"

"It will definitely help him—"

"If you let him go, you have to promise you won't make him go back to his father."

"Now, *that* I can't—"

"He's a child abuser," I said. "He's the one who should be in jail."

"One thing at time—"

"Did you see his eye? And his lip? His own father did that to him."

The officer looked at Mom like he was expecting her to stop me, but her face was somewhere between mother bear and news person. She showed no signs of putting a halt to my tirade.

"All right," the officer said. "I promise you we'll look into it. The doc said your knee needs to stay on ice for a while, so why don't you start from the beginning."

I did. At a corner table in my mind, I wished Ruthie was there. She could tell a story a lot better than I could.

*

It was almost dark by the time the hospital released me with the promise that I would see my orthopedic surgeon on Monday. When the I-don't-really-have-time-for-you ER doctor took off the ice pack and checked, he said the swelling had already receded some. I couldn't say. I was afraid to look.

They tried to give me pain meds, but I opted for the ibuprofen Mom had in her purse and left the hospital a free woman without a rap sheet. I wasn't as worried about my knee or my criminal record as I was about Rafe.

I couldn't even eat the soup Mom fixed for me, and if I hadn't been wrapped in both ice and a hot blanket, I would have been up pacing the family room. Mom tried everything from a fire in the fireplace to a cup of chamomile tea to calm me down (chocolate wasn't even offered), but all I could think about was Rafe, pacing a jail cell where nobody was offering him anything.

Mom was handling it all with blue-eyed calm and a lot of hair tucking. I was sure I was about to drive her nuts, and then the phone rang. My attempt to roll off the couch to get to it was met with a particularly rough hair tuck and the phone being put on speaker.

"This is Officer Meadows," the voice said. "I thought you might like an update."

Julio Jimenez, aka Lizard, was charged because he did, in fact, "borrow" Old Man Stutz's car. I felt bad about having to tell the police that he'd picked me up in it, but the boy really was a moron. The judge, Officer Meadows said, would probably go easy on him since this was his first offense.

Who'd have thought? Rafe really must have been doing a good job keeping him in line up 'til now.

DeLeon, aka Tank Shermann, was picked up, questioned, and released. His statement confirmed the alibi I'd given Rafe for Thursday night. The only question was why he hadn't come forward with his information before. Uma was going to be surprised by that.

"What about Rafe—Raphael?" I said.

"Mr. Diego has been cleared of all charges. It helped that he led us to the people who stole Mr. Stutz's home furnishings before his body was even cold."

How did Rafe know who and where they were? It was becoming more and more clear that Rafe lived in a world that was as foreign to me as Saudi Arabia, and probably just as scary. I really wished he didn't have to live in it.

"What about the other thing?" I said. "You didn't make Rafe go back to his father, right?"

I thought Officer Meadows snickered. "You didn't actually think I was going to call you without the skinny on that, did you?"

Mom grinned and mouthed the word "no" at the phone.

"Mr. Diego did make a statement pertaining to his father's abuse, and Mr. Diego senior has been taken in for questioning. I don't know any more than that except—"

"Where's Rafe now? You didn't put him in foster care?"

"At the moment I believe he is in the custody of Mrs. Shermann—"

"Tank's mother?" I said. And Uma's? I tried not to let that drag my heart down. Rafe was safe, and that was all that mattered.

*

The snow was already melting when I woke up the next morning. I could see it dripping off the roof as I lay in bed wondering what was going to happen when I tried to move my leg. It hurt the same way it had on Tuesday, and it turned out to be okay then. Maybe I would be lucky a second time.

Or maybe I should get busy saying, "Please, please, please."

Actually, I felt more like saying thank you. Mom and I had stayed up late making s'mores in the fireplace—a celebration of everyone's freedom—and talking about ... everything.

I tried to remember it all now, but the words themselves had been lost in the sleep I'd finally fallen into around one o'clock. The feeling, though—*that* was still with me, the warm safeness that filled me when Mom was nodding at me, firelight dancing across her face, erasing the "lines and wrinkles" she was always complaining about.

She'd looked just the way she had when I was little and would come to her lap for what she used to call a "pit stop." I never stayed longer than about sixteen seconds—I had stuff to do—and she never tried to hold me there.

I saw now that she must have known early on that I wasn't

going to be into cuddling and pink and shopping for sweaters with kittens on them. She probably knew who I was before I did, and even though my father had taken me over for the past six years, I knew as we twirled melted Hershey's around our fingers that she was still one of the only people who knew the real me.

It gave me a spurt of courage. I tossed the covers aside and was about to take off my brace so I could inspect my knee when I heard the front door slam—harder than we were supposed to slam in the Brewster house.

"Did you see this?" I heard my father growl as he very obviously marched through to the family room.

He hardly waited for my mother's sleepy "See what?" before he bellowed on.

"She made the paper. Front page of the sports section. Wonderful."

I heard paper slap on wood—the Sunday *Gazette* hitting the coffee table.

His next bellow was, "Cassidy!"

"Trent, honestly, she's exhausted," Mom said.

"Cassidy!" he yelled again, this time closer.

Before I could even think about swinging my legs over the side of my bed, he was in my room, my mother right behind him. He was still in his overcoat, like he'd driven in from Denver for the sole purpose of yelling at me. Mom didn't look like she'd been to bed at all.

Dad threw the newspaper on my bed, but I didn't look at it. There really was no need, with him spewing out the article about me, probably word for word. The longer he went on, the lower his voice got, until it was down to its finest point for the final stab.

"You know what this means, don't you?"

I did, but I was sure it wasn't the answer he had in mind.

"You've clearly made your choice, Cassidy. After everything I've said and done, you've still 'decided for yourself.'" He deposited a glare on my mother before he turned on me again. "Well, it's definitely over now. You've ruined any possible chance you had left of getting back into basketball. I might as well cancel the appeal hearing—I'm not going to fight in a battle I know I can't win."

I stared at my knees. The most athletic part of your body, Ben had said, and the most vulnerable. I felt both.

"I want to hear it, Cassidy," Dad said. "I want to hear you say you have no problem with the fact that you have wrecked what could have been a great career. I want to hear it in your own voice."

My voice? My *voice*?

I looked up from my knees. "Dad, I don't have a voice," I said. "Why did I need one? You always told me what to do, when to do it, how to do it, and how well I just did it." I swallowed, hard. "If I say what I think my voice wants to say, you're not going to hear it, so what's the point?"

I watched the color completely drain from my father's face until it matched his white hair and he was no longer "striking."

"I suppose there is none then," he said. And he left my room.

"Are you okay, Cass?" Mom said.

"Yeah."

"Then I'm going to go ..."

I nodded, and she closed my door and hurried down the hall.

"Good luck with that, Mom," I whispered. Please, please, please.

*

I heard the up-and-down murmurs of a fight behind closed doors, and then the strained silence, during which I took a shower so I wouldn't have to hear any follow-up. I was pretty sure Dad was gone when I got out. Mom was somewhere talking softly—probably on the phone—and the air was free again.

I was starving by then and ventured out in the direction of the kitchen. I stopped cold when I found Mom and Ben in the family room.

"Good morning, Boss," Ben said. "I hear you had a busy day yesterday."

For the first time *since* that "busy day," the voice of the ER doctor barged into my head and brought the Frenemy with him. "You might have blown the graft but I can't be sure," he said. I kicked both of them aside and sank onto the couch.

"I did everything I could not to mess it up," I said. "But I had to do it. I had to be there."

He nodded without grinning. "Let's see what we've got."

The bending-touching-frowning tests he did didn't show that I'd torn the graft completely, but he still wasn't sure it wasn't damaged.

"The ER doc was right, you do need another MRI. I know you hate to go back into that storm drain ..."

"It's okay," I said.

"I'm going to make more coffee," Mom said.

When she'd padded into the kitchen, I let Ben put my brace back on me. "Are you disappointed in me?" I said.

His face came up quickly. "Why would I be?"

I shrugged. "I've messed it up twice now. That doesn't exactly make me your poster girl anymore."

Ben patted the brace for me to lower my leg. "Let me tell you something, Boss," he said. "I admire the tremendous commitment you've made to becoming a great athlete. But what inspires me more is your commitment to becoming a great person."

"I wish my father thought that," I said.

He gave a grim nod. "I wish he did too. But it looks like it's up to you now."

I was thinking about that when he'd left and Mom was washing out the coffee pot. She and Dad *must* have had it out if she was cleaning everything that didn't move. I propped my leg on the opposite kitchen chair and picked my words carefully.

"Do you think I could go ahead with the appeal without Dad?"

She stopped scrubbing. "Seriously?"

"Bad idea?"

"No." She left the rag on the counter and sat down to face me. "I was actually going to suggest it. Unlike your father, I don't think this incident with Rafe necessarily has to work against you."

"Do you think I can do it, though? I'd have to talk in front of a whole bunch of people, right? I'm not sure I even know what to say, or how."

Mom leaned toward me, hair untucked. All the lines in her face showed today.

"What you said earlier about not having a voice? I don't think that's true, Cass. What was that I heard yesterday when you were telling that police officer how it was going to be? I don't think Rafe's friends came to *you* to help him because you don't know what to say or how to say it." She took my shoulders in her hands. "You're right—your father has spoken for you for years. He probably could still represent you as an agent—for basketball. But your scoring average is not who you are—your sport doesn't complete you—it's not your identity. And I think that's what you need to tell the appeals board, because that's what's going to show you what Cassidy Brewster is made of."

I looked into her eyes for a long time, until I had every crease memorized.

"Will you make sure he doesn't cancel the hearing?" I said finally.

"Done."

"And will you be there?"

"A truckload of chocolate couldn't keep me away," she said.

"Thank you," I said. "Thank you, thank you, thank you."

*

I was dying to see Rafe and make sure Officer Meadows hadn't been feeding me a line about him being at Tank and Uma's just to get me to shut up. But I couldn't go to school Monday, because Dr. Horton's office got me in for an MRI. If it turned out I needed more surgery, it probably wasn't going to matter what happened at the appeal hearing.

I was shooing the Frenemy out for about the third time that day as Mom and I turned the corner onto our street.

"Whose car is that in the driveway?" She lowered her sunglasses. "It can't be."

"Oh my gosh," I said. "Is that Gretchen's car?"

Mom slowed down like we were doing surveillance, but it was definitely the green Mazda. And Gretchen was sitting in the driver's seat.

"Have you even talked to her since—"

"No," Mom said.

She pulled up next to the Mazda and turned off the engine.

"What are you going to do?" I said.

"What we always do," she said. "Break out the chocolate."

We all got out of our cars and exchanged the most awkward greetings ever. Mom somehow got us into the house without anybody smacking anybody. I noticed that Gretchen's hair wasn't as full and luscious as it used to be, and that she was so thin, the bones in her wrists stuck out like knobs on kitchen cabinets. Mom left us in the family room while she went to make hot chocolate, and I was frantically searching for something to say when Gretchen blurted out—

"I know you must hate me, Cassidy. I hate me too."

Now I *really* didn't know what to say, but she didn't seem to need for me to say anything. Everything came out like she'd practiced long and hard.

"I heard what happened, and I had to come over, because I just want to say I am so, so sorry for what I did to you. You have absolutely no idea." She piled her hair up to let it drop, which it did in a mere listless shadow of its former self. "I had this mindset then, like 'I can fix anything. I'm in control. I know more than the people who are teaching me.' I really did want to help you—and your family—but I did it the wrong way. Totally the wrong way."

I still couldn't respond. She'd said everything I would have said anyway.

"I didn't come here to ask you to forgive me." Gretchen's voice was winding down. "I just had to tell you that if I could undo it, I would."

A noisy group of answers called out in my head. *You can't*

now, can you? Feels pretty lousy to lose everything, huh? You blew
my chances, so why don't you just blow right out of here?

I slammed the door on all of them — because there wasn't one that didn't sound like something my father would say. It never solved anything to hear them. It sure wasn't going to solve anything to say them. And besides —

"Y'know what?" I said. "All that stuff you said about your-self — it fit me too, back then."

"I don't get that," she said.

"I had a mindset too, like the team couldn't do anything without me and I had to be in control, and I couldn't just wait and do it the right way." I looked at her with my whole self wide open. "Doesn't it just totally bite to find out that stuff?"

"Yeah." Her face was still fighting something. "And if you admit it, you still lose everything."

It was my turn not to get it.

"I'm so close to getting back into med school, Cassidy."

"That's good, isn't it?"

She looked at me, misery pouring from her eyes. "Not when I have to give up everything to make it happen."

"You mean Aaron?" I said.

She only half nodded. "Not just Aaron. My own self-respect. And you."

"Don't worry about me," I said. "Because, y'know what? I forgive you."

Her swollen eyes widened. "Why would you?"

"Because one mistake doesn't make you who you are."

Gretchen shook her head. She didn't believe a word of it.

But I did.

CHAPTER SIXTEEN

When Gretchen left, it felt like she took a chunk of the past with her, a chunk I was more than happy to let go of. I didn't even ask Mom what went down between the two of them when she walked Gretchen out to her car. All I wanted to do was look ahead.

So I read the RL stories over again. I went to the Center like always the next morning, and did the exercises I could. I chatted it up with Boz during first period and at lunch, where I told him and Ruthie everything that happened over the weekend. I had to keep going forward.

Funny how just a few weeks before, I would have considered that moving backward.

But fifth period was going to be hard, I thought, as I headed to the art room after lunch. I hadn't seen or talked to Rafe since Saturday, which had to mean he was back with Uma and that they, too, were going forward. It was all right, really. They came from the same world. He needed Uma now—she understood where he'd been. I was totally okay with it.

Uh-huh. Then why did I feel like I might fold if I didn't hear—

"Hey, Roid."

There he was, right inside the art room, wiggling his eyebrows and greeting me like he had a shopping cart and a sales flier waiting just for me. Although, Walmart didn't usually hire people who looked like they'd just gone a couple of rounds on Smackdown.

"Hey," I said. "Are you okay?"

"I'm always okay."

"Liar. Seriously—are you?"

"That would be a yes. Except for sharin' a room with Tank. The dude snores like a Harley."

I almost melted into a puddle, right there in front of the chalks and paintbrushes.

"So—are *you?*" he said.

"Am I what?"

"Okay."

"Yes."

"Liar." Rafe looked down at my knee, and I saw something different in his eyes. "Did I hurt it?" he said.

"I don't know."

"Aw, man—"

I shook my head at him. "No. I'd do it again in a heartbeat."

The bell rang, and Mrs. Petrocelli-Ward pointed at us, wrist jingling.

"Just because you're artists doesn't mean you have to be flakes. The bell has rung. Have a seat."

Rafe wiggled his eyebrows at her. It got him nowhere.

*

The next hurdle I had to get over was seeing Uma. As it turned out, I didn't have to jump very high.

The weather was warm, and that was such an oddity for a Colorado April that Ms. Edelstein announced that we were having study hall outside. The minute we were out of the building, Uma broke from the kindergarten line we were in and threw her arms around my waist. I looked down at the top of her head with what I knew had to be total bafflement.

"Thankyouthankyouthankyouthankyou," she said.

"I guess you're welcome," I said.

She tilted her head back to look up at me, mascara streaming down her face, as well as the front of my shirt. "You saved Rafe's life."

Rafe took hold of her arm and peeled her off me. "She gets it, Uma. Don't go emo."

I laughed. "Okay, so I saved him for you. You can owe me."

She shook her head and gave Rafe a look so full of sheer longing I could feel it in my own soul. "You tell her," she said to him. And then she turned and headed back to the building.

"Where are you going, Uma?" Ms. Edelstein said.

"Bathroom."

I looked at Rafe. "Should I go after her?"

"No," he said.

I was considering it, though, when Ruthie came up on the other side of me.

"Will you be okay sitting out here?" she said.

We'd reached the track by then, and Tank and Ms. Edelstein were already settling in on the bleachers. Ms. Edelstein pulled her red pencil from behind her ear. Did she go anywhere without those papers?

"It's okay," I said to Ruthie. "Why?"

"Aren't those, like, those girls?"

I looked where she was pointing. Coach Deetz stood at the other end of the track with that obnoxious whistle in his mouth, while the entire girls' varsity basketball team loped past him and rounded the bend to come toward us. He always made us run outside on days like this.

"What girls?" Rafe said.

"Girls I used to know," I said. "I need to sit."

Rafe and I parked on the second-to-the-bottom row so I could prop my leg, and Ruthie sat behind us and was soon immersed in the inevitable paperback. I felt a pang when I realized it was *The Scarlet Letter*. I was ready to bury my own face in a book, just to keep from watching the long legs that took the track like antelopes. Especially Kara's.

"Hey, Roid."

I turned to Rafe. Okay, for lack of a book, he would do.

"Yeah?" I said.

"What you said to Uma—you were right. I owe you."

"I didn't mean it like that," I said. "I was just trying to get her to stop crying."

211

"No—for real. You risked it all for me. I'm scared to ask what your old man said about it."

"Don't," I said.

"Yeah, well, I wish I could do something to, I don't know—be there for you like you—"

"Oh, nuh-*uh*."

I glanced back to see Ruthie staring round-eyed at the field. "What?"

Ruthie used the book to cover the track-ward side of her face. "Look at that one girl—that Asian girl."

"Dude," Rafe said.

"*What?*"

Rafe physically turned my head to face the track. Selena was just passing us, and Emily. If she got any closer to her she was going to—

"Did you *see* that?" Ruthie said.

I did. I saw Selena step into Emily's path, just as Em's foot came off the ground. To keep from landing on her, Emily had to jerk sideways. When her foot went down, it went down flat. And so did Emily.

Selena turned and ran backward a few steps, and then stopped. She was on Emily, hand down to help her up, before I could decide whether I'd actually seen what I'd just seen.

And whether it was the first time I'd seen it.

I stared at my knee brace.

"Did she do that on purpose?" Ruthie said.

Before I could answer, Rafe crooked his elbow around my neck and pulled me in so he could talk into my ear.

"I've seen that chick before," he said. "That Asian chick."

"She goes here," I said.

"No—"

"Enough with the PDA down there," Ms. Edelstein said in her usual dry voice.

Rafe let go, but he kept his voice low and close. "You remember that day I hit on you outside LaSalle's office?"

"You were hitting on me?"

He gave half an eye roll. "Yeah. It worked so well on you, I tried it on her—same place—about two weeks later."

I rolled *my* eyes all the way. "I bet you got farther with me than you did with her. What was she doing at LaSalle's office anyway? The girl's, like, the perfect student." I put my hand to my forehead. "Tell me you didn't say you and she were there for the same reason."

"If a line works for me, I stick with it."

"No way it worked with Selena."

"Nah. She said she wasn't a loser—she was there to take *down* a loser. The chick's a—" He shrugged one shoulder. "A snot."

Thoughts suddenly lined up in my head so brightly and sharply that I had to close my eyes to keep from being blinded by them.

Coach Deetz is totally biased. If somebody else hadn't tipped LaSalle off, you never would have gone down for it.

That's what Selena said that day in the cafeteria. I'd been so stung by her calling me a druggie and saying she would never play on a team with me again, I'd missed it.

"Rafe, will you help me walk down there?"

He let one eyebrow go up. "You gonna take her down right here? You oughta at least wait until after school."

"I'm not going to fight her," I said. "I just have to talk to her. Now."

"Then let's do it."

Selena was on the grass stretching when I hobbled over to her. Rafe stood at the edge of the track like a bodyguard.

"How did you know?" I said.

She looked up with a jerk, but she recovered quickly to the smooth, cold face I knew so well.

"How did I know what?"

"How did you know Coach Deetz wasn't the one who went to Mr. LaSalle?"

Her eyes shifted to the left. "What are you talking about?"

"That day in the cafeteria when you came up to me. If you knew so much, why didn't you just say, 'If Kara hadn't tipped him off ... '?"

"Kara?" Selena turned abruptly to her other leg, but not before I saw her realize her own mistake.

213

"It wasn't Kara, was it?" I said. "It was you."

"What difference does it make who it was? It was the truth."

"Only you didn't know it, Selena. You just made it up."

She whipped her head around to look at me. Her eyes were in paper-thin slits. "Fine. But I was right about you."

"I know," I said.

But I was wrong about Kara. So wrong.

I could still hear her crying, *I don't even know what I did!* Because she didn't do it.

The top half of my body folded over my legs, and I buried my face in my hands.

"Roid, what's goin' on? Hey—Roid."

Rafe was at my side, but I couldn't answer him. All I could cry was, "I was wrong! Oh my gosh, I was wrong!"

I vaguely heard Ms. Edelstein say, "Is she okay? Cassidy—what is it? Is it your knee?" And then I felt hands, warm and damp, on my back. Ruthie's hands.

"Dude—you want me to call 9–1–1?" Tank said.

I pulled my head up in time to see him motioning to Rafe with his cell phone—and Selena hurrying away.

"No, moron." Uma hurried to us and gave Tank a swollen-eyed look before she went to her knees in front of me. "You need something?" she said. "You want me to call somebody out?"

"That Asian girl," Ruthie said.

"No!" I shook my head at them all, gathered around me like they were about to do an intervention. "I just realized I made a really bad call about somebody and—I just messed up, okay?"

"I hate it when I do that," Uma said.

"What else is going on?"

I looked at Ms. Edelstein, who was surveying me over the tops of her glasses. "You've looked like you're about to receive a life sentence ever since you walked in the door today."

"It's the hearing," Ruthie said.

"Ruthie—" I said.

Ms. Edelstein shushed me. "What hearing? What am I missing?"

I was suddenly too emotionally wasted to do anything but nod at Ruthie—who started with Genesis and told Ms. Edelstein and all of Loser Hall about what I was going to be up against the next afternoon. Nobody even seemed to take a breath until she was through. Even when she was, none of them said anything. Every face looked as hopeless as I felt.

Except Ms. Edelstein's. "All right," she said. "Enough with the gloom and doom. Why do we think Cassidy can't do this thing? She stood up to all of you, didn't she? You were the scariest bunch of hoods I'd ever been stuck with until she came in." She glanced at Ruthie. "Not you," she said. "I just thought you'd taken a vow of silence."

"Now we can't shut her up," Uma said. And then she smiled at Ruthie. She actually smiled.

"You can do this," Ms. Edelstein said to me. Her eyes took on a gleam. "Just stand up there and pretend you're telling Loser Hall where it's at."

*

When I got to the Center, Ben greeted me with a grin and gray-eyed sparkle.

"The MRI was negative for a new tear," he said. "Just some inflammation. It shouldn't put you too far behind schedule if you want to play in the fall." He did his wonderful head tilt. "It's all up to you, of course."

"Actually," I said, "it's kind of up to what the board decides."

"And doesn't that come back to you convincing them they'd be nuts not to let you participate? Which, compared to the things you've already been through, should be a slam dunk."

"Cute," I said.

I got started on my calf stretching, but I couldn't get my mood to stretch with it. Even with everybody cheering me on—Mom and Boz and Rafe and Ben, and all of Loser Hall— didn't it still come down to me convincing the board that I didn't know I was taking steroids? If I could have proven that a month ago, I wouldn't have been ousted in the first place. They might say I was now a better person than I'd been back then, but the fact remained that I had no proof that I had not been told that what I was taking was an illegal substance. The idea was truly in their heads that I was a user. Changing their minds was going to be like unringing a bell.

I stopped to rest my now screaming calf. I guessed I could stand in front of the board and tell them what I'd told Gretchen. Somehow, I didn't see that working. All I could do now was say pleasepleaseplease. I wondered if the widow in the RL story was that eloquent.

The minute I got home, I checked to see. And then I fell asleep with RL hugged to my chest, and the words "please, please, please" still on my lips.

CHAPTER SEVENTEEN

om picked me up right after school to drive me to the hearing. The sun was sparkling on the snow on the peaks, and not a single cloud marred the sky. I wished my mind could have been as clear. Seeing Mom helped.

"I thought about bringing you a change of clothes," she said. "Maybe make you look older or something. But then I thought, no, you should just be you." She reached over and squeezed my good knee. "I can't imagine why you'd want to be anybody else."

I gazed out the side window and wished I was just going to the Center to moan over how many squats Ben made me do.

"Is Dad coming?" I said.

For the first time since I got in the car, Mom pushed her hair behind her ear. "I told him it was still on."

From the way she accelerated through the yellow light, I was pretty sure she'd told him a few other things too.

"If it weren't for me, would you and Dad ever fight?" I said.

She pulled her eyes from the road for an instant to stare at me. "We don't really fight over you, Cass. We fight over some fundamental differences between us that come out punching where you are concerned. You don't need to worry about that—especially not today." She picked up her purse from the console and put it in my lap. "I brought a bar of seventy percent."

"I love you, Mom," I said.

"Loved you first, Cass," she said.

The woman who was obviously in charge, judging from the way she threw her shoulders back when she told people what to do—which seemed to be everyone—told us to sit in the front row so I could come up to the speaker's chair when they called me. Yeah, they might have made it more nerve-wracking, but I didn't see how. Especially with Mr. LaSalle sitting across the aisle from us. He must have gotten a fresh buzz cut for the occasion, because his scalp showed angry pink as he cracked his knuckles like he had way more important things to do. He could have skipped the whole thing, and that would have been fine with me.

Four other people assembled and sat at the front table. One of the women had bleached hair and drawn-on eyebrows, and the other owned several chins and wore her glasses on a chain like she was afraid they were going to get away. I wouldn't have put it past the man beside her to try to steal them; he kind of looked like a grown-up version of Lizard. The final board member, another guy, was the last to join them. He was the only one who looked directly at me, with his head lowered to reveal the front half of his very bald head. It was like being stared at by a skull.

"I think I'm gonna throw up," I whispered to Mom.

"Seriously?" she whispered back.

I shook my head. But it would have made a good excuse to get out of there.

Once Head Lady got things started, there was no escaping. While she read the decision Mr. LaSalle had written on March 9, every glare from the front table was directed at me. I was sure I couldn't have felt guiltier if I'd actually *been* guilty. Mr. LaSalle's report would have earned about a C for structure in Mr. Josephson's class, but he got his point across: I was a deliberate drug user and I needed to be shunned.

Next, Head Lady read the official appeal. She wasn't two sentences into it before I knew my father had written it, filled as it was with words nobody used in normal conversation and statements you would only argue with if you wanted your head bitten off. It was like he was right there, pointing his entire self at the five people on the board. I guessed in a way he was. I felt about as much warmth and security as I would if he'd actually been sitting next to me.

Now the looks the board gave me ranged from quizzical to annoyed. Chain Lady squinted through her glasses. Lizard Look-Alike made notes on a pad. Skull sighed so hard through his nose I could see his nostrils flaring. Dad might have been great in court, but his words on a page didn't seem to be convincing anybody. Why had I thought I could do this on my own?

When she was finished reading the appeal, Head Lady jerked her head in my direction.

"We want to hear this in your own words, but a few people have come forward on your behalf and we're obligated to hear them."

It didn't seem like I should turn around and look to see who they were — not with everyone at the table shuffling around like all these "people who had come forward" were an extreme inconvenience.

Head Lady consulted her file. "Ms. Edelstein, is it?"

"Yes," said a familiar voice behind me.

"Isn't that your study hall teacher?" Mom whispered to me as Ms. Edelstein hurried up the aisle.

Actually, I thought it might be an imposter. The woman who took the speaker's chair wasn't holding a stack of geometry papers and a red pencil.

There was a mumble of introductions, and then Ms. Edelstein was speaking. Her voice had its usual dry edge.

"My sixth-period class is a study hall for at-risk students," she said. She paused to give Mr. LaSalle a dark look. "It's a class Cassidy Brewster should never have been placed in, because the only thing she is at risk for is losing sleep over other people's problems. However, I'm glad she was placed in my class, because she has turned kids around in there that I wouldn't have given you two cents for four weeks ago. Every single student in there — and we are talking everything from

219

a potential suicide to a hardcore graffiti artist—has had his or her life changed because of this young woman."

Chins-and-Chain was nodding, and I felt my shoulders rising from their sag.

"Have you ever seen evidence that she has continued to use steroids?" Skull said. "Rage, for instance?"

I sucked in my breath as my past meltdown scene with Ms. Edelstein in the hall outside Room 109 flashed through my mind.

But she shook her head. "Cassidy doesn't do 'rage.' Righteous anger, yes. And if I were her at this moment—" Her eyes found mine. "I would be angry too."

Head Lady thanked her politely, and Ms. Edelstein left the chair with a smile for me. Chins-and-Chain was still bobbing her head. Lizard Look-Alike was still scribbling on his pad. I didn't know what it all meant, except that I owed Ms. Edelstein. I owed her big time.

"Mrs. Petrocelli-Ward?"

I did start to turn around then, although I didn't need to because P-W's jewelry jangled as she swept up the aisle and took the speaker's chair. No way. No freakin' way.

"In what capacity do you know the student?" Head Lady said.

"'The student'?" Mom muttered. If her hair had been tucked any tighter, she would have pulled it out by the roots.

"I'm Cassidy's art teacher," P-W said. "She has become one of the top students in my class."

Lizard Look-Alike raised his pencil. "What does her being an artist have to do with whether we should let her play basketball?"

In spite of my current agony, I could barely smother a grin as P-W turned on him. "A true artist is a well-disciplined individual, sir. Otherwise, she could never turn out work like this."

She nodded to somebody in the back, and suddenly the white wall behind the table was alive with a photograph that, once someone else dimmed the lights, showed Rafe and me standing next to our Legal Wall. My heart turned over.

"Impressive." Blonde-With-Eyebrows leaned forward to

gaze at it. Until now I'd assumed she was napping with her eyes open. "This is hers?"

"Hers and that of the boy there with her. This represents hours of work and dedication, and mine is not the only class where she shows that kind of commitment."

"I'd like to speak to that," said yet another voice from the back of the room.

There was *absolutely* no way. Mr. Josephson could *not* be there. I stifled a groan. Every inch of ground Ms. Edelstein and Mrs. Petrocelli-Ward might have gained for me was about to be lost.

Head Lady ran her finger down her file. "Mr.—"

"Josephson. Randall Josephson."

He strode to the front like the boardroom was his classroom and the five people at the table merely students who didn't understand the assignment. P-W stood to give him her chair, but he shook his head and held up what appeared to be several typewritten sheets.

"Is that a prepared statement, Mr. Josephson?" Head Lady said. "Time doesn't really allow—"

Mr. Josephson cut her off somewhere around the knees. "I don't think there is anything any of you have to do this afternoon that is more important than making sure this young woman gets a fair shot at her future."

"I would agree with that," Blonde-With-Eyebrows said.

Chins was nodding. Lizard Look-Alike made a circle with his hand and said, "Go ahead. Let's hear it."

Mr. Josephson wasn't two words into it before I realized he was reading my essay on *The Scarlet Letter*. The one where I told the entire story. I could hear Boz's suggestions in there, but the words were mine, and because of Ruthie, I hadn't missed a detail.

"'Since that day,'" Mr. Josephson read at the end, "'I have walked the halls of my school with a large invisible *L* on my chest. In a place where I was once hailed as a star, an athlete who brought honor to the school, a leader among my peers, I now stand on a scaffold every day and suffer the humiliation of failure and betrayal and broken dreams. Some of that I brought on myself. I should have discussed any medicine I was taking with my parents. Maybe I knew deep down that the secrecy I was sworn to was suspicious and wrong. That was my mistake, and I'm trying to learn from it. But I wonder—do I have to wear this scarlet letter for the rest of my life?'"

Mr. Josephson raised his eyes to the room. "It is signed, 'Cassidy Brewster.'"

The room was silent. Even Mr. LaSalle had stopped working his knuckles. I looked at Mr. Josephson through a film of tears and mouthed the words, *Thank you.*

"We appreciate your coming forward, Mr. Josephson," Head Lady said. "We'll take your comments under advisement."

She held out her hand as if she expected Mr. Josephson to put the paper in it. But he crossed to me and placed it in my lap.

"I knew you had it in you," he said.

There was a blue A+ at the top.

Mr. LaSalle stood up. "May I say something?" he said, and he then proceeded to talk before anybody could tell him not to. "I don't argue with the fact that this student—"

"Cassidy," my mother said.

Head Lady blinked.

"Her name is Cassidy," Mom said. "I'd appreciate your not referring to her as 'the student.'"

"Amen to that," said Chins-and-Chain.

Mr. LaSalle's entire head turned red, down to the roots of his haircut. "Fine. I don't argue with the fact that *Cassidy* is a stellar student, she's had a turnaround, blah-blah-blah ... but the policy is clear. You take steroids, you're out. Period. End of story."

Lizard Look-Alike raised his pencil again. "But we've heard evidence that the stu—Cassidy—wasn't aware the medication she was taking *was* steroids."

"What evidence?" Skull said. "She wrote a nice paper, supposedly telling all, but it's still just her word."

"Thank you." Mr. LaSalle threw up his hands as if that decided it, and sat back down.

"Is there a problem back there?"

Head Lady was craning toward the rear of the room, where words were being exchanged in hoarse whispers. As much as I would have loved to have seen them just then, I hoped all of Loser Hall hadn't shown up. I really didn't want them to watch me go down—and it was obvious now that that was where I was headed after all.

"What's going on?" Head Lady said.

"She didn't know she had to get on the speakers' list," someone answered.

"Who?"

"Look, I've heard all the character witnesses I care to hear," Skull said.

"I'm not—I have proof," still another voice said.

Another voice I knew.

Gretchen's voice.

*

Gretchen looked so cobweb frail as she told her story, I was afraid she might blow away before she finished. As far as Skull seemed to be concerned, it wouldn't have mattered. While I was wrapping all my hopes around her testimony, he was visibly busy *unwrapping* them.

Even when Lizard Look-Alike stopped scribbling on his pad and Chins kept nodding and Head Lady and Eyebrows took to giving each other "aha" looks, Skull leaned his chair back and shook his head.

"How is Ms.—"

"Holden," Gretchen said.

"How does Ms. Holden's statement give us any more than we already have?"

"It corroborates Cassidy's testimony," the blonde woman said.

"And we're supposed to just believe the person who provided her with the stuff in the first place?" Skull shrugged. "It's not like she's under oath."

"What would satisfy you, Mr. Blake?" Head Lady said.

"Because we all want Mr. Blake to be satisfied," Mom said under her breath.

Gretchen stuck up a tentative hand.

"You want to add something?" Head Lady said.

"I just want to say that by coming forward with this, I've given up my chance of having my med school suspension removed."

"Well, aren't you just the noble one?" Skull said.

Head Lady gave him a withering look, but he still said, "I'd like to see some hard evidence." He let the front legs of his chair down. "Look, if we're going to override a district policy, we have to have more than he-said-she-said."

"If you're looking for something in writing—"

"We had something in writing—"

"The *student's* writing. Oh, excuse me, 'Cassidy's'—"

"Ms. Holden, we don't allow the use of cell phones in here."

Gretchen looked up from the phone she was frowning at, fingers flying. "I do have something in writing."

Disbelief twisted Mr. Blake's face.

"I still have the text message," Gretchen said. "The one Cassidy sent me the day she tested positive for steroids."

Chins propped her glasses on her nose. "You saved a text from over a month ago?"

I heard it in my head before Gretchen even said it: Aaron saying *She doesn't even take the time to delete her text messages.*

"Here it is," Gretchen said.

I saw her bony hands shaking as she handed the phone to Mr. Blake. He blinked at the screen, and then up at me.

"Do you remember the text you sent her on March eighth?" he said.

The Lizard Look-Alike man leaned over to read with him. Chins put out her hand and wiggled her fingers in a "give it." Both Head Lady and Eyebrows looked at me with glimmers of hope in their eyes. It was that that opened my mouth for me.

"I said something like, 'They're saying those pills you gave me are steroids. Were they?'"

The man who no longer seemed like a Lizard to me looked at Mr. Blake. "That hard enough for you?" he said.

Before Mr. Blake could answer, Head Lady threw back her shoulders and stood up. "Thank you, Ms. Holden. We appreciate you coming in." She looked at me. "The board still needs to confer and give our decision, so unless you have anything to add, we'll go ahead and ask everyone to step out."

It was over then? I didn't have to stand up in front of those five intimidating people and defend myself after all? Could it really be that everyone else had spoken *for* me?

I should have been just short of cheering at that point, or at the very least melting into a puddle of relief. But something weighed on me and wouldn't let me stand up and flee before they could change their minds. Something that pressed my mother's words into my mind.

I looked at her now, and I could see it in her eyes again. *What you said about not having a voice? I don't think that's true . . .*

"Excuse me — I apologize for being late — "

As Ruthie would say, oh, nuh-*uh*.

Dad charged up the aisle, swinging his briefcase like he was flying into a courtroom. "My apologies. I'm Trent Brewster, the defendant's father. I hope I'm not too late to speak for my daughter's case — "

"You are."

The five gazes that had been locked on my father flipped to me. Probably because I was on my feet. And using the voice I'd only used when I was standing up for Rafe. The voice in my head said it was time to stand up for me.

Dad's face had long since come to a point. "Cassidy, sit down."

"No, Trent," my mother said. "You need to sit down."

Head Lady leaned around Dad and looked at me. "If you want to say anything, Cassidy, now is the time."

I didn't look at either of my parents, though Mom did squeeze my hand as I headed for the speaker's chair. I could do this. I could — even though when I turned to face the audience, my breath caught in my throat.

There wasn't an empty chair in the room. They were filled with the rest of my teachers, most of my art class, Boz, and all of Loser Hall, including Lizard. Rafe wiggled his eyebrows at me, and I wondered how that hadn't always been the most supportive thing a person could do.

But it was the people standing in the back who caught me and hung onto me. Coach leaned against the wall, wearing the shirt and the Mickey Mouse tie he always put on for our games. Standing beside him was Kara. My heart halted in my chest.

"Cassidy?" someone said.

I sank into the speaker's chair and looked at Head Lady.

"Did you want to make a statement?" she said.

Chins was nodding. "Go ahead, honey. I want to hear what you have to say."

I suddenly wished I knew her real name.

I closed my eyes, saw what I needed to see, and opened them again.

"I really appreciate all the things Ms. Edelstein and Mrs. Petrocelli-Ward said. And Gretchen — I know she risked a lot to come forward."

I looked at Dad, who was seething on the edge of the chair my mother had ordered him to sit in.

"And my father for making the appeal on my behalf. They've said almost everything that needs to be said. Except for one thing."

I turned to the board. "I made a stupid mistake. And even though it isn't the mistake Mr. LaSalle says I made, maybe you're right to take basketball away from me."

I heard a unanimous gasp, but I pushed on.

"I've hurt a lot of people I love. My family. Coach Deetz. My team." My eyes lingered on Kara. "The best friend I ever had."

I looked away so I wouldn't cry.

"There isn't any punishment you could give me that would undo that," I said. "Maybe I *have* helped some other people since I was taken out of the sports program — but only because of what I've learned from *not* being able to play basketball." I shook my head. "Don't get me wrong — I want to play with my team again, if they'll even have me." I didn't dare look at Coach Deetz. "But if that means turning back into the person I was before ... I shouldn't be allowed to do it."

226

I went back to my seat beside Mom and sank into the arm she put around me. Head Lady said something about taking a recess so the board could make its decision, and people moved and whispered all around me. But all I really knew was that I'd found my voice.

And that was all I needed to know.

*

"I don't get you," Dad said.

"How could you?" I said. "I'm only now getting me myself."

"That makes no sense."

I wasn't sure I could ever make it make sense to my father, and I definitely wasn't going to try to do it right now. I looked over his head at the knots of people that dotted the board-room. All I wanted to do was touch every person in there that I loved and say thank you. And thank you. And thank you. I just didn't know where to start.

A voice behind me made that decision for me.

"Brewster."

I turned in almost slow motion. Coach Deetz looked down at me, and I realized with a pang that I had forgotten how tall he was.

"Thanks for coming," I said, and then my heart twisted. "Or—oh—did you come for the other side? I mean—"

"Don't be a moron, Brewster," he said. "I've always been on your side." He ran his hand over his shaved head. "Besides, I had to bring Gretchen."

"I'm sorry?"

"I gave her a call when I heard about the hearing. She said no at first, but after she talked to you ..." He gave me a look he'd never given me before. It was person to person, not coach to star player. "I guess you can pretty much talk anybody into anything now," he said. "She called me this morning and asked me if I'd bring her."

I turned to look for her, but he brushed my arm. "She was pretty upset. But let me just say this, Brewster."

"What?" I said.

"I still have to abide by district policy, but if the board says you can play again, you're welcome back on the team."

There should have been a surge of excitement. I waited for it, as I'd been waiting for it for weeks. But it caught on a snag somewhere inside me. Just the way my gaze caught on Kara.

She was standing apart from everyone, long arms hugged around her, looking at the floor as if she wished it would swallow her up. I knew that feeling well.

"What about the team, though?" I said. "Are they going to want me?"

Coach followed my gaze with his. "She came to vouch for you in case you needed her. 'Course, you ended up with people coming out of the woodwork to do that." He nudged my arm with his knuckles. "And you didn't do bad yourself."

"Bad" didn't even come close to how I felt. I maneuvered around Coach, and I gave Boz, who was heading my way, a hold-on-a-sec signal. By the time I got to Kara, she was hugging herself so tight her fingers were white against her rib cage.

"Coach told me why you came," I said. "I just want to tell you—thank you."

She nodded, eyes still directed at the carpet. I got that. I wouldn't have wanted to look at me either. But even if she never did again, I had to say it.

"I'm sorry, Kara. I know you didn't tell Mr. LaSalle—I know now it was Selena. Only—" I pressed my throat to push down the tears. "I never should have believed you did it in the first place. I should have listened to you. I'm sorrier for that than for any of it."

She started to lift her chin. Please, please, please, don't let her tell me to—

"Folks, if we could reconvene quickly." It was Head Lady, leading the rest of the board into the room.

I turned back to Kara, but I saw only her back as she walked away from me.

*

"Mr. LaSalle," Head Lady said. "We want you to know that we

appreciate your diligence in upholding district policies concerning athletics. That goes a long way in teaching our young people that the example of performance enhancement they're being shown in professional sports is not one they should follow."

I sagged against Mom, but on the other side, my father nudged me.

"I hear a 'but' coming," he whispered.

"Having said that," Head Lady went on, "the board feels there is reason to believe that Cassidy Brewster was not aware that she was ingesting anabolic steroids and that it would be a detriment to her education and training to prohibit her from participating in the basketball program at Austin Bluffs High School."

Her mouth continued to move, but if anybody heard the rest it was a miracle. The room erupted into cheers and whistles, and I heard one voice wriggle its way to the top of it with, "All right, Roid!"

"It's over, Cass," Mom said as she put her arms around me. "It's finally over."

I nodded against her hair, and felt the pats on the back and the squeezes on the arm that should have sent me over the moon. She was right, I thought as I looked over her shoulder.

Coach was moving out the door with Kara. It was all over.

CHAPTER EIGHTEEN

When I woke up the next morning, I smelled coffee, so I knew Dad was up. I listened harder and heard him moving around in the kitchen. I knew it was him and not Mom by the way the water turned on full force and then off with a punishing squeal—and the way the refrigerator door closed and made the salad dressing bottles rattle. I could even hear the impatient rustle of the newspaper as the chair scraped the floor. He was still mad. "Disconcerted," as he had put it last night. A spoon attacked the sides of a mug in even, metallic blows. That wasn't "disconcerted." That was an anger I'd never heard from my father before.

I stayed where I was and waited for the Frenemy to creep in. I'd actually been waiting for her ever since Dad insisted that I ride home with him from the hearing. Being in the front seat with him again was like experiencing déjà vu: *Let's review— you could have lightened up on the self-deprecation; it worked, but you had a fifty-fifty chance that it wouldn't, and I didn't like those odds.* I really had no idea what he was talking about.

"I just told the whole truth, Dad," I'd said. "Not doing that was what got me there in the first place."

I expected both the Frenemy and a full-out critique of *that* logic, but Dad had moved me on, as usual right to where I didn't want to go.

"What does your PT guy say about your progress?" he said.

It surprised me that he hadn't called Ben and given him the third degree himself, until I remembered Ben saying he and my father didn't have "conversations."

"I'm back on track," I said.

"Which means you'll be ready to play when?"

"Five months."

"Any chance of going at it a little more aggressively?"

"Tryouts aren't even until November," I said.

"Tryouts?" Dad made a face at me as he looked over his shoulder to change lanes. "You've got to be kidding me."

I shook my head. "By that time I'll have been off the court for longer than anybody else. I'm going to try out again."

"Deetz said that?"

"No," I said. "That was my decision." As of that very moment. And then I made another one.

"I know I can play again—and I know I'll be good because it's part of me," I said. "But I don't know if I'm going to."

It was the first time in my sixteen years as Trent Brewster's kid that I ever saw him without a comeback. I watched him grope for words like a drowning person fights for air. When he did find some, any blasting I'd ever gotten from him was going to be a puff in the face in comparison.

"I'm sorry," I said. "I knew this was going to make you mad, but—"

"I am not 'mad,'" he said, though his face was the shape of an ice pick. "I am just completely disconcerted."

There hadn't been so much as a whisper from the Frenemy. I slid out of bed now and crossed to the beanbag and crunched the stuffings under my feet as I stood on it to raise the blinds. A weak light whispered good morning and went back to turning the face of Pike's Peak a dawning pink. The promise of a bright day outside—in spite of the dark one that was going to take place inside.

Dad seemed to have finally settled in with coffee and the paper. At least he wasn't charging in here to ream me with the words he must have found during the night. Not yet anyway. I nestled into the beanbag and slid out RL.

It was the voice that made all the other voices make sense every time I had a decision to make. I was about to make a huge one, and although the Frenemy was not putting her two cents in, my hands shook a little as I lay the leather book on my lap.

Okay, so — yeah, I knew Yeshua wouldn't come right out and say, "Cassidy, do this and you're good to go." I wasn't sure I would have followed his instructions if he had ever done that anyway. I guessed figuring it out was the only way I could live it.

The sunlight brightened the page that found me, and I almost expected the words to squint. How weird was that? How weird was *I*? Weird enough to let the page press into me.

Yeshua was hanging out with people as usual, and this one guy who was pretty much rolling in money — and he was a city official, so who knew where some of that dough came from ... Anyway, the guy said, "Good teacher, what do I have to do to get eternal life?" Yeshua said, "Well, first of all, don't be calling me good. The only one who's totally good is God — just so we're clear."

That I could totally believe.

Yeshua then said, "All right, you know your commandments, yes? No sex outside marriage, no killing, stealing, lying. Be good to your parents — all that." And the rich guy said, "I have always kept the commandments. I'm squeaky clean."

Huh. I wished I could say that about myself.

Yeshua said, "Okay, then there's only one more thing you need to do: sell absolutely everything you own and give the money to the poor. That's your ticket to a life with God. You'll have more than you've ever dreamed of having. Do that and then come follow me."

Whoa. That's like — huge.

Yeah. The guy didn't see that coming. He was mega rich, and the thought of having to give all of that away to people he considered to be pretty much pond scum was depressing. His wealth defined him, and there was no way he was letting go of it. Without it, he was afraid he'd just be nobody. He couldn't do it.

I nodded and went on.

When Yeshua saw the near panic on the man's face, he said to the rest of the group, "Do you know how hard it is for somebody who's got it all to enter the world God wants us in — what he calls his kingdom?"

I could imagine the follower-friends shaking their heads, just as I was swinging mine back and forth.

"I gotta tell you, it's easier to get a camel through the eye of a needle than for me to get a person to let go of all his falseness and come into a full life with the Father." The group shuffled uneasy feet and swallowed lumps in their throats. *"Then who even has half a chance?"* one of them said.

My question exactly.

"Nobody has a snowball's chance in the furnace," Yeshua said, *"if you think you can do it on your own. But if you trust God to define you, to show you who you are, you have all the chance you need."*

I started to lean back and close my eyes to try to figure that out, but the book pressed me on.

Pete, one of Yeshua's follower-friends, wanted to make sure he was getting it right. He said, "We gave up all our stuff, basically our whole lives, and have stuck with you, right?" And Yeshua said, "Absolutely, you have. You're never going to be sorry either. Nobody who gives up what's keeping them from being who they truly are in God's eyes—even if that means their closest relationships or their social status or whatever—will lose out on what's really important. The gifts of truth will multiply in ways you can't even dream of, and not just here on earth but in the life to come."

The page let me close my eyes this time, and RL waited like a feather in my lap. Nothing pressed me or nudged me or Frenemied me—maybe because there was nothing to figure out. I didn't say please, please, please ... maybe because the right words were already thank you, thank you, thank you. I didn't try to picture what my next move was going to look like, because I knew I wouldn't see it. I wouldn't know it until I got there—to the place where Yeshua would be waiting.

*

I went through the morning doing everything the same way I'd been doing it. Boz and I bantered back and forth in first period. I pretty much hung out by myself until lunch. I was headed for our corner table to meet Ruthie when three long-legged girl bodies planted themselves in my path. My stomach fell to my knees when I saw that it was M.J. and Hilary and Kara.

I tried to read their faces, but everyone seemed to be wearing a mask. Through hers, Hilary said, "Coach told us what happened at the hearing."

I couldn't tell what that meant to her. I didn't want it to matter what it meant to any of them, but it did. Because if they turned me away, my decision was made. I said the only thing I could.

"I'm sorry, you guys."

"For what?" M.J. blinked her dark eyes at me and so peeled back a piece of her mask. "I never thought you were a druggie—no matter what Selena said."

Hilary shook her mop of red hair. "I didn't either. Not really."

At that point, Kara still hadn't said anything. It seemed to be taking all her energy just to swallow.

"You thought we thought that, though, huh?" M.J. dodged the swat Hilary aimed at her. "I'm just asking."

Hilary rolled her eyes at me. "So, like, why else would you not want to hang out with us, right?"

I felt my own eyes bulge. "You thought *I* didn't want to hang around with *you?*" I said. But as soon as the words left my lips, I wanted to bite them off. I looked at Kara again. "I guess I messed that up too."

A screaming silence fell. Even M.J. didn't try to fill it in. They were waiting for me to fix it. Just like they always had. Only now, I knew I'd never really been able to.

"Coach said you could play again."

I looked, startled, at Kara. She was looking back with her blue, blue eyes.

"Yeah," I said. "But I'm not sure I am."

"It's because of Selena, huh?" M.J. leaned in. "Just so you know, Coach put her on probation for attitude. She might not even be on the team next season."

Hilary put her hands on her hips. "I do *not* get why you wouldn't be, like, ecstatic to be back on the team."

"I do."

234

Again I looked at Kara. Her face still showed nothing.

"You can't be on a team with people you can't trust," she said. "And if you can't trust them off the court, you can't trust them on it."

She couldn't have sounded any more like the former version of myself if she'd been playing a tape recorder. When she opened her mouth to go on, I wanted to beg her not to. I didn't want to hear any more of the old me.

"So I was thinking," she said, "that maybe you'd want to go to lunch with us."

I stared at her, and then stared some more, as the blue, blue eyes filled with Kara tears.

"You sure?" I said.

"Yeah," she said. "We gotta start somewhere."

"Okay!" M.J. said, like she couldn't wait to escape from Awkwardville. "We can take my car."

"Y'know what—no," Hilary said. "I don't want to lose my appetite before we even get there, and your driving makes me nauseous."

"Hello! Rude to me! Where are we eating anyway?"

The two of them bantered on as if suddenly five weeks had been wiped away. They hadn't been. They never would be. And tempting as it was, I didn't want them to be. I watched as they headed for the door, weaving their way among kids with cafeteria trays and brown bags ...

I whipped around toward our table, mine and Ruthie's. She was just settling in with a thick book and a package of Oreos.

"I can't go, Kara," I said.

"Why not?"

"Because I don't want to ditch my friend—"

"That girl you always eat with," Kara said.

I nodded and began a slow backing away. "I really want to go, but—"

"Why can't she come with?"

I looked from Kara to Ruthie, who was peeking over the top of the fairies, trying not to look like she was searching for me.

"Yeah," I said. "Why not?"

"Does your old man know you're here?"

"Yes," I said. "Just don't ask me if he *likes* it that I'm here."

"He hates my guts," Rafe said.

"He's not that crazy about mine either right now."

"'Cause of me."

"Mostly because I haven't decided whether to go back to basketball. I'm pretty sure I am, but 'we'll see' only seems to be okay when it's the parent who's saying it."

Rafe wiggled his eyebrows. "Your old lady likes me, though."

"She's not my old lady," I said. "She's my mother. Which reminds me — you probably shouldn't call your own mom that when you see her."

His eyes darkened. "*If* I see her."

"What are you talking about?" I pointed to the ticket sticking out of his pocket. "You're gonna get off the bus in Tucson, and she's gonna be waiting for you just like she said, and you're gonna have this great spring break together."

The wonderful lips twitched. "Whose world are you talkin' about? It's not like we're gonna bond in a week. I haven't seen her in two years."

"Only because your dad wouldn't let you. She's your mom, genius. She's probably not even gonna want you to come back here."

Rafe took an unexpected interest in the Greyhound sign over my head. "Do *you* want me to come back?"

"Okay," I said. "That ranks up there with the ten stupidest questions anybody has ever asked. If you stay in Arizona, who's gonna drive me nuts calling me 'Roid'?"

I knew I was suddenly chattering like a freaked-out canary, but how else was I supposed to react when he was suddenly looking at me like — like that?

"I'm not calling you that anymore," he said.

"Why not?" I said.

"Because I wanna call you something else."

"What?"

He shrugged. "I don't know. Babe — My Woman."

"You're serious," I said.

"Yeah."

"You want us to be—together? To*gether* together?"

"You don't."

"Yes, I do!" I said—because I knew at that very moment it wasn't a decision I had to wait to make.

Slowly, slowly, the wonderful lips went soft into a smile.

"There's just one thing, though," I said.

"What?"

"You are *so* not calling me babe—and *definitely* not your 'woman.' How gross is that?"

"Dude—what then?"

"Keep calling me Roid," I said. "Because I don't ever want to forget."

Something about bus number something going to Tucson squawked over the intercom. My mouth went dry and Rafe's crumpled.

"I'm already missing you," he said.

"Yeah," I said.

The wonderful lips brushed mine before I watched him swagger to the bus, shoes swallowed by his pant legs.

*

I didn't leave the bus station right away, even though Dad had informed me it was a "rough place." Personally, I thought it was the most romantic place I'd ever been, and I wanted to gather up the details so I could savor it.

Besides, there was something I needed to do there.

I picked a row of peeling vinyl seats where it looked like a lot of people sat to wait to leave, maybe for places they, too, were unsure about. The initials some of them had carved into the armrests were so much like the homemade engravings in RL, it had to be a sign. Especially after what I'd read in it the night before.

I'd been expecting another story, but when the book pressed into my lap, Yeshua didn't have one for me. Instead, for once the voice told me exactly what to do.

You've come a long, long way in our time together, it said.

Like everyone else who knows me, you still have far to go. But you're on your way. Continue on the Way with Yeshua. Read his Word in the Book.

I knew it was talking about the Bible. I'd known that from the very first story.

I gave a little cry. "But I like the way *you* say it. I understand you!"

You'll understand. Yeshua will make sure of that. But it's time for you to leave me for someone else who isn't where you are. Let someone find it the way you did.

So here I was, in a "rough place" — where someone who wasn't where I was might find it. I pulled RL from my bag and hugged it to my chest. One more time, it pressed against me as it had done so many times before. There must be one more thing it had to say.

I let it open. Once more there was no story. Just a bunch of scribblings.

"What?" I said. Out loud. "What's this supposed to tell me?"

I searched the page again. Others before me had left their initials, like the ones carved on the covers. Still others had done drawings or written out verses. But two things stared at me, just the way the important words always did.

"If you ever want to talk about what you learned from RL," someone had written, "call me. Meanwhile, I'll be praying for you."

It was signed Jess K. and had a phone number next to it.

"I'd totally love to share too," someone had written underneath. "And I'll never stop praying. Bryn C." Beside it was her email address.

I could almost hear their voices, calling to me, saying, *We've been where you are — come, follow. We'll be there.*

I dug in my bag for a pen. My hands were still and calm as I added my voice to theirs. *Cassidy B. I'm there too.*

Only after I'd added my email address and written their names and information on my hand, the way Ruthie did — only then did RL let me close its covers.

I was sure I heard it sigh as I placed it softly on the seat, and then I went out to find the rest of me.

ABOUT THE RL BOOK

Cassidy was pretty quick to figure out that when she opened the leather RL book, she was reading stories from the Bible, and I'm sure you were too. They aren't the actual Scriptures, of course, but they are inspired by what Eugene Peterson did in *The Message*, which was to use modern, everyday language that makes you realize the Bible is for and about you. Jesus spoke in the street language of his day, so it only makes sense that we should be able to read his words that way. In fact, Eugene Peterson was inspired by a man named J. B. Phillips, who in 1947 wrote *The New Testament In Modern English* so his *youth group* could understand the Bible and live it. How cool is that?

Of course, no matter what translation of the Bible you read, it doesn't actually "talk" to you the way RL carries on a conversation with Cassidy. Or doesn't it? Scripture is the Word of God, and a Word is meant to be spoken. When you really settle in with the Bible:

- *doesn't it make you ask questions?*

- *doesn't it answer the questions that pop into your head?*

- *doesn't it seem weirdly close to the exact things you're going through now, even though the stories were told thousands of years ago?*

- *doesn't it sometimes say something you didn't see the last time you looked at that very same part?*

Reading the Bible really is like having a conversation with God, and I hope RL helps you open up your own discussion with our Lord, who is waiting for you to say, "Can we talk?" Comparing what Cassidy reads to the actual passages in the Bible might help you get started. All of them (with one exception from Psalms) are found in the Gospel of Luke, who even more than Mark, Matthew, and John showed the love and sympathy Jesus had for the people who didn't fit, the people who others said were weird, sinful, and not to be hung out with. Luke also shows how much Jesus respected women. It seemed like just the thing for our RL girls—and for you.

THE SCRIPTURES

WHO HELPED

One of my favorite steps in the process of writing a book is working with experts who know things I don't. I mean, seriously, how much time have I spent playing basketball or doing graffiti? (Answer: not much, and none.) These are the pros who helped me make *Tournaments, Cocoa & One Wrong Move* feel like real life.

Jennifer Risper, former Vanderbilt University women's basketball player, currently playing professionally in Slovakia, whom I met by divine appointment in the restroom of a Mexican restaurant. Watching her play, having her (try to) teach me how to do a layup, and talking for hours about her experiences as player and patient (she has suffered two shattered ACLs) brought Cassidy Brewster into her own as a young woman. (Any similarities between Jennifer and Cassidy are purely coincidental.)

John Painter, RNC, MSN, FNP (in case you're actually interested, that stands for Registered Nurse Certified, Masters of Science in Nursing, Family Nurse Practitioner), and former basketball player. John helped get Cassidy—and me—through that first scene, as well as through physical therapy.

Lucas Daughtery, BS, ATC, Cumberland University (Certified Athletic Trainer), who literally showed up on my doorstep as the guest of a friend and spent an entire afternoon putting Cassidy through the paces in physical therapy. All three of us were exhausted when we were through!

My Colorado Springs Consultants—Abby Wertenberger, Bree Mielke, Rachel Moore, Chelsea Baird, Evelyn Wyss, Lauren Haynes, Hannah Tackett, and Katherine Brickley—who as teens growing up in the Springs helped me to see the town through teenage eyes. Because they are budding novelists themselves, their descriptions of things like Pike's Perk and the Black Forest Coffee Haus were exquisite. I hope I did them justice.

I also relied on several nonfiction books written by authors far wiser than I in the ways of young female athletes:

Warrior Girls, by Michael Sokolove (Simon and Schuster, 2008)

Games Girls Play, by Caroline Silby with Shelley Smith (St. Martin's Griffin, 2000)

The Female Athlete's Body Book, by Gloria Beim and Ruth Winter (Contemporary Books, 2003)

Turn the page to check out an excerpt from the next Real Life book, Limos, Lattes & My Life on the Fringe.

CHAPTER ONE

I was used to the responses I received when I walked down the hall at school.

I could always predict that the Kmart kids—not *my* name for them—would cut a wide path around me, like being intelligent made me an alien. Make that tall, gawky, black, and intelligent. They didn't get me, and I was really okay with that.

And it was also a safe bet that the Ruling Class would ignore me, even though I was in every honors class known to adolescence with them. And that the few African Americans in my school would say, "Hey, Tyler," with Crest-commercial smiles and then move on because we really didn't have much in common beyond the color of our skin. According to them.

My actual friends—a group I referred to in my mind as The Fringe—were also predictable. From them I could expect things like, "You're looking enigmatic today, Tyler." At which point any passing Kmart kid would scurry away as if vocabulary were a contagious disease.

I had come to expect all of that. It was like the raspberry Pop-Tart I ate for breakfast every day. It might not be that interesting, but at least I knew what I was getting.

But then there was that day in April when the snow had all melted for the first time since late November and I had walked to school without a ten-pound down jacket. That was the day it changed—the way people were looking at me, I mean. Three steps from my locker on the way to the lunchroom, I was already wondering what high school I'd been teleported to.

I hiked my black-and-white plaid messenger bag over my

shoulder, stuffed with all the research I'd done the night before on Andrew Jackson for my group history project. I was thinking about what an egotistical fool the man was and how we could possibly present that in our report, since Mr. Linkhart was from Mississippi or someplace and probably thought Jackson should be canonized as a saint. My head was totally wrapped around that when three girls in too-tight sweaters and too-skinny jeans planted themselves right in front of me. I tried to steer around them, the way they would have steered around *me* any other day, but they shimmied themselves into that path, too, and stared at me. It was like they were waiting for me to, I don't know, transform into another life form.

"Excuse me — what do you want?" I said.

Apparently that was hilarious, because they spewed giggles and looked at each other and giggled again, all the way down the hall. I decided that couldn't possibly have anything to do with me, and I proceeded another five steps toward the cafeteria where two thirds of my group was supposedly waiting with their own bags bulging with fascinating facts about our seventh president. I was thinking they'd probably want to mooch off of *my* facts, as well as my lunch money, when another trio of girls slowed down to gape at me and then sidled off, tittering. I've never "tittered" in my life, but I knew even the crowd who saw school as a hindrance to their social lives didn't collapse into that kind of hilarity without a reason, however lame it might be.

I took a detour into the girls' restroom and examined my face in one of the mirrors generations of girls had clouded with clandestine cigarette smoke. My brown eyes stared back at me as if to say *What are you looking at?*

I expected to see ink smeared across my cheek, or at the very least a large wart blossoming on my forehead. But I looked the same as I had that morning when I brushed my teeth. Hair cut into a close cap on what my mother referred to as a "nicely shaped head" — like that was every girl's idea of the perfect complement — skin still the color of pancake syrup, mouth still big enough for several people, nose still the only accusing hint that all my ancestors had not come from Africa. There was nothing in the mirror that all those kids in the hall hadn't seen before. Definitely nothing worth "tittering" over, unless you counted the map of red lines in the whites of my eyes from studying until midnight. Did they think I was on drugs? Were *they* on drugs?

"Oops," somebody said from the doorway.

I looked at her from the mirror. Alyssa Hampton. Pretty blonde girl, if you liked big teeth. Half the males in her senior class apparently did.

Another girl came in behind her and nearly plowed into Alyssa. Hayley Barr, a junior famous for her thick ponytail. The two of them were normally attached right about where their jeans hugged their hips. Jeans that cost more than the entire wardrobe of those six girls I'd seen in the hall. Combined.

"Hi, Tyler," Hayley said, in a voice about two keys higher than her usual voice. "You going to lunch?"

She looked at Alyssa and, to their credit, they visibly stifled the laughter that was so clearly about to explode out of them.

"I usually go to lunch," I said. "Why? Are they serving botulism again today?"

They did explode then, and I knew it wasn't my humor that sent them diving into a stall. Together.

Seriously—what was making me such a source of endless amusement?

I transferred my bag to my other shoulder and hauled Andrew Jackson's life story back into the hall, where I set out again for the lunch room. But when I saw my second cousin Kenny at the drinking fountain, I swerved and caught up to him before he could take off to join the other professional slackers at the Jiff-E-Mart.

"Do you have any idea why every girl in this school suddenly thinks I'm funnier than Tina Fey?" I said.

He raised his head and blinked. I could tell it took him a full five seconds to recognize me, which made sense. We hadn't actually spoken since Christmas dinner.

"Who's Tina Fey?" he said.

I should have known. Whenever I did try to have a conversation with the boy, he never had any idea what I was talking about. I'd suspected for some time that he was hatched from an egg every morning.

"I don't think you're that funny," he said.

A girl materialized. Candace, Kenny's older sister.

"Come on, Kenny," she said, wrapping her fingers around his arm. "You don't want to get into this."

"Into what, Candace?" I said.

"Into nothing." With her hands on Kenny and her eyes warily on me, she dragged him away.

All right. Enough. I charged down the hall, through the looks and the snickers and the snippets of conversation, like I was traveling in a tunnel. I headed straight to the table in the corner by the "salad bar" nobody ever ate from, and when I arrived, I knew at least things were still normal over here.

Matthew sat, as usual, with his enormous feet propped on a chair, which meant the teacher/cop of the day hadn't been by yet to tell him to get them off. Scrawny Yuri was across from him, frowning at the ingredients printed on an energy drink bottle. Deidre, the only senior in our group of juniors, was standing up, digging through a vintage purse suitable for a bag lady, which probably contained items she hadn't seen since seventh grade. She was talking. Nobody was listening. I sank into my plastic chair next to her and plunked my own bag on the table.

"Does anybody know what's going on?"

"Are we talking globally?" Matthew said. "We're pretty sure Pakistan's harboring Osama Bin Laden. We have a black president—"

"Mercury's in retrograde," Deidre said into her purse.

"No, I mean here," I said.

Yuri looked up from the drink bottle and squinted at me through his wire-rimmed glasses. "Who cares what's going on here?"

"Not me, usually," I said. "But people I don't even know are walking up to me and losing it."

Deidre dragged her eyes from the bottomless bag and pulled her dark I-refuse-to-tweeze eyebrows together over her yes-I'm-Italian-is-that-a-problem nose.

"They know something you don't?" she said. "Hard to believe."

"Maybe it's about that," Matthew said.

"About what?" I said. Matthew's currently raven-black hair hung over his eyes, so it was hard to tell what, if anything, he was seeing.

"That." He jerked his square chin toward the opposite wall of the lunchroom.

I followed his jerk. Our cafeteria was long and narrow and an even uglier green than any other part of the over-fifty-year-old school. To make it look even longer—and uglier—rectangular tables were placed in rows all the way from one end to the other. Green, yellow, and orange plastic chairs that always started out tucked into the tables at the beginning of lunch period were quickly scattered and regrouped and often overturned, until by the end the place looked like those prison scenes you see in movies where the inmates start banging their cups and somebody gets thrown into the chow line. One teacher-monitor was only enough to keep that to a minimum.

One of the advantages of being a junior or senior at Castle Heights High was getting to sit at the round tables that skirted the room. We—that would be The Fringe and I—had claimed ours in September, and like most groups we were pretty territorial about it. Which meant we seldom ventured to the other end where the bulletin board was hung. The Ruling Class had their three tables down there so they could preside over the significant events posted on it. Homecoming king and queen. Roles in the current theatrical production. Starting lineup for the next sporting event. If I'd had the slightest interest in any of that, I might have wandered past it now and then. Since, however, I could very possibly live my entire life successfully without ever going to a homecoming dance or cheering at a basketball game, I'd never even glanced in that direction.

But at the moment, everybody else in the student body

appeared to be absolutely fascinated by it. The crowd in front of the board was four people deep.

"Let me guess," Deidre said. "They posted the results of the 'Most Shallow' competition."

"Oh." Matthew sat upright in the chair. "Do you think I won?"

Deidre shook her head. "Although I have known puddles deeper than you, Matthew, I'm sure you didn't."

"Shucks," he said to Yuri.

Yuri cocked a colorless eyebrow that matched his hair. "Define 'shucks.'"

"That can't be it," I said. "If my name ever appeared on that board it would be for 'Most Unknown.'"

"Isn't that an oxymoron?" Matthew said.

"Is that what they call *this*?"

We looked up at a wildly curly brunette who'd appeared at the salad bar and was poking the tongs into a stainless steel pan full of brown lettuce.

I studied her for a few seconds. She didn't immediately fall into any of the categories of people I passed in the halls. In fact, I didn't think I'd ever seen her before. It had to be tough being a new kid in April, when all the friend slots had long since been filled. It had been hard enough for me at the beginning of sophomore year, seeing how most of the friend slots here had actually been filled back in preschool.

"Do you know what's going on down there?" I said to her.

She gave the lettuce another dubious look and moved on to the anemic chopped tomatoes.

"I think they posted the nominations for prom queen," she said. "I'm not sure — this is only my second day here."

Yeah, I was good.

"How's that working out for you?" Matthew said.

She passed on the tomatoes too and dumped a spoonful of grated cheese onto her plate. "Is there a microwave we can use?"

Matthew laughed out loud. Yuri scrutinized her as if she were speaking one of the few foreign languages he didn't know.

"No," I told the girl. "We're lucky to have electricity. Where'd you move here from?"

"France," she said.

Deidre stared. "Seriously?"

"My family lived there for five years."

She brought her plate of cheese close to the table, and for the first time I saw that she had incredibly blue eyes, even though her skin was as dark as mine.

Deidre kicked Matthew's feet off the extra chair. "Join us," she said, "if you can stand Mr. Crude."

"My stuff's over there," she said. "Thanks, though. Most people here aren't this friendly." She glanced toward the bulletin board again. "They're kind of mean, some of them."

"What do you expect from the low end of the food chain?" Matthew said.

Yuri just glowered.

"No, seriously." The girl lowered her voice. "A bunch of them are up there laughing their fannies off because somebody's in the top four for prom queen that evidently isn't queen material."

"Did she just say 'fannies'?" Deidre said to Yuri.

"Trust me," I said, "nobody made it to that list that wasn't supposed to be there. We have people who oversee those kinds of things."

"The principal does that?"

Matthew snorted from under his hair. "He never comes out of the main office. Nobody's seen him since the Clinton administration."

I shook my head at the new girl. "A bunch of juniors and seniors run everything."

"You'll know them by the vacant look they get in their eyes when you use words of more than three syllables," Matthew said.

"Except 'Abercrombie,'" Deidre said. "They know that."

Yuri was still glowering. "It's all inbreeding."

The new girl had yet to crack a smile. It was time to find out which way she was leaning before we said much more.

"Were you in student government at your school in France?" I said.

She shook her head and pushed a few strands of curly hair behind her ear. "I was homeschooled."

The three of us exchanged glances.

"What?" she said.

I cleared my throat. "Just a word of warning. Those kids aren't usually outright mean until somebody does something 'different.' Otherwise, they don't really have to be because they're already in control."

"So start by not telling anybody you've been home-schooled," Deidre said.

The blue eyes blinked. "I don't get that. And I definitely don't get the prom queen thing."

Deidre patted the empty chair. "You absolutely should sit with us. You've found your people, right, Tyler?"

"Huh?" I said.

I'd heard the words, but most of them hadn't sunk in. My eyes and my mind and the sick feeling in the pit of my stomach had wandered back toward the bulletin board. Now that entire half of the cafeteria was alternating between ogling our end of the room and doing some variation on a disbelieving guffaw.

"Tyler?" Deidre said.

"Who is it—do you know?" I said.

The girl shook her head.

"Will somebody go look?"

"Oh, can I please?" Deidre said. "And can I also poke a fork in my eye?"

"Why do we care who it is?" Matthew said to Yuri, who answered, "We don't."

The new girl edged away. "Listen, thanks for talking to me. I better go eat."

"I'll walk with you," I said.

"Oh, yeah," Matthew said. "She could get lost in here. It's a veritable labyrinth."

He gave the whole table an elaborate shrug. I followed the girl down the aisle, past the freshmen and sophomores who had also sorted themselves into a caste system early on in their high school career — if not sooner, since they'd all basically been born in the same hospital. Normally louder and more obnoxious than the crowd at a tractor pull, they practically went into a coma as I went by.

What? I wanted to say to all of them.

But the closer I got to the board, the surer I was that I already knew "what." My mouth felt like sawdust, and my stomach had completely shifted to the feeling I hadn't had since my first day here a year and a half ago, moments before I made up my mind that fitting in was not my life goal. Even the cafeteria food couldn't wreak this much havoc on my insides.

Still, I kept my head up and, as my father always said, my eyes on the prize. There was no doubt that the object of everybody's attention was a pink sheet of paper stapled to the center of the board and surrounded by a frame of fake roses. Could they have made it any cheesier?

A small sea of people who were just getting in on the fun parted as I took the final steps. Nobody breathed a word, except the one girl who needlessly said, "Shhh!" The silence had the clear sound of people holding back hysteria.

The new girl had been right. It was the list of prom queen nominees, voted on in junior and senior homerooms that very morning and narrowed down by none other than the prom committee, a subset of the Ruling Class.

Alyssa Hampton was the first name. No surprise.

Hayley Barr was the second. To be expected.

Joanna Payne, the third. Ya think?

And there below them, in the same font, the same color, the same size — as if it belonged there — was the fourth one.

Tyler Bonning.

When the room could hold its breath no longer and ripped open in a roar, I realized I'd just read the name out loud.

"Tyler Bonning?" The new girl half-yelled to me over the din. "Is that you?"

"Yes," I said. "That's me." I turned to her and plastered a manufactured smile onto my face. "Hilarious, isn't it?"